By the same author

JOHN MORTIMER

Titmuss Regained

VIKING

VIKING
Published by the Penguin Group
Viking Penguin, a division of Penguin Books USA Inc.,
40 West 23rd Street, New York, New York 10010, U.S.A.
Penguin Books Ltd, 27 Wrights Lane, London W8 5TZ, England
Penguin Books Australia Ltd, Ringwood, Victoria, Australia
Penguin Books Canada Ltd, 2801 John Street, Markham, Ontario, Canada L3R 1B4
Penguin Books (N.Z.) Ltd, 182–190 Wairau Road, Auckland 10, New Zealand

Penguin Books Ltd, Registered Offices: Harmondsworth, Middlesex, England

First American Edition
Published in 1990 by Viking Penguin,
a division of Penguin Books USA Inc.

1   3   5   7   9   10   8   6   4   2

LIBRARY OF CONGRESS CATALOGING IN PUBLICATION DATA
Mortimer, John Clifford.
Titmuss regained/John Mortimer.
p.   cm.
ISBN 0-670-82333-3
I. Title.
PR6025.07552T58   1990
823'.914—dc20   89-40801
Printed in the United States of America
Set in Ehrhardt

For John and Myfanwy Piper

Today

What would the world be, once bereft
Of wet and of wildness? Let them be left,
O let them be left, wildness and wet;
Long live the weeds and the wilderness yet.

'Inversnaid'
Gerard Manley Hopkins

CHAPTER ONE

About a mile to the north of the village of Rapstone there was an
area of mixed woodland and uncultivated chalk downs. The
woods included some beech, birch, field maple and yew. The
grassland, owing to the centuries of peace it had enjoyed from
the depredations of farmers and builders, was rich in plant and
insect life. The violet hellebore and the bird's-nest orchid did
well there and gentians and wild thyme proliferated. The Duke
of Burgundy's fritillary and the chalkhill blue butterflies were to
be seen, as were the trapdoor spider, fallow and muntjac deer,
badgers, foxes, adders and slow-worms. At the foot of the hill
there was a stream said to be haunted by two kingfishers,
although their nesting-place had never been found.

One afternoon in April a Volvo stopped on the road by the
stream. An observer standing on the crest of the grassland might
have seen, indeed did see, a young couple, hand in hand, climb
the hill towards him. They were a good-looking pair. The man
had heavy, regular features, fair hair which covered the tops of
his ears and a moustache. At serious moments his face could
assume a look of sullen brutality, but now he seemed cheerful
enough. The girl with him was sturdily attractive, with white,
slightly protruding teeth. Such clouds as there were hung high
in the sky. The early sunshine gave promise of a hot summer,
never to be fulfilled.

Half-way up the hill the observer saw the couple stop and
stand still, facing each other. They had chosen a patch of clear

scrub where the turf was soft and springy, much undermined by rabbits. They did not kiss or touch each other, but the girl laughed, causing a colony of fat pigeons to tumble out of the trees in alarm. Then they prepared to make love.

They did this in a businesslike way, with an efficiency born of experience. They moved deliberately but seemed to be under pressure of time, like soldiers at a military tattoo racing against the clock to assemble a gun. Buttons and belt buckles were undone and shoes kicked off and they then fell to the ground in one movement, as though they were under fire. Only then did they embrace, but as soon as their mouths joined they were interrupted.

'Can't you lot read? There's notices where you came in. This place is reserved for nature!' The man standing over them was short, square and bristling with anger. Hair covered the lower half of his face so profusely that his eyes seemed in a perpetual panic at the danger of being overgrown. With his green sweater and leather patches, his beret, knapsack and stick, he had the appearance of a soldier beating the countryside for terrorists. His name was Hector Bolitho Jones. 'I,' he told them, 'am keeper and warden of the Rapstone Nature Area.'

'Tell him,' the girl muttered, avoiding the eyes of the infuriated warden as she stood up, straightening her skirt. 'Tell him who you are.' But her companion remained motionless, staring up, unamused.

'You know what we get on this natural downland which has never known pollution by any form of artificial manure or pesticide of any nature whatsoever? You know what you may be laying on there? Do you have any idea what you may be crushing?'

'We're going,' the girl said. 'We wouldn't want to stay here, anyway.' And once again she advised her lover, 'Tell him who you are.'

'Just on a stone curlew's nest. I don't suppose you realized that, did you? In your ignorance. The stone curlew habitually

6

makes its nest on the ground. On the natural chalk. You could have got that from our fact-sheet at the area entrance. If you lot can read.'

'We're moving, anyway.' The girl, glancing down, found another button and did it up.

'That'd be a bit late if you've laid on a stone curlew's nest. If you've smashed the eggs or frightened away the mother. You might have had a death on your hands then, mightn't you? As if you lot cared!'

The man didn't move but spoke for the first time. 'Why don't you shut up and mind your own bloody business.'

'It's not *my* business!' Hector Bolitho Jones raised his voice as though talking to the deaf or to a foreigner. 'It's S.C.R.A.P.'s business. S.C.R.A.P owns this ground, the Society for Conservation, Rural and Arboreal Protection. S.C.R.A.P.!' he shouted, so that his voice echoed across the woods and set the pigeons off again. 'I suppose that means nothing to you?'

'Of course it does.' The man got slowly to his feet, on which he towered over the small, infuriated Jones. 'It means I'm your boss. I just happen to be at H.E.A.P., the Department of Housing, Ecological Affairs and Planning. It may come as news to you out here in the sticks, but we have just taken over the S.C.R.A.P. Nature Areas with a view to privatization!'

'After all the government money you've had poured into you!' The girl, who seemed to understand such matters, looked at Hector Bolitho Jones accusingly.

'So you'd better keep a civil tongue in your head. If you value your job, that is.' Her friend was even more threatening.

Hector Bolitho Jones drew a breath. His chest swelled and his beard bristled. He was about to start on a lengthy speech about stone curlews being the business of all of us, together with rain forests, the black rhino, badgers, otters, the greenhouse effect, lead in petrol, seal slaughter, mink coats, fox-hunting, hedge destruction and non-organic farming. He looked at his audience and decided, like a Victorian missionary facing a hostile couple in war-paint with rings through their noses, that a sermon would be a waste of breath. 'I don't care who you are,' he said. 'I give you five minutes to get off this Nature Area.'

'And if we don't?'

'You'll find yourselves mentioned in S.C.R.A.P.'s annual report.'

'Oh, Christ.' The man smiled coldly. 'You're scaring us to death.' He was strong, with muscles that stretched his neat grey suit, clothes which looked too formal for courting in the countryside. For a moment he seemed about to strike the warden but, surprisingly, he took his girlfriend's arm and they walked away down the hill towards the road where their car was waiting. Hector Bolitho Jones watched them leave with undiminished hostility and only when the lovers had driven away was he satisfied that he was once again in command of a small kingdom where nature might pursue its uninterrupted course.

'What're you going to do?' In the car the girl, whose name was Joyce Timberlake, twisted the driving-mirror and leant sideways to repair her lipstick. 'You going to get him the sack?'

'Probably not worth it.' Her companion drove with one hand, the other was lying coldly on her thigh. 'But it's not something I'm going to forget either. You can be sure of that.'

Hector Bolitho Jones, true to his word, did mention the sacrilegious behaviour of the lovers in the Nature Area in a report to his masters at S.C.R.A.P. Months later, watching television, he saw an interview with Ken Cracken, M.P., on the subject of planning permission for a theme park in the Lake District. He at once recognized the fair moustache, the wary and hostile expression of the youngish man who had become, with a rapidity which alarmed many older politicians, Minister at the Department of Housing, Ecological Affairs and Planning, a position only junior to that of the Secretary of State himself, the Right Honourable Leslie Titmuss.

CHAPTER TWO

'What a swine God was!'

While the forces of nature were in collision on the chalk downland, and Ken Cracken and his girlfriend, who was also his
personal assistant and political adviser, were being expelled from
the paradise of the Rapstone Nature Area, a woman of eighty,
her legs and arms shrunk as though from enforced starvation, lay
waiting, with growing impatience, for death. Grace Fanner was
unaccustomed to being kept waiting for anything. Her bedroom
in Rapstone Manor was dark and gloomy, its windows curtained
by the spreading yew tree in front of the house; patches of damp
stained the wallpaper which was decorated with lighter squares
from which pictures had been removed and auctioned off as
Lady Fanner's overdraft climbed to dizzier heights. She lay now,
an unpaid-for and half-drunk bottle of champagne beside her,
her diminutive body scarcely swelling the coverlet on the bed in
which her husband Nicholas, over a decade before, had met
death with the polite but puzzled smile with which he had
greeted all his visitors.

'I've been reading the Bible.'

The Rector of Rapstone, Kevin Bulstrode, known to many of
his parishioners as Kev the Rev., looked at her as though this
activity were a sign of mental weakness, like astrology or studying
the measurements of the Great Pyramid.

'Not the Old Testament?' he asked nervously.

'*Particularly* the Old Testament. What a swine God was,
most of the time.' Lady Fanner said this with a tight smile of

admiration. 'Smiting people in a way I've hardly ever done. Right, left and centre.'

'I don't think we see God as so much of a smiter nowadays,' Kev the Rev. explained. 'We see Him more as the depth of our being.'

'Certainly the depth of *my* being,' Lady Fanner agreed. 'Smiting away like that. Bully for Him!'

'The God that's within us all' – Bulstrode was still patient – 'is above all things a God of love.'

'God is within *you*?'

'I'd certainly like to think so.'

'It seems' – Lady Fanner looked at the clergyman with ill-disguised contempt – 'a most peculiar place to put Him. The tide's gone down.' She put out a matchstick arm and her hand trembled as it felt for the glass on her bedside table. 'Pour!'

'Are you sure that's absolutely wise?'

'Pour!' she repeated in a voice which rose towards an enraged squawk. Her eyes widened with anger and the Reverend Kevin obeyed her immediately, although he could have sat still and left her impotent and thirsty. Being unused to pouring champagne he sent the liquid bubbling up over the top of the glass. Life, Lady Fanner thought, had deteriorated in Rapstone. The previous Rector, the Reverend Simeon Simcox, although a life-long Socialist, could at least pour a glass of champagne without letting it overflow and ruin the furniture.

'I read the Book of Job.' She lifted the great weight of a half-filled glass to her lips and pecked at it in the manner of a blue tit at a bird-bath. 'God certainly gave that poor bugger a hard time. Boils!'

'I think you'll find that He has grown a little more civilized down the centuries. As, perhaps, we all have.' Kevin Bulstrode did his best to sound reassuring. 'I don't think the Old Testament God should be taken as a model of behaviour.'

'Oh, I do. I quite definitely do. I'd love to see my son-in-law afflicted with boils. That is if the Right Honourable Leslie

Titmuss hasn't got plenty of them already. As a young man, I hate to remember, he appeared to suffer from terminal acne. What my poor Charlotte saw in him, I really can't imagine. But then Charlie was such a beggar in the looks department, she couldn't be much of a chooser, could she?'

'I always heard your daughter Charlotte was a bit of a saint, Lady Fanner. Didn't she die in a C.N.D. demonstration at Worsfield Heath?' Kevin sounded like an old-time army padre, remembering those who fell on the Somme and at El Alamein. His head was bowed and his hands locked between his knees.

'She was run over there. In some foolish demonstration.' Once again Grace Fanner pecked at the liquid in her glass and then waved it wildly in the air, trying to restore it to the bedside table, an operation which her visitor just saved from disaster. 'At least she caused the terrible Titmuss extreme embarrassment. He was something rather pompous in the government at the time. Having a wife who went to bomb protests was worse than tucking up with a tart in Mount Street.'

'Did he do that?' His nose was twitching and Grace Fanner thought how eager the little cleric was for gossip. No doubt that was why he came to visit her; though her gossip was mainly about a vanished society and persons long dead.

'Did he do what?' She was tired and testy.

'"Tuck up" . . . with whoever you said?'

'Oh, no. So far as I can tell he didn't tuck up with anyone. Leslie Titmuss wouldn't have the gumption. On his way up from being the spottiest and commonest little boy in the village to Minister of Something Incredibly Boring he thought it might help his career to marry my daughter. Well, Charlie put him right about that. We've got to give her the credit. Bloody near scuppered his miserable career, my Charlie did.'

She smiled proudly and then fell silent for so long that the Reverend Kevin thought she had gone to sleep or died. Her eyes were closed but her brain was whirling. She was thinking, not of Leslie Titmuss, her son-in-law, or of Charlotte, her dead daughter, but of their son, Nicholas, who once used to visit her, riding over on his bike and listening, while she fed him cocktail biscuits and let him take sips of her champagne, to her long, involved stories about the South of France and the old days at the Café de Paris. She would ask Nick, 'Do you know who I mean by Nancy Cunard?', at which the schoolboy would smile tolerantly and nibble at a Twiglet. Sometimes, in the long winter afternoons, she would show him her photograph albums or the old Molyneux dresses she kept hanging like tattered banners in her wardrobe. All that had ended when the toad Titmuss, dressed for Westminster, with his hair slicked down like a counter-jumper, had burst in and accused her of being drunk and of corrupting his boy with stories of useless people whom she had probably never known anyway. Titmuss's driver had packed Nick's bike into the boot of the government Rover and the boy, silent and tolerant of all adult outbursts, had been driven away, never to visit his grandmother again at Rapstone Manor.

'If he thinks I'm going to leave this house to young Nick so *he* can plonk himself in it,' she suddenly called out, 'the toad Titmuss has got another think coming.' She opened her eyes to see Kevin Bulstrode creeping, as though from the bedroom of a fractious child he hoped was now safely asleep, towards the door. 'And where do you think you're going?'

'You will excuse me.' The Rector was stopped in mid-flight. 'One has certain duties.'

'Oh no, one hasn't. Not until Sunday and they're not exactly full-time then, are they? One sits down and one tries to think of something nice to say about me at my funeral.'

He obeyed her. In fact he had spent many unprofitable hours thinking of any kindly words that could be used at Lady Fanner's obsequies without inducing cynical and incredulous smiles on the faces of the attendant mourners. 'Positive', 'always knew her mind', 'a genuine character', 'one of the Old Brigade': these were about as far as he had got. 'Never one to suffer fools gladly'. He reflected that on his duty-visits he always seemed to be cast as the fool who wasn't suffered gladly.

'The Titmuss family shan't have a brick of Rapstone Manor. Not a stick of furniture. Not a lavatory-paper holder, if I have anything to do with it.'

'Lady Fanner. Isn't that a matter for your lawyer?'

'Jackson Cantellow! That idiot who spends his time bawling out the Hallelujah Chorus with the Worsfield Choral Society. Of course not. It's a matter entirely for me. You know what I'll do?' Her smile was suddenly girlish, set in a pale, skull-like face that had once been beautiful. 'I'll leave the whole shooting-match to the anti-bomb brigade. That should teach Titmuss!'

CHAPTER THREE

The town of Hartscombe lay about five miles to the south of the Rapstone Valley. In the days when Grace Fanner was about to dispose finally of her property it had changed from the town it was when she was carried over the threshold of Rapstone Manor by her stumbling husband. This ceremonial was insisted upon by Grace, mainly for the purpose of impressing those of her former lovers who were present. It had also changed since the days when the Right Honourable Leslie Titmuss had been a silent and deeply mistrusted boy at Hartscombe Grammar. It was then a small and sleepy riverside town. Streets of brick and flint houses, some half-timbered, a few square and Georgian with surprisingly large gardens, led down to the river where swans hissed at the children who threw bread to them, and punts and skiffs for hire were moored under the bridge. There were grocers' shops where hams hung from the ceiling, a draper's where the change travelled on an elaborate system of overhead railway, the Copper Kettle Tea-Room – a popular place of resort after visiting Boots Lending Library – and a cinema, built in the thirties, where the patrons were entertained by a magnificent organ which rose from the floor in a haze of purple light and played a selection of golden oldies. Double seats were available in the back rows for couples who wished to show extra friendliness. Hartscombe's pride and main source of employment, however, was the building where Simcox ales had been brewed for generations. Its brick had worn to a dusty pink and dray horses used to stamp and jangle their brass on frosty mornings outside the yard gates. The cinema had now been torn down to make way for a pedestrian precinct through which the wind howled, blowing the cardboard remains of Chinese take-aways against the concrete plant-tubs. In it the shops sold life insurance, shoes, electrical appliances and such essential objects as scented and upholstered coat-hangers or His and Her embroidered knicker-bags. A thriving business undertook to supply jacuzzis and gold-tapped bidets to converted barns and former labourers' cottages. There was a health-food bar and a herbal cosmetic boutique. There was not a butcher, an ironmonger or a fish shop. Behind this disappointing market-place, an almost exact replica of those implanted into the hearts of hundreds of once-healthy towns in Southern England, towered a huge supermarket and a concrete multi-storey car park, to enter and leave which required an advanced knowledge of computer technology. The brewery building had been sold and converted into flats for upwardly mobile executives and money managers who commuted on the motor-ways to London, a city which, when Leslie Titmuss was a boy, many Hartscombe inhabitants had never visited. Simcox ales were now brewed in a new factory in the industrial zone and their Fortissimo lager was held to be responsible for the youthful violence that brought some sort of life to the shopping precinct on Saturday nights.

It was into this new Hartscombe, which had been dragged, without too many screams of protest, into the age of prosperity, that the Right Honourable Leslie Titmuss was driven a week or two after his former mother-in-law had told Kev the Rev. what she thought of her former son-in-law. He felt, he could never help feeling, like a king returning to his own small kingdom. Had he not, a despised and laughed-at boy, who earned his scant pocket-money cutting down nettles and doing odd jobs in the Rapstone Rectory garden, fought his way up and over the Hooray Henrys, bank managers and country gents in his local party to become the M.P. for Hartscombe and Worsfield South, which seat he had held by an impregnable majority for twenty-five years? Was he not the candidate who had first preached the gospel, learnt he used to say from his father, a clerk in the Brewery, of respect for thrift, a constant appreciation of the mystical power of money and a deep suspicion of those who wished to hand it out to the undeserving poor? Armed with this simple creed, which had since become the accepted doctrine of his party, Leslie Titmuss had helped to change the face of England. After years of toil he had cut the ribbon that threw open the shopping precinct and had given planning permission for the new trading estate. And if the old-fashioned landlords in his local party complained that the new motorway cut across their fields or that lorries on the way to the trading estate blocked the lanes and frightened the laying birds, so much the worse for them. They had been, some of them, those whooping little snobs who had pushed him into the river for wearing a hired dinner-jacket, redolent of mothballs, at his first Young Conservative dinner dance in the Swan's Nest Hotel.

He walked by the river, having sent his driver to cope with the mysteries of the car park. Hartscombe Bridge was as yet unaltered, although another four-lane span would soon have to be built to accommodate the increase in traffic. The big pink and white, gabled Edwardian riverside villas still looked raffish – places where long-forgotten actresses and retired army officers had once lived in decorous sin; their windows still stared out at the island, flooded each year, with its bungalows and tangled gardens. The footpath, after the boat-houses, still led past flat meadows where cows stumbled down to the water. It was part of the scene of Leslie Titmuss's youth but as he walked he didn't think of standing barefoot in the squelching mud among the rushes or trying to catch tiddlers in a jam-jar. His childhood was a prison from which he had long escaped. Once over the wall he had wanted to put as much distance as possible between himself and that place of confinement. Although he made much of his father's values for political purposes, the memory of the old

man's life filled him with horror. The complacent acceptance of
a job with no prospects, the self-satisfied assurance that the good
things in life were not for the likes of him or of young Leslie,
the nightly routine of polishing off his tea, telling his wife that it
was 'very tasty' and falling asleep in the armchair – this was
the expected fate the young Titmuss had escaped by courtesy
of a head for accountancy and the voters of Hartscombe and
Worsfield South.

So he walked, a man now in his fifties, with a long, dark
overcoat flapping round his knees in spite of the spring sunshine.
He strode energetically, with no particular pleasure, as though
always late for a vital meeting. His hair had receded, leaving an
expanse of bony forehead; he was pale with a pallor inflicted by
overwork. He rarely smiled, although he was known to make
unexpected, often wounding remarks which were thought to be
jokes. Although he walked rapidly, his pale eyes missed nothing
of the riverside scene. The area, he saw, was ripe for development. There would have to be some pretty radical changes made
if Hartscombe were to meet the challenge of Europe. In Leslie
Titmuss's world nothing was allowed to stand still for very long.
Having made that decision without difficulty, he rang at the
door of one of the older riverside houses which bore the brass
plate of Cantellow & Bagley, Solicitors and Commissioners for
Oaths.

'I am afraid Lady Fanner is not well, not at all well. You will
be dropping in to see her, I suppose?'

'You suppose wrong,' Leslie answered.

Jackson Cantellow was a man who had conducted a long love-
affair with his own voice. So delighted was he with its rich and
rumbling tones that his account of his client's ill-health came out
as a recitative. 'Skin and bone,' he intoned with apparent enjoy-
ment. 'Skin and bone, I'm afraid. And that's the best that can be
said of her condition. I'm told she eats nothing.'

'But makes up for it by drinking?'

'Her bills for champagne at the Simcox off-licence. Phee–

nominal!' Cantellow hit a low note and then pursed his lips and put a finger to them. 'Tales out of school.' He seemed tempted to slap his own wrist.

'I expect you will tell me what I need to know.' The politician did not stoop to remind Jackson Cantellow how many of his clients were gambling on getting planning permission for various expensive projects, still less to hint at how many of such applications might be looked on favourably by his department.

'Lady Fanner, I'm told, eats nothing.' Jackson Cantellow's conversation proceeded by constant repetition, like an oratorio.

'What's that mean?'

'It means that I wouldn't expect her to last until . . .' He rolled his eyes to the ceiling. 'Until September.'

'September's a long time ahead.'

'Well' – the solicitor had chosen the month more for the resonance of its syllables than for any medical reason – 'she may go, of course, at any moment, but she always had this extraordinary energy.'

'For destruction?'

'As one of the family you knew her, of course, as well as anyone.'

'I'm not one of the family. I never felt one of the family. I suppose my son is, though. What's going to happen to the house?'

'The house?' Cantellow did his best to look innocent, as though he had never heard of Rapstone Manor.

'It's about all she has left. I suppose she's made a will of some sort?'

'I'm sure you wouldn't expect me' – Cantellow looked down modestly, as though he had been propositioned – 'to divulge the contents of any testamentary document of a client who, in spite of being a shadow, a shadow is how I would describe it, of what she was, after all a great beauty, rather before your time, of course, is still, to all intents and purposes, alive, so they tell me. The Rector visits regularly, although I believe he finds the task painful and sometimes humiliating. You wouldn't expect me to divulge anything further, would you?'

Leslie Titmuss didn't answer but kept his eyes fixed on Cantellow in the pale stare which he used to send his permanent staff out of the room in terror.

'Of course you would assume she had made wills. Various wills. In fact in her later years will-making has come upon her as a sort of disease.' Cantellow looked at his visitor. Surely he had now said enough, more than he should have, to satisfy his curiosity? But Leslie still stared at him and said nothing.

'Some of the wills were notably eccentric. Perverse, I might say. Particularly the last. Let us devoutly hope it will be the last.' Jackson Cantellow felt he had to fill in the silence and immediately regretted it.

'Now you've told me she hasn't left the house to my son, Nick.'

'I didn't say that!' Cantellow retreated in a panic. 'You mustn't put words into my mouth. I didn't say *what* she had done. The question, at any rate, is purely academic. It's really quite pointless to speculate. It's always a pleasure to see such a distinguished member of the Cabinet in the constituency, Mr Titmuss. But now if you'll excuse me . . .' He looked, in vain, for some important papers on his desk.

'Did you say *academic*?' Leslie pounced on the word and worried it as a terrier might worry a rat. 'Why did you say academic?'

'Well, shall we say not of enormous *practical* importance, in the circumstances.' Cantellow now knew he had said too much.

'The circumstances being, I suppose, that the whole caboodle is in hock to the bank. She's drunk away the equity and they'll foreclose as soon as her Ladyship is boxed up.'

'I didn't say that.' Cantellow looked pained at the idea that he could possibly have used words so brutal.

'You never could hold your tongue.' Leslie stood up now that the meeting was over. 'You've told me exactly what I needed to know. I'll find my own way out, Cantellow. All I can say is, thank God you're not my lawyer. I might as well conduct my private business on the "News at Ten".'

After his visit to the lawyer's office Leslie Titmuss was driven out of the reconstituted Hartscombe and deeper into his past. The car turned towards the Rapstone Valley. It passed the gates of the Manor but didn't stop. The next village was Skurfield, an untidy collection of houses strung out along the road, a grey place of corrugated-iron sheds, chickens roosting in the wreckage of old motor cars, pebble-dash walls and bungalows built with concrete blocks. Isolated from its neighbours stood 'The Spruces', a small, detached house with a scrubbed appearance, its privet hedge neatly trimmed and white paint shining against its red brick walls. Although there was no plaque to record the event, this was the house where, bellowing his lungs out in the upstairs bedroom, the Right Honourable Leslie Titmuss had first seen the light of day. It was the home of his mother Elsie, now over eighty, who spent her days dusting and polishing the labour-saving devices her son sent her and which she never used. She had resisted all his attempts to move her into larger and more luxurious accommodation.

'This place was good enough for your father,' Elsie said as she poured tea for her son, 'and it's good enough for me to end up in. Shouldn't I take a cup to the poor man outside?' She looked out pityingly towards the driver of the waiting Rover.

'He's used to waiting. I wanted to talk about something.'

'If you'd told me you were coming, I could've done you a steak and kidney. I know how you love your steak and kidney.' Elsie Titmuss had been in service as a cook with the Stroves of Picton Principal. Her pies had been the delight of the neighbour-hood shoots.

'Old mother Fanner, it seems, is on her way out at last.'

'You never had no time for her, did you, Leslie? May God forgive her.'

'God can do what he likes. I see absolutely no reason to forgive her. Ever. But if we manage to get hold of her house for Nicky . . .'

'Rapstone Manor? Whatever would young Nick do with that?'

'I don't know. Live in it, I suppose. Eventually. Anyway, that family owes my son something. I suppose you'd agree with that?'

'His mother should never have gone out with those bomb women. Not when she had a child to think of.' Elsie lifted the teapot, snug in its knitted cosy, and refilled her son's cup. They sat in silence for a moment, in comfortable agreement on the subject of the wickedness of Mrs Charlotte Titmuss, now long dead.

'Anyway, when Nicky gets it . . .'

'You seem quite sure of that.'

'Oh, yes. Absolutely sure. Well, there's rooms there. Floors of them. We could make a nice little conversion for you, Mother. There'd be a place for someone living-in, to look after you.'

'Living-in!' She spoke with contempt. 'I've done enough living-in not to want anyone else doing it for me. Livers-in take advantage. I know that. I've taken advantage in my time.' The memory clearly caused Elsie Titmuss satisfaction.

'We could make it very comfortable for you. Living in the Manor. Isn't that what you'd like?'

'Leslie Titmuss!' In her days as a cook, Elsie had been greatly desired by all the male inside- and outside-workers and, it was said, by members of the Strove family also. When she looked at her son she was a still pretty and flirtatious octogenarian. 'I'm not going to have it. Not from her Ladyship or from you or anyone. And I'm not leaving this house, not till I join your father in Rapstone churchyard. Don't move me out of here. Will you promise me?'

Leslie wasn't smiling but he thought, at the time, that he meant it when he said, 'I promise you, Mother.'

So the immediate future of the big house at Rapstone remained unsettled, which was what gave Leslie Titmuss his great opportunity, and also what brought him more trouble than he had had since the days when he first entered politics and was pushed unceremoniously into the river during his first Young Conservative dinner dance.

'Fallowfield Country Town. A proposed development of ten thousand houses. It will entail a new commuter high-speed rail-link and the construction of a spur to the motorway. Architect-designed town centre, with civic buildings, sports and leisure complex. Multi-storey shopping facilities with extensive car parking. Pedestrian walkways and traffic-free zones. Site: between the towns of Worsfield and Hartscombe, making use of hitherto undeveloped areas such as the village of Skurfield and the Rapstone Valley' – Ken Cracken was laughing as he read out these specifications in his room at H.E.A.P.

At a desk in the corner Joyce Timberlake, his political adviser, wearing a neat black suit and glasses, was evolving a scheme, to be discussed with her opposite number at the Home Office, for the sale of specified National Trust houses for use as privatized youth custody centres.

'What's so funny about that?'

'The Rapstone Valley. It's the Secretary of State's back garden. That's what's so funny.'

'His back garden? Leslie sold his place in the country, didn't he? Doesn't he have a flat in Waterside Mansions?' Joyce made it her business to know most things. Leslie Titmuss had disposed of the big house he had bought at Picton Principal, where his mother had once cooked, shortly after Charlotte's death. To have had a wife suspected of being an anti-bomb Worsfield Heath woman, coupled with farming interests, would have been, he felt sure, too much for his political career. So he had managed, with some skill and much expedition, to disown them both.

'He's still involved in Rapstone. His mother's house is in the next village. And his old mother-in-law lives there. I wonder how they'd like to wake up next to Tesco's in Fallowfield Country Town. It might be interesting to hand our Leslie a political hot potato. See where he drops it.'

'You want to be a bit careful of Leslie,' Joyce warned him. 'He's used to winning.'

'Oh, he won't know who handed it to him. It'll come as a planning decision. Through all the normal channels. Anyway, there's another excellent reason for laying down a bit of concrete on the Rapstone Valley.'

'What?'

'It's where that bearded lunatic made us get up off the grass.'

'You mean,' Joyce asked, although this was the sort of matter they hardly ever discussed at work, 'when you were hot to trot?'

'Yes.' Ken Cracken wasn't smiling. 'That's what I mean exactly.'

CHAPTER FOUR

'So you're a widow?'

'Well, not really.'

It was a word Jenny Sidonia never used, not under any circumstances. The fact that Tony Sidonia with his sad, dark eyes – the eyes, his ex-girlfriend Sue Bramble had once said, of a lemur after a passionate weekend – his untidy greying hair and his untidier tweed suits and unbuttoned collars, his exhaustive knowledge of the Renaissance Popes, his long, anxious face and his rare smile, eagerly awaited, had left her never to return was something which, like most unpleasant facts, she chose to ignore. She didn't forget it; she hid it away in some remote cupboard of her mind, like an unwelcome Christmas present, and couldn't always remember exactly where she'd put it. Tony was with her because she thought about him constantly and she never thought about him as dead. Above all she'd never seen herself as a widow. A widow was a ridiculous figure, dumpy, dressed in black, sexually frustrated and on the look-out for another man. 'The Merry Widow' – that was something she would have hated to be.

'Not really what?'

'Not really a widow.'

Her neighbour was pale and stared at her with colourless eyes. He had been asking her questions with great intensity but he didn't seem to be interested in her as a woman. She was used to men looking at her hopefully as they went through their old routines or pretended to be fascinated by her in order to excite some sort of interest in themselves. The strange man on her left asked, 'What sort of an answer is that?'

'I'm sorry.' It was something that Jenny said a lot, smiling, although she didn't feel any need to apologize.

'I mean about your husband. Is he dead or isn't he?'

It was, she supposed, a fair question. Tony had given her so much and most of all a sense of fairness. He had brought her standards of truthfulness and decency. Now that the question was put to her so bluntly she had, in all honesty, to answer it.

'He's dead,' she admitted and was struck again, as she was whenever she allowed herself to be, by the bleakness of her situation. 'I suppose you could say that.'

'Well' – the man beside her attacked his food, satisfied – 'now we know.'

On the other side of the table the Master of St Joseph's, in whose lodgings the carefully calculated lunch-party was taking place, looked at the couple with glee. It had been a brilliant idea to sit the Secretary of State next to Jenny Sidonia. She had, above all things, a talent for making men feel that they had her entire attention, even though her thoughts were far away in some private and distant country of her own. Although fragile, she always managed to look healthy, her eyes shining, and she appeared to be continually amused, even when her thoughts were sad. Sir Willoughby Blane wasn't above squeezing the knees of many of the ladies he sat beside at lunch and he sometimes received unexpected encouragement; but he had never dared lay a straying hand on Jenny. Her good looks were awe-inspiring, even to a marine biologist who had made a lifetime's study of the prawn and who regarded human beings as only a little more developed than the minor crustacea. Jenny had been invited to that sunny Sunday lunch-table not to be flirted with by the Master but to charm the Secretary of State and later, when they were strolling round the great mulberry tree, the Master might do a little trade with the Right Honourable Leslie

Titmuss on the matter of government support for an addition to the college, to be christened – whatever else? – the Willoughby Blane Biology Library. Politicians like Leslie were, so Sir Willoughby felt, alien beings, creatures from outer space, far from the crumbling walls and the soggy lawns of Oxford. Some heads of colleges would flinch at the name of Titmuss; they would mutter despairing imprecations and hastily change the subject as though the topic were somehow obscene. Not so the Master of St Joseph's. He prided himself that he could do business with a potentate so foreign, rather as the government boasted it could do business with the Soviet President. Whatever our differences, he was prepared to say, we're both practical sorts of chaps, aren't we? No doubt the transaction would be easier after Mr Titmuss had spent luncheon in close proximity to Jenny Sidonia.

'Why do you get asked here?' Leslie was interrogating her as though she were under suspicion; but, away from the subject of her personal tragedy, Jenny seemed to find the experience comic. 'Are you anything to do with this lot?' The people round the table – Hector and Gudrun Lessore, an ex-ambassador and his wife, a Liberal peer, someone in publishing, her Honour Judge Phyllis Durst and her silent husband, a smattering of dons and their wives – were all older than Jenny and yet, when she came to look at them, she supposed they were her friends.

'They're my friends,' she said.

'They don't look your sort.'

'What do you think my sort is, exactly?'

'A bit better than this, I should have said.'

Their fellow guests deliberately avoided looking at the Cabinet Minister, rather as people avoid staring at those disfigured or in some way maimed. Before Leslie arrived they had been denouncing his government, but now he was among them they talked about books, or the theatre, or the heads of colleges who weren't present.

'It must be terrific to be the wife of a head of college,' Judge Durst said. She was a highly perfumed lady whose flat, pink face emerged like a cutlet from an elaborate, white ruffled collar. 'You get put next to all the male heads at dinners.'

'And what if you're a male head of college?' Willoughby Blane asked her in his old aunty's posh Edinburgh accent, his bald head on one side, his hands clasped across his stomach.

'That must be terrible. You get put next to their wives!'

'Willoughby often asks me to his lunches. And Tony . . . That's my husband. Of course, Tony taught here,' Jenny explained patiently to Leslie Titmuss.

'*Was* your husband.'

'What?'

'You mean Tony *was* your husband.'

'Oh, yes. Of course.' For once it seemed simpler to say it. 'When he was alive.'

Leslie nodded and for a moment they sat silent. Jenny wondered whether to turn to the ex-ambassador on her left, but he was involved with the Lady Judge and it didn't seem altogether right to abandon her pale neighbour, who looked lost. To leave him now, she suddenly felt, would be like ditching a blind man you have helped half-way across the street.

'Why're *you* here?' she asked him. 'Apart from the obvious reason.'

'What's the obvious reason?'

'Well. Willoughby's always on the look-out for someone who'll help the college.' Jenny was in no way a party to the Master's ploy; he had used her as an attractive antelope tied up to lure the tiger within range of the rifle. 'And I'm sure you have terrific influence and all that sort of thing.'

'I'm here because of my son,' Leslie Titmuss said. 'Young Nick is up. About to do his finals, in fact. And I didn't have to offer to build another wing on the place to get him in here, either.'

'I'm sure you didn't. About to do his finals? That must be exciting.'

'Finals in English? I don't think that excites me much.'

'Perhaps it excites your son.'

'He knew English before he got here. Even I know English. I don't know why he can't learn something that'll help him get on.'

'Get on where, exactly?'

'Well, to where I've got. Somewhere near it. Nothing wrong with that for an ambition, is there?'

'No. No, I'm sure not. Nothing wrong at all.' Jenny was used to men who begged her for reassurance and, if possible, praise. She gave it generously, knowing what was expected of her, so that at the end of such a lunch as this, she felt physically tired and her arms seemed to be exhausted from massaging so many egos. The man beside her clearly needed no such therapy. He was convinced that where he had got was everybody's distant, usually unattainable, goal in life.

'I told him, I can't see how reading English is going to be the slightest help to the economy. It's not going to produce jobs. It's going to do damn all for the prosperity of the country. Isn't that what these places should be for?'

'Is it?' She looked at him, smiling, feeling that she owed it to Tony Sidonia's memory to take some sort of a stand. 'I'm not *absolutely* sure about that. My husband spent his life with Renaissance Popes. I don't suppose that did much for the economy.'

'Renaissance *Popes*?' Leslie looked at her, incredulous.

'Of course, they behaved appallingly, but for some reason he felt able to forgive them. He was awfully good at forgiving people. He said you had to do a lot of that, when you took on ecclesiastical history.'

'Ecclesiastical history,' Leslie said with disgust. 'What luxury!'

'Luxury!' Jenny was suddenly angry, as she had it in her to be. The accusation was absurd and entirely unfair to Tony. The extraordinary man beside her spoke as though her husband had devoted his life to fast cars, drugs and exotic women and hadn't

28

spent his holidays in the Vatican Library in order to produce *Humanism or Indulgence? The Papacy 1492–1534*. 'What's *not* a luxury? Learning how to operate some sort of giant computer so we can all have our bank balances flashed on the screen every moment of the day and get pre-cooked Thai dinners sent round without even having to go down to the shops? Is that how Tony ought to have spent his life? Well, I'm sorry but I really can't agree with that.'

'I don't expect anyone round this table would. Not until they wake up to the world we're living in.'

'Jenny!' Sir Willoughby called to her like some disapproving nanny who has spotted two children, invited to make friends, about to pull each other's hair in a corner. 'Will you be at Covent Garden on Monday?'

'I don't think so. What is it?'

'Placido. In a brand new *Ballo*. This Greek producer woman,' the Master remembered, 'has set it all in Stalin's Kremlin. Should be rather fun.'

'The love duet!' The Lady Judge sighed unexpectedly on the Cabinet Minister's left. 'Don't you simply adore *Un ballo in maschera*?'

'Never seen it,' Leslie told her. 'I'm not a great one for dancing.'

'Dancing?' Gudrun Lessore, the ex-ambassador's wife – a large, glacial woman Sir Hector had met when posted to Iceland and had brought home rather to everyone's regret – was the only one daring enough to ask.

'Yes. I know nothing about your ballet, *In maskera*.'

'The garden!' The Master stood, as though announcing the treat for which they'd all been longing. 'What about a small, digestive turn around the mulberry tree? It really is looking rather fine.'

Then, as they trooped down the narrow, dark staircase of the lodgings and out into the sunshine, Jenny, walking beside Leslie, took his arm. What did it matter if he couldn't tell a Verdi opera from a ballet, even if he confused *Traviata* with *Les Sylphides?* She had seen him surrounded by faces which just, only just, concealed their owners' mockery and contempt. They had a story to tell, which would be laughed at in all the country houses and at all the high tables they visited, about the incredible Philistines in control of their government; but then government was, perhaps, always a matter for Philistines. She put her arm into his as a sign that she disapproved of their cruelty and because she imagined, wrongly as it so happened, that Leslie had been made to feel awkward and miserable by it. Her sense of fairness was outraged and she lavished the sympathy on him which her late husband had even been able to feel for the Borgia Pope. It was a moment, as they went down the dark staircase together, which was the start of all their troubles.

'You and I –' The Master now had his hand on Leslie's arm, a contact which he found, unlike the gentle touch of Jenny Sidonia, irritating and which he wished to shake off as rapidly as possible. 'We both look at education in the same way, from an entirely practical point of view.'

'Practical? I thought you specialized in shrimps?' Leslie Titmuss was nothing if not well informed.

'Crustacea. The whole range from the lobster to the woodlouse. Not forgetting the minute pelagic copepods, useful little blighters, who swim in mile-wide shoals and guide whalers to the most profitable fishing-grounds.'

'Didn't you read my Birmingham speech? We've come out in favour of the whale.'

And your concern for the larger cetaceous mammals, Sir Willoughby thought, may, I suppose, distract attention from your plans to concrete over the South of England. It is the smallest possible concession you can make to the growing, and irritating, army of greens. What he actually said was, 'There's scope for a study of labour-intensive prawn cultivation. On a strictly commercial basis, of course. Now *there*'s a valuable food source for you!' He was one of those who believed that Leslie's political supporters never entered a restaurant without ordering prawn cocktail, followed by steak 'and all the trimmings', to be topped off with a liberal helping of Black Forest gâteau. Delighted by his private gastronomic joke, he giggled in his most aunty-like way. 'Labour-intensive food production. Isn't that the name of your game? Now, all that know-how needs proper technological back-up, which is why we at St Joseph's feel that the Blane Library is going to be so enormously cost-effective. Most of the information would be computer-stored so it won't have to be an *enormous* building.'

'I saw my son this morning. We had a drink together. In the Randolph.'

'Did you? Oh, good. Now *we* know, *you* know, *I* know, that enough food can be produced to feed the ten thousand by a couple of men and a computer. Particularly in coastal waters. Farming land is just a luxury nowadays. And I'm sure you chaps have plenty of other uses for it.'

'Getting on all right, is he? Nick doesn't tell me much.' Across the low wall which bounded the Master's gardens was the wider territory open to the undergraduates. They lay together, kissing, rolling over like baby seals, pretending to read their notes, pretending it was summer, listening to their ghetto blasters. Leslie couldn't see Nick among them. Where was he? Shut up in his room doing – what exactly? He had boasted, around the corridors of power, when Nick had got into Oxford. No doubt his boy would join the Union and the Conservative Association; the political and business contacts which Leslie had made with such difficulty would come easily to his son. He expected to hear in the mutter of conversation before Cabinet meetings, 'Your Nick's invited me to come down and speak at Oxford. Suppose I'd better keep in with a new generation of Titmusses.' He had prepared speeches, apparently half angry and envious, in reality proud and even adoring, which he would make to Nicholas: 'I never had a head start like I'm giving you,

Nick. I had to fight my way up, every inch of the way. I'd've saved years of hard work if I'd've had your chances. You've got it with jam on, son, and don't you ever forget it.' But because Nick showed no sign whatever of taking advantage of his position, as he seemed to have joined nothing, made no speeches, invited no Cabinet Ministers, these carefully prepared sentences seemed inappropriate. So they had sat that morning in the hotel bar with Leslie, determined to be one of the boys, nursing a pint of bitter, and Nicholas staring, secretly smiling into a Coke, and they had shared long periods of silence.

'I may have some good news for you soon, Nicky.'

'What sort of good news?'

'Something you may be coming in for. A house.'

'A house?' Nick looked at his father, amazed, as though he were offering him something totally impractical, like an ocean-going yacht or a château on the Loire.

'It's somewhere you always liked. Somewhere you were always taking off to. On your bike.'

'I don't think I need a house.'

'Not yet awhile. But in time, of course. Well, there're not many better investments.'

'What would I do with a house? I don't know where I'm going to be. I don't know that at all.' Nick still smiled.

'You never know what you're going to need. I wanted you to know. Something's going to come your way. That's all I can say about it.'

'I don't know what this place is doing for Nick,' Leslie told the Master of St Joseph's later as they walked across the garden. 'Hardly what I expected.'

'I've made inquiries about him, of course.'

'I hope you've found out more than I have.'

'He's a hard worker. I do hear that about him. And well liked. Everyone seems to agree about that. Young Fanner is very well liked.'

'Fanner?' The Minister stood still beside the great mulberry tree. The laughter and the thumpings from the ghetto blasters and the subdued gossip of the other guests walking behind him died away. He seemed to be listening to other voices, coming at him from the past. 'Why the hell do you call him Fanner?'

'Stupid of me.' Sir Willoughby smiled. 'I'm sure some of his friends call him that. I must have heard it somewhere. Is that not part of his name? Not double-barrelled, is it?'

'It certainly isn't.' The Minister's tone was icy, and help for the Blane Biology Library faded into the distance. 'There's absolutely nothing double-barrelled about my Nick.'

CHAPTER FIVE

'I'm bored with dying. Let's have a cocktail party,' Lady Fanner said. 'For God's sake, let's organize a cocker!'

The Reverend Kevin Bulstrode had flirted, during his first curacy, with the idea of joining a mission to Central Africa. He had felt a calling to care for the sick, educate the children, comfort the persecuted in some distant land, but fear of being hacked to pieces by machetes on a hot, African night had deterred him. He had set his eyes on a less adventurous path and become the Rector of Rapstone. Now, as he sat by Grace Fanner's bed trying to decipher the spidery numbers in her ancient address book and dial them for her, his thoughts turned with longing to any dangerous spot on the Zimbabwe border. The fragile but alarming old woman demanded his full attention. She telephoned the Rectory day and night to call him to her bedside. He had a terrible fear that, unless he obeyed her, she might contrive to leave her bed in a final burst of manic energy and appear, her nightdress fluttering against her skeletal body, in church to interrupt the service. Visiting the dying was no doubt a pastoral duty, but he hadn't taken orders to become the unpaid secretary, champagne pourer and telephone operator to an old woman whose accounts of high life in the thirties, at one time entertaining, had been so often repeated that he now knew them all by heart.

'Betsy von Trump. Isn't she there? It's Kensington somewhere.'

'It's ringing. There's no answer.'

'Probably tucking up with some lover-boy. Who's next?'

'Jack Annersley-Vachell.'

'Well, he can't be dead. Not Jack. That wouldn't be his line at all. Telephone up, why don't you?'

Kevin's finger got to work again. The instrument whined. Jack Annersley-Vachell, whoever he might have been, was no longer obtainable.

'What do I say to these people, if I get hold of them?'

'Tell them to come down for a cocker, of course. If they don't get their skates on I'll be gone, and most likely the house'll be gone with me. Tell them that. If I know Jack, he'll go anywhere for a glass of Bollinger and a couple of cheese straws.'

Grace Fanner was right about one thing. Rapstone Manor was going with her. Centuries ago, at the time of the Civil War, when the Cavalier Fanners fought the Roundhead Stroves of Picton Principal, their lands stretched far from the valley and down to the riverside near Hartscombe. A Fanner cousin, a man with a head for politics, had joined the Parliament army as a wise insurance against the King's defeat, which had therefore brought no loss of family acres. At the Restoration a number of Strove farms were added by a grateful monarch and the eighteenth-century Fanners could ride for almost a day without leaving their boundaries. Gambling during the Regency, and a vague lack of interest in money in later years, had considerably reduced the family's estate and by the time Grace's husband had died it was owned by farmers who had once been Fanner tenants. Only that sacred area of wood and chalk downs, bought by S.C.R.A.P. as a place of safety for the stone curlew and the Duke of Burgundy's fritillary butterfly, remained unavailable for commercial exploitation.

But still, as Grace planned her final party, the cultivated land and pastures around her looked much as they had done in her husband's, and his father's and grandfather's day. Only the garish yellow fields of oil-seed rape were different and the old farm-labourers' cottages, converted with open-plan kitchens and extensions containing granny flats and saunas, had been sold off to bankers and men in satellite television. And they, appearing at weekends in their waxed jackets, driving their Range Rovers, were loudly eager to maintain the rustic appearance of their neighbourhood.

Market forces, however, were sweeping up the Rapstone Valley and secret plans were being made to change it as it had not been changed since the Fanners, with a commercial sense not much apparent in their subsequent history, had fought on both sides in the Civil War. The scattered farms had, without anyone paying too much attention, amalgamated and formed a consortium. They had approached Kempenflatts, the builders, a firm which had done well erecting multi-storey car parks, communications systems factories and office blocks. Kempenflatts had long wished to attract new business, change their image and 'go into the countryside'. Accordingly they formed a wholly owned subsidiary, Fallowfield Enterprises Ltd. Fallowfield was prominent on the list of subscribers to all societies out to protect the environment and contributed largely to Friends of the Planet, Friends of the Maypole (The Folk Art Preservation Society), Friends of the Rain Forests and Friends of the Leopard. It extended the hand of friendship to the farmers of the Rapstone Valley and paid them a handsome sum for an option to buy their land in the event of planning permission being granted for the building of Fallowfield Country Town. If all went well and the scheme were finally to be approved by the Secretary of State, the farmers would make half a million pounds an acre, a sum unattainable by slaving over oil-seed rape or battery hens.

These seismic movements in the countryside had not yet touched Rapstone Manor, and its small area of surrounding parkland, as Lady Fanner planned her cocktail party and Kev the Rev. made telephone calls to people, most of whom seemed to be either dead or in hiding. When he had, at long last, managed to escape from her bedside and the nurse, whose services added so considerably to Lady Fanner's overdraft, was downstairs making tea, the invalid, stimulated by champagne and telephone calls, suddenly jerked herself out of bed. The sitting-room! It was a long time since she had seen it but was it, could she be sure it was, in a fit state for a cocker? Was it warm, was it comfortable, were the cushions plumped on the sofa and was the chandelier sparkling? It must be as it was when they had their first parties, before the war ended and everything got so dull. She had to make sure. Her small, white feet, dangling from the bedside, searched in panic for her slippers. Then, with her lips pursed and her hands held out in front of her as though the room were dark, she made the long journey to the door, which seemed enormously heavy as she tugged it open.

Heaven alone knew how she got down the stairs. She was like a marionette operated by a drunken puppeteer. She floated, she stumbled, she almost fell in a pile of dislocated limbs. By an extraordinary effort she crossed the marble hallway and pushed open the sitting-room door. She switched on a light and what she saw caused her to cry out and bite her knuckles.

There was no chandelier, dim or sparkling; a dusty bulb dangled from a wire in the middle of the ceiling. Everything of value had gone, including the Georgian bookcases, the console tables, the Chesterfield, the claw-footed wing-chair in which Sir Nicholas had sat after dinner and infuriated her by falling asleep. What remained, mostly wickerwork covered in chipped white paint, she seemed to remember from the conservatory or the garden. What she didn't remember were the bedside conversations with Jackson Cantellow during which he had given her the news, which she had done her best not to hear, that a great deal of furniture had to be sent to auction to satisfy the ever more anxious demands of the caring West Country Bank.

She stood, swaying, wide-eyed and dismayed, until she saw, on a table which had lived somewhere quite different (the scullery, the potting-shed?), her old wind-up gramophone. It was among a clutter of unsaleable objects, broken lamps, cracked decanters and family photographs. She had used it often, particularly to play her favourite record made by Pinky Pinkerton, her immaculate spade from the Café de Paris, who had sat at a white piano and added, in his black treacly voice, a special verse for her in 'You're the Top!'. She made for this beloved object and clung to it. In her head she sang, in a high, girlish voice, her own particular words:

> You're the top!
> You can trump the A–ace.
> You're the top!
> You're the Lady Gra–ace . . .

but no sound came from her. She managed half a turn of the handle and then fell, as though the wires which held her up had been dropped at last.

When Grace Fanner died, her few friends and numerous relatives felt that some invaluable subject of gossip and entertainment had been removed from their lives. Her funeral was well attended and the Reverend Kevin Bulstrode conducted the service with considerable relief. He made use of all his long-prepared phrases and said that she was 'a genuine character', 'one of the Old Brigade' and 'never one to suffer fools gladly'.

She was buried in Rapstone churchyard and whether her grave would look over damp fields and dripping woodlands, or at the bleak prospect of a multi-storey car park and another pedestrian shopping precinct, was a matter which the Right Honourable Leslie Titmuss, as the Seceretary of State for Housing, Ecological Affairs and Planning, would eventually have to decide. Lady Fanner's future was in the hands of H.E.A.P.

CHAPTER SIX

'Some people. People with plenty of money who can enjoy the privileges of living in the "green field areas" will talk a lot about not disturbing the peace and tranquillity of the English countryside. Strangely enough these are often the same whingers and belly-achers who criticize the government for not providing enough houses, who accuse us of lack of compassion, or of not being "fair". Well, if they're so keen on fairness, why don't they want to share their little corner of England with ordinary folk who have worked and saved enough to buy a decent, newly built house of their own in these privileged areas? [Applause.] "Oh, no," say the green welly brigade of the Countryside Clubs and the Rural Preservation Societies, "we want the government to be fair, but please, not in our back garden!" [Laughter and applause.] My old father had a word for their sort. Dogs, he would have called them, in the manger. [Prolonged applause.]

'I would say to them, I would say this. Don't come to me in your tweed hats ... [Laughter.] ... and lecture me. I know all about England's green and pleasant land. I was born there! [Applause.] In a little two-up and two-down where my father died and my old mother, bless her, still lives. We didn't take in *Country Life*. [Laughter.] We didn't have a herb garden or breed up pheasants for the pleasure of their ritual execution. We didn't have a woman from the village in to do the washing. My mother did that herself in the old copper.

[Applause.] I got to know about country life by cutting down nettles in the Rectory garden for sixpence a day and a glass of ginger-beer, if the Rector's wife was feeling generous. [Laughter.] My mother got to know about country life by cooking steak and kidney pie for the local big-wigs. And it's no reflection at all on this five-star eatery, ladies and gentlemen, to say that my mother could have taught them a thing or two when it comes to steak and kidney! I knew what the English countryside meant to me. It meant damned hard work and a decent home for anyone with the determinaton to save up for it. [Loud applause.] That's more than the rich Socialists who live in their converted farmhouses will ever understand. Here's what I would say to the Rural Preservation Society which means the Keep the Other Folk Away Society. Oh, we shall have whiners, ladies and gentlemen. We shall have whingers. We shall have petitions and we shall have protests and we may get a vote against us in the House of Lords. But a wind of change is blowing through the English countryside. And let me say this to you. While I'm at H.E.A.P. there shall be very few No Go areas for the operation of the free market economy. Thank you.' [Prolonged applause mixed with 'Hear, hear!', 'Sock it to them!' from the partially intoxicated lady wife of one of the guests, and a solitary attempt to start the singing of 'For he's a jolly good fellow', quickly silenced by the Chairman, who rose to thank the Secretary of State for his wise and genuine understanding of the problems of the construction industry.]

Leslie Titmuss sat at the top table, with a winged collar sawing at his neck like a blunt execution, and, his speech over, he thought about the past. He thought about it particularly because the Chairman of the United Construction and Developers Association (U.C.D.A.), who was making such a gracious speech of thanks, was that same Christopher Kempenflatt who had led the baying band of ex-public schoolboys who had pushed the young Leslie into the river. It was Kempenflatt also who had, many years ago, invited the young Titmuss to go into a property business with him, a venture which had left Leslie with enough money to devote the rest of his life to politics and Kempenflatt temporarily in debt. It goes without saying that neither man mentioned these past events, although no doubt they had not forgotten them.

'It was a tremendous speech,' Kempenflatt said as he sat down to renewed applause beside his guest. 'They loved every word of it. I hope you've enjoyed the evening.'

'I always enjoy a speech.' Leslie never tired of the way he could affect an audience.

'Because you're so good at it.'

'I have an uncanny knack of bringing out the baser instincts in any gathering. That's what the Leader of the so-called Opposition said about me.'

'That's not true.'

'Isn't it? I rather hoped it was,' Leslie Titmuss said seriously, and Kempenflatt paused, a lighted match in his cupped hand on the way to his cigar. Then he laughed at what he could only assume was a joke. 'Well, you certainly gave them what they wanted to hear.'

'I like it better, though, when I give them what they *don't* want to hear. And they have to take it. That's when politics begins to get interesting.'

Kempenflatt, a big, square-shouldered man, an old rowing Blue fast going to seed, tried to establish a little more common ground with the Secretary of State that he would need when Fallowfield Country Town came up for planning permission. 'I'm sorry to hear about poor old Grace.'

'Are you? Can't say I am.'

'Well, I suppose it was a merciful release.'

'About the only merciful thing she ever did.'

'I forgot. Your wife never got on with her mother.'

'Lady Fanner thought her daughter ugly and me common. I needn't tell you what we thought of her.'

'What's going to become of the house?' As soon as he had asked it, Kempenflatt regretted the question. His guest of honour looked at him, stony-faced and silent. Ken Cracken, Leslie's second-in-command, whom Kempenflatt called a 'personal friend', had advised him to say nothing about the proposals to 'develop' the Rapstone Valley until he gave the word that the time was ripe. Ripeness was clearly not yet.

'She's only just cold in the ground,' Leslie said reproachfully. 'Isn't it a little early to be talking about that?'

'Smashing speech that Leslie made at the U.C.D.A. dinner,' said Joyce Timberlake.

'Yes. The old boy was terrific. From our point of view.' Ken Cracken put his hands behind his head, leant back in his desk chair and looked at his political adviser with every sign of satisfaction.

'What's that meant to mean?'

'Just that now he's said all that, he'll find it very difficult to backtrack. Even in a difficult case.'

'What sort of difficult case?'

'I mean difficult. For him personally.'

'He doesn't know yet? About that new country town at Rapstone?'

'He hasn't said anything. And I'm not telling him. Yet. I'm worried about Leslie, though. He seems to have got culture.'

'You mean he's read a book?' Joyce, who had a degree in the History of Art from Exeter, was often contemptuous of the Secretary of State's reputation for reading nothing but Green Papers and Cabinet minutes.

'Worse than that. He asked me about the ballet.'

'Oh, Christmas!' Joyce, even as a political adviser, sometimes went too far. 'I don't fancy seeing him in tights!'

'The funny thing' – Ken Cracken didn't laugh, but then he rarely did – 'is that he asked what was so amusing about the ballet, *In Maskera*. I was able to tell him it wasn't a ballet at all.

42

It's an opera.' Ken's friend Christopher Kempenflatt often invited him to his firm's box at Covent Garden and so he was not altogether uninformed about such matters. 'You know, he has been behaving rather strangely.'

'Why? What did he say when you told him that? About the opera, I mean?'

'He said, "Bastards!" And that's all he said.'

'What on earth is it?'

'Well, I suppose it's a flower.'

'It looks dead.'

'It looks laid out. Embalmed.'

'In that awful little plastic coffin.'

The women speaking were Jenny Sidonia and her friend Sue Bramble. Sue had been, was perfectly well known to have been, the girlfriend of Tony before Jenny married him. They had, however, liked and trusted each other for a long time. Sue had told Jenny she was absolutely right for Tony, and Jenny had felt that the other woman, five or six years older than herself, had understood her husband whereas she could only love him. Now, in the London flat Jenny had bought when she sold the spiky, Victorian Gothic house in North Oxford in which she had been happy, they had their heads together. Sue was blonde, freckled, slightly sun-tanned — even in the most unlikely weather — went hunting and smoked like a chimney. Jenny was dark, delicately boned, ivory-skinned, amused and slightly aghast as she looked at the object which they were examining, nothing more or less than a single orchid lying on a bed of velvet in a see-through box, tied up with gold ribbon.

'It's got some sort of pin up its bum,' Sue discovered.

'Perhaps it's a corsage.' Jenny made the appalling suggestion.

'A what?'

'Well. Something you pin on. For going out to dinner. Don't some men send them to some women? Before they take them out, I mean?'

'Some men? I don't think,' Jenny's friend said with certainty, 'that Mr Sidonia would ever have sent a girl anything like that.'

'Tony wouldn't,' Jenny agreed.

'Well, who would?'

Jenny said nothing.

'Have you any idea?'

'Some idea. Yes.'

'Not that ghastly little politician?' Sue, who was not easily shocked, sounded as though she would rather have heard that her friend was considering an evening out with a bisexual Californian drug addict with sado-masochistic tendencies.

'Well, he's not so little. Quite tall, as it so happens.'

'I don't believe it.'

'Why don't you? I told you he telephoned. He said, would I like a bite of dinner?'

'Typical.'

'What?'

'"A bite of dinner". How typical of him to say that.'

'You can't say it's typical. You don't know him.'

'Aren't I lucky!'

'Probably.' Jenny looked gloomily at the orchid lying in state.

'You didn't say you'd go?'

Jenny nodded guiltily and Sue asked, '*Why*, in the name of God?'

'It was that lunch at Oxford. They were laughing at him because he didn't know about opera.'

'There must be millions of people who don't know about opera. But you don't have to go out to dinner with all of them.'

'I suppose I was sorry for him.'

'But that's the worst possible reason.'

'Yes,' Jenny admitted it, contrite.

'What on earth would Tony have said?'

'I suppose he'd've said it was a bit of a joke.'

'He'd certainly have laughed. Tony would.'

'But not to his face. Tony wouldn't have done a thing like that. It was awful really. Poor Mr Titmuss was looking round

44

the table and he had no idea he'd said anything wrong.' Jenny was carefully removing the orchid from its box. Sue looked at her with growing incredulity. 'You're not going to pin that thing on you?'

'Well. I suppose I'd better.'

'Why on earth?'

'I don't want to seem rude.'

'You take my advice. There are times when seeming rude's the best possible thing to do.'

Later, when Jenny Sidonia was changed and ready, Sue, looking out of the window of the flat, saw a large black car draw up.

'Something's arrived.'

'He said he'd send a car for me.'

'It looks like a hearse.'

'I think it belongs to the government.'

'That's so much worse! Oh, Jenny, what *have* you got yourself into?'

So, feeling apologetic, Jenny went off on her first and, her friend sincerely hoped, her last date with Leslie Titmuss.

CHAPTER SEVEN

Hector Bolitho Jones, warden of the Rapstone Nature Area and servant of the Society for Conservation, Rural and Arboreal Protection (S.C.R.A.P.), had not always been green. It would be true to say that he came of a shooting family. Hector's father had been a gamekeeper on the Rapstone Manor estate; he was a large, gentle Scot who occupied a cottage which had been expanded after his death. Part of it now housed the Area's audio-visual instruction material; the other half was used as living accommodation for the warden. When Hector was a boy, in the long-gone days of rabbit pie and outside lavatories, when many of the cottages were still inhabited by woodmen, gardeners and farm workers, he had followed his father about his work and at an early age he could name the wild flowers, identify the butterflies and predict the weather with astonishing accuracy. He had also assisted in the more bloodstained part of his father's profession. He took strangled rabbits from snares, he baited rat traps, he hung up on a branch, like a gallows, those magpies which the gamekeeper had shot for poaching pheasants' eggs and wanted displayed as a dire warning to other criminally minded birds. He would go out with old Jones on moonlit nights and stalk deer in the depths of the woods and, at that time, he had no objection to venison steaks or even a dish of deer's liver for his tea. He helped beat the woods when the pheasants were old enough for execution and piled up the corpses of birds shot by the Fanner family and their guests. He was a stocky and unusually silent child who shared his father's devotion to animals. The difference between them was that, while old Jones's concern was to provide the wild creatures he cared for with a dramatic and splendid death, the young Hector wished above all to preserve their lives. It was this devotion to animals which had caused him to rage at Ken Cracken and Joyce Timberlake who had, when returning from a lunch in the country with Christopher Kempenflatt, felt the urgent need to be alone on a hillside.

Hector had worked hard at school and, to his father's considerable pride, taken a degree in forestry at Worsfield University. When the Rapstone Nature Area was set up he seemed, as a local boy who had been born in these woods, an ideal candidate for warden. The public career of Hector Bolitho Jones was upwardly mobile.

His private life was not so successful. Whilst a student he had met a girl named Daphne Bridgewater at the folk club. She had come from a large family, was naturally gregarious and studied sociology. She thought that Hector, with his large, perpetually anxious eyes, was deeply concerned about a number of causes. She was also, as she would have been the first to admit, the sort that went for beards and Hector's had sprouted profusely since his first year at college. They went on several hunt sabotage expeditions together and for long walks in the country. When she suggested that they visited Rapstone Wood at bluebell time and lay down together on the misty blue carpet, however, he wouldn't hear of it. 'There's wildlife there,' he said, 'and who are we to disturb it?' At the time she liked him all the better for his caring nature.

When they were married and living in the extension to old Jones's converted cottage, and especially after their daughter, Joan (named after Joan Baez, a heroine of the folk club), had turned four and was old enough to play in the woodlands, Daphne became disenchanted with her lot as a warden's wife. The trees seemed to grow rapidly and crowded round their home, shutting out light from the kitchen windows. Hector was away from early morning until long after nightfall, in the woods or clearing scrub on the grassland. In the shadowy kitchen there was always some animal recovering: a tiny fox cub, perhaps, that had to be fed milk from a baby's bottle, or a young caged barn owl with a broken wing. Hector seemed more and more reluctant to leave the Nature Area and his passion for rain forests (everywhere felled to make way for beef cattle) ruled out a Whopperburger after the pictures at the multi-screen in Worsfield. Above all she grew weary of his conversation, which came to consist almost entirely of grim warnings of environmental doom.

'That hair-spray of yours,' he said. 'Do you want to kill off *all* our oak trees, Daphne? Can't you be made aware, dear, of the death and destruction you're causing, penetrating the ozone layer like that?'

'I don't think your oak trees are going to drop dead because of one little hair-spray.'

'That's not the point. The point is, we've got to set an example.'

'Oh, have we? We don't hardly see anybody to set an example to.'

'It's the attitude. That's what I object to. There's forests the size of Europe disappearing all the time. And what are you doing about it? Spraying your hair, that's all. Adding to the terrible toll of destruction. Sometimes I wonder, Daphne. Don't you care at all?'

'Not when I can't do much about it.' Daphne took a gulp of the homemade wine which they drank to avoid chemical additives and longed for a long, cool gulp of Fortissimo lager in the bar of the Olde Maypole in Hartscombe.

'That is exactly the type of attitude' – Hector sighed and looked up at the ceiling – 'which is going to lose us the black rhino.'

'Oh, bugger the black rhino!' Daphne's patience with her marriage was running out.

'What's that, Daphne?' Hector spoke very slowly and softly; he

48

sounded enormously calm, a sure sign that he was nothing of the sort. 'What did I hear you say?'

'I said, bugger the black rhino. And I shan't be all that sorry to see the last of the whales, either.'

'I took you, Daphne,' Hector said, after a long and disapproving silence, 'for a genuinely caring sort of person. It seems I took you wrong.'

'Listen, Hector. There's men sleeping in cardboard boxes by the canal in Worsfield. There's old ladies with all their worldly goods in plastic bags, kipping down in the bus shelters in Parkinson Avenue. There's a couple turned out of their home for being behind with the rent as are sleeping rough in the pedestrian walkways. What use is the black rhino to them? That's what I'd like to know!'

'It doesn't have to be any *use*, Daphne. It's a form of wildlife and has rights which we have to respect. I think I'm off out now. I might get a sight of the badgers. At least they're creatures you don't catch polluting the atmosphere with hair-sprays!'

'Sod badgers!' Daphne Jones said after her husband had gone out. And then she did something which she had promised to confine to Christmas and her birthday. She lit a cigarette.

People, Hector Bolitho Jones reflected as he walked through the woods in which fallen branches were left undisturbed as a home for a variety of insects, people, no doubt about it, were what caused all the pollution in the world. People drove cars with lead-filled petrol and felled rain forests. People, unless watched incessantly, dug up orchids and primroses, they frightened the foxes, lit fires in the bracken and threw plastic bottles into the undergrowth. He emerged from under the tall beeches to the top of the downland and, looking down towards the stream, he saw two more of them, no doubt also intent on intruding on to the gentle privacy of the animals. His boots thudded through the brambles and scrub as he strode to the attack. The man wore a city suit and looked older than the small, fragile woman, elegant in black and white. They were townees, he felt sure, who once again would have no respect for the nesting birds. And as he tramped forward he began to call, hoarsely, so that his voice sounded, from a distance, like the calling of rooks.

Hector Bolitho Jones saw them turn away and stood still, triumphant, his feet planted firmly and apart on his patch of uncultivated downland. He had been too far away to recognize a local boy made good and thought that whatever polluting activity they wanted to get up to they now had to do it somewhere else.

Jenny Sidonia's first dinner with Leslie Titmuss had been an occasion of some embarrassment. They had gone to an expensive restaurant where minute quantities of monkfish and prawns, accompanied by a wisp of dill and a small puddle of pink sauce, decorated the octagonal plates. (The Secretary of State had asked his Junior Minister to recommend somewhere to eat; he now decided that it was the last time he was going to take Ken Cracken's advice on anything.) Jenny felt that the orchid, pinned to her dress, hung there like a dead weight. The conversation was equally heavy and when they had talked about the lunch in Oxford, and failed to mention the confusion about the *Ballo in maschera*, it was apparently exhausted. In the long silences Jenny wondered how soon she could ask for a taxi home, but whenever she glanced furtively at her watch the hands scarcely seemed to have moved.

'Your job,' she tried desperately, 'must be very interesting.' She hoped this trite remark would switch on an endless speech during which she could retire into her own world and close the door.

'So far to go,' he said, 'before they grow up.'

'Who grow up?'

'People.' Leslie looked morosely down at his plate. She wondered if she were to be numbered among the un–grown-ups and thought such a description of herself might well be justified.

'They expect the government to wipe their noses, see they wear their vests in the winter. Do everything for them.'

'I don't think I expect that.'

'Of course you don't. Oh, and make sure they have a nice view of empty fields from their bedroom windows. So they can pretend there's no one else in the world except them. They're very keen on the rights of Patagonian Indians but they won't allow the right of an English builder to put up a few houses within ten miles of their view. That's what's got to change. Am I boring you?' He asked the question perfectly seriously, without a smile.

'No,' she said. 'No, of course not.' If only, she thought, I had some talent for being impolite. If only I could say, Naturally you're boring the pants off me, Mr Titmuss. For God's sake, pay the bill and let's get out of this dimly lit place where the waiters pad reverently up and serve out these plates of nothing very much as though it were some religious ritual. Please, Mr Titmuss, let me go home and make myself toast and marmalade and go to bed. Aloud she said, 'It's very interesting.'

'I don't think it interests you at all.' He managed to make her feel guilty. She resented this, even though she tried to look fascinated as she said, 'Planning and all that sort of thing. I know so little about it.'

'Don't bother. It's something we want to get rid of.'

'But perhaps' – she felt she owed him a little discussion, for politeness' sake – 'you can see their point.'

'Whose point?'

'People who live in the country. After all, that's what they went there for. Peace and solitude. You can understand that.'

He looked at her in silence and she nerved herself for the impact of another public address. Instead he said, 'Is that what you'd really like, Jenny?'

In the short time she had known him she couldn't remember his having used her name before. It was as though he had moved one step nearer her and it made her nervous.

'What?'

'Peace and solitude. Living in the country all the time.'

51

'Oh, yes,' she said truthfully. 'Sometime, perhaps. That's what I'd like. Tony and I were always planning to do it. When he lived by writing and didn't have to teach any more.'

Leslie Titmuss seemed to be thinking this over carefully and the silence grew to a disconcerting length until relief flooded over her as he said, 'What do you think we have to do to get a bill here? Drop dead?'

When it came she saw that he was adding it up, checking the items, even making an inquiry about a minute plate of scarcely cooked vegetables, the price of which was finally deleted by the head waiter with a pencil stroke of unutterable contempt. Tony Sidonia had never read a restaurant bill in his life; he used to go on talking, teasing her gently, making her laugh as he dropped money on to the plate with the bill on it. 'Waiters have got to live,' Tony used to say. 'Anyway, it's the duty of people who can afford restaurants to be cheated a little.'

When the argument about the bill was over and Leslie had left a tip of punitive size, he smiled at her and said, 'You look hungry.'

'Well, yes. As a matter of fact, starving.' She was angry about the fuss over the bill, irritated by the restaurant, annoyed with herself for having been weak-minded enough to accept this bizarre invitation. She thought that by being uncharacteristically rude she might nip what looked like becoming a most unsuitable acquaintance in the bud.

'Good. Then we ought to go on somewhere.' He seemed delighted by what she had said. 'It won't take long.'

'I really need an early night.' It was true. The strain of dinner with Leslie Titmuss had exhausted her.

'I told you. It won't take long at all. The car's outside.'

Sitting behind his driver, she cursed her own fatal tendency to agree. What did 'going somewhere' mean? A terrible club, perhaps, with hostesses and a cigarette girl in fishnet tights where he'd buy sweet champagne and go on talking about town and country planning until her eyes closed and her limbs ached with tiredness. He couldn't think for a moment that she'd go back to his flat with him, somewhere, he'd told her, extremely convenient on the Embankment, with a porter who'd smile knowingly as they got into the lift. It was true that he had made no move towards her, leaving as much space as possible between them in the back of the car, but could that be because he was sure his opportunity would come later? Was he arrogant enough to think that? Was he not arrogant enough to think anything? Well, if he imagined she'd put one foot into the entrance hall of Waterside Mansions, or whatever it was called, he was suffering the strangest of illusions. However much ruder would she have to be, she wondered with some dread, before she was shot of him forever? Then she saw that they were not at the entrance of any mansion flats, but surrounded by the bright lights of a street running into Leicester Square. She hadn't heard his muttered instructions to the driver and now the car stopped.

'Wherever . . .?'

'At least we'll be sure of a decent helping!'

It wasn't dark, like the unmentionable club she had imagined, but brilliantly lit, decorated with bright pink plaster pillars and murals of scenes on the Costa Brava, which made her eyeballs ache. Piped music and the fairground smell of frying oil pervaded the place. They sat at a table with a fully loaded ashtray and Leslie asked her, 'What would you say to a couple of eggs and a large go of chips? We might as well live dangerously.'

'I think it'd be wonderful,' she said.

'It was the worst thing he could do.' Sue Bramble looked horrified when Jenny described the evening to her. 'It made you like him.'

'Well, it did almost. It was so sensible.'

'Jenny! How could you have done it?'

'Easily. You know it doesn't matter what I eat. I mean, I don't get fat or anything.' This fact, Jenny knew, was one that Sue, who often dined on white wine and cigarettes, found intensely irritating, but then she was beginning to get tired of her friend's grim warnings about the disaster of Mr Titmuss.

'What on earth did you talk about?'

'Well, nothing very much. We didn't stay that long.'

In fact they had talked about his dead wife.

'Charlotte used to like this sort of thing,' he said. 'Fish and chips, eggs and sausage; all with plenty of sauce. She'd've eaten sauce sandwiches if I'd let her. She thought that was "terribly working class". She was very keen on anything working class, was Charlotte. Coming from where I did, I couldn't see the attraction.'

'Where did *she* come from?'

'Oh, the decaying gentry. She was the girl from the local manor house. The sort that's desperately in love with their ponies until they discover some lad who works round the stable and likes sauce sandwiches.'

'So that was you?'

'Not me. I suppose I was the next best thing. By the way, you can take that flower off if it's worrying you.'

Jenny unpinned the orchid and put it down between the sauce and the mustard where it stayed after they had left, forgotten. 'You're not married to her now?' Asking about himself, she knew, only involved her further; but she was curious and wanted to know.

'Oh, no.' He looked solemn. 'Charlotte passed away.'

In his family, she thought, everyone 'passed away', the most terrible illness was 'feeling poorly' and death itself was 'a merciful release'. She watched as he dipped a long, golden chip into the yoke of his egg and thought how near we all are to childhood.

'I'm sorry.'

'I thought you'd understand. That's why I told you.'

'Because I'd go for people who like lots of tomato ketchup? I have to say, Tony couldn't stand it.'

'No. Because he's dead too.'

She stared at the wall, at a garish señorita with a carnation between her teeth, dancing some sort of clumsy fandango against an electric blue sea. They were the words, it seemed, that her new acquaintance always wanted to make her say.

'Yes.'

'We're alike, aren't we? Both married to people who're dead.'

Was death what they had in common? Not much, surely. The world was full of widows and widowers with absolutely no links between them. 'Does that make us alike?' she asked, giving him another opportunity to approach her.

'We're both alone.'

'Well, not quite alone. Friends count for a good deal. Don't you think?' What she said sounded to her as trite as 'he passed away', or 'it was a merciful release'.

'Friends?' he asked. 'I suppose I've never really tried them. That's why I asked you to dinner. Hope you enjoyed it?'

'I enjoyed the second dinner very much.'

He paid the bill then, without any argument, and she was driven home.

'What about in the car?' Sue asked. 'Did he leap on you?'

'Nothing,' Jenny told her truthfully. 'Not even a kiss on the cheek.'

'Well, thank God for that, at least.'

'Yes,' Jenny said. 'Thank God for that.'

There was then a long silence from Leslie Titmuss. Jenny spent her days in the art gallery, having been lucky, she told herself, to find a job among beautiful things, although many of the works on the stark white walls of the room in Bruton Street were not, she had to admit, particularly beautiful. She sat behind a desk smiling at the visitors, cataloguing paintings at prices which would have bought her the longed-for house in the country, something which, as the empty days and late nights of her London life dragged on, she wanted more than ever. In the evenings she went to dinner parties and was put next to men thought to be likely partners for her, men unhappily married, divorced, or, and here her hosts always assured her that such was not the case, gay. She was usually relieved when this turned out to be the fact, and then she could talk easily, laugh at their jokes and suffer no fear of attack. The heterosexuals were more difficult. They either hinted at past successful seductions and assumed, without any encouragement, that because they had been placed next to Jenny they would spend the night with her, or they poured out their souls to her, described the way their children were being brought up to hate them, or the greed of their ex-wives and the inferiority of their ex-wives' present husbands. In neither case did they ask her anything about herself, and never mentioned the fact that her husband was dead.

'Tracked you down!' She was yawning one morning in the gallery over the proof of a new catalogue, and looked up to see Leslie, his dark suit and pale face striking an unusual note of realism among the art works. 'I rang your flat and there was a girl there. She didn't want to tell me where you worked.'

'Your Mr Titmuss,' Sue said, 'is so horribly persistent. He just wouldn't get off the phone until I spilled the beans. Can you ever forgive me?'

'Oh, yes,' Jenny said later. 'I forgive you.'

'What've we got here?' Leslie Titmuss asked, looking about him. 'Portraits of bath-towels?'

'I'm afraid it's the New Abstraction.'

'Dull, isn't it?'

'Yes,' she had to admit. 'Very dull.'

'Well. I've come to take you away from it all.' He spoke as though he were a rich Victorian squire offering to save a girl from long hours in the sweatshop. 'What would you say to a breath of country air?'

'It would be wonderful. But I can't possibly.'

'Who says you can't?'

As though summoned by the Secretary of State's peremptory questions, the proprietor entered the gallery. He looked, as always, nervously exhausted, his grey hair ruffled, his bow-tie askew and a scratch on his cheek, which was, perhaps, a war wound from the battles of his love life, which involved the constant unhappiness of at least five people. He lived in fear of women, in fear of his landlord and in the faint but constant hope that he would discover, in some villa owned by an insane old lady who had once been the artist's mistress, an unknown Modigliani which she would give him for love and make his fortune.

'Mark. This is Mr Titmuss. Mark Vanberry.'

'Not *the* Mr Titmuss?' Mark's perpetual guilt was such that his heart missed a beat whenever he saw a policeman. The sight of a Cabinet Minister caused him instant terror, which he did his best to suppress.

'*A* Mr Titmuss, anyway,' Leslie told him.

A member of the government, Mark began to calculate, who might have some say in the funding of the arts and in the buying of pictures for countless offices. He said, 'I'm so glad you dropped in. This is a very patriotic show. We're entirely given over to the British Abstract stuff. We got an absolutely *super* notice in the *Guardian*. Does it interest you at all, Mr Titmuss?' Mark looked proudly at the monotonous canvases.

'Not in the least. We were just saying how dull they all were.'

'Dull?' Mark was pained.

'Nothing abstract about life, is there? I suppose my job might be a deal easier if people were no more complicated than bathtowels. I want to take your assistant away from you.'

'You want to take Jenny?' Mark sounded deprived.

'Only for a day in the country. Don't you think she could do with a breath of fresh air?'

'Well, yes.' Anxious to appease this overbearing and undoubtedly influential man, Mark said, with an air of great concern, 'You do look a little peaky, Jenny.'

'She doesn't look peaky at all. She looks glorious. All the same, she'd appreciate a day in the country.'

'Perhaps we can spare her.'

'Of course you can spare her. You're not going to get much trade with these things, are you?'

'I really do have work to do.' Jenny resented having plans made for her as though she wasn't there.

'I suppose they might make room for one of the small tea-towels in the Oslo Embassy,' Leslie speculated. 'Very abstract sort of people, the Scandinavians.'

'Oh, do please go, Jenny. We can manage here easily, just for today. And it would do you good,' Mark pleaded and she fell, once more, a victim to her reckless longing to help the underdog.

When they were in the car she asked what country they were going to.

'My country,' Leslie Titmuss said.

CHAPTER EIGHT

It hadn't been a good summer, but as they turned off the
motorway and took the road to Hartscombe the rain stopped,
heavy gun-metal clouds were dragged away and a shaft of
sunlight lit the church tower and the swollen river. When they
reached the Rapstone Valley the whole sky lightened and, switch-
ing down her window, Jenny smelt the wet countryside. She saw
a stream at the foot of a chalky hillside which led up to a beech
wood, and asked Leslie to stop the car. They got out and walked
down a path where the bracken and the white lace on the cow
parsley were steaming like drying laundry.

'It's beautiful!' Jenny was looking up the hill. The wind from
behind her blew a dark veil of hair across her face.

'It's where I was a kid,' Leslie Titmuss told her. 'I didn't
think it was beautiful then.'

'But now?'

'I suppose so. Anyway, it's been designated under the Nature
Areas Act.'

'Then it must be beautiful.' She pulled the hair away from
her face and laughed at him.

'They always said there were kingfishers by that stream.'

'Truly?'

'I don't know.' The rook call grew nearer and sounded
distinctly human. 'I never did have the time for bird-watching.'

'There's a man up there.' Jenny was worried. 'He seems to be
shouting at us.'

'Well, for God's sake. Who does he think he is?'

'Who is he?'

'Jones! Looks after this place. Obviously they don't give him enough work to do.' And Leslie added, lacking his Junior Minister's taste for anonymity, 'Doesn't he know who he's talking to?'

'No.' Jenny put a hand on his arm. 'Don't let's have an argument. Not here.'

'We can't let him shout at us.'

'Please. Let's go.'

'All right. Anyway, I wanted to show you something.'

They drove on up the valley, between a fold in the hills and then high over fields and little woods. They turned down an avenue of decrepit lime trees, planted, it was always said, to celebrate a young Fanner's return from the Peninsular War, and through an open gateway into a long drive across a park, in which the deer were lit dramatically as the clouds blew away from above them. They came to the empty Manor with its jumble of architectural styles, its pillared portico and its stone green with age, as though it had at some point in its history emerged from under the sea.

'What's this?' Jenny asked.

'Well, a house.'

'I think I can see that.' She laughed at him.

'I just thought you might like to look it over.'

He's like an estate agent, she thought, as he took a key from his pocket and opened the heavy front door, trying to sell me something. 'Well,' she humoured him, 'I suppose it might suit me. How many bedrooms, did you say?'

'I think about ten. A lot for the servants, of course. When they had servants. Most of the rooms haven't been used for years.'

'Ten?' She was still laughing. 'It might just do me. There's a gun-room, I hope. And billiards. And a place for the butler to clean the silver.'

'Oh, yes. There's all that.' Standing in the black-and-white marble paved entrance hall, looking up the wide staircase that twisted away into the shadows, towards a domed ceiling on which falling angels had been badly painted, she felt an extraordinary peace come over her. It was all a huge, a ridiculous, joke; but for some absurd reason she would have liked to live there, quietly perhaps, in one of the rooms, causing no harm to anyone.

'This is the sitting-room, madam.' He pushed open some high double doors, playing the part in which he seemed to know she had cast him. 'Madam might be quite cosy in here.'

She went through, on the echoing boards, into what seemed to be a sort of stateroom containing nothing but a table and some old garden furniture. Through the tall windows she saw the deer again, moving in and out of the shadows.

'Will you be taking it?' he asked.

'On my wages from the gallery and the nothing much Mr Sidonia left me? Well now, why ever not?'

'Didn't your husband leave you anything very much?' Leslie Titmuss was concerning himself with an old wind-up gramophone he had discovered on the table and blowing the dust off a record.

'Tony didn't have anything to leave, except the house in Oxford. I bought my flat with that. Money bored him.'

'What a luxury, to be bored by money!' Quite unexpectedly a deep voice and a tinkling piano came to them through a fusillade of scratches.

> You're the top!
> You can trump the A–ce.
> You're the top!
> You're the Lady Gr–ace . . .

'What on earth's that?'

'My ex-mother-in-law's favourite song. She liked it because it was about her.'

'It's *her* house!' How could she have been so stupid, so intoxicated by a rare day out in the country, not to have understood at once what he was up to?

'Yes.'

'Your wife lived here.'

'Not for very long. Or very happily.'

'You used to come here with her?'

'As little as I could manage. I told you, the old lady hated me.' He switched off the gramophone, causing Pinky Pinkerton, Lady Fanner's beloved singer, to skid into silence.

'What about her father? Did he hate you too?'

'Sir Nicholas? He was a country gent. He wore an old tweed suit and gave his tenants blankets and pounds of tea at Christmas.'

'He sounds rather nice.'

'He was the sort that went out with the dinosaurs.'

'The sort of country gent?'

'The sort of Conservative. We've got rid of them all now. Swept them into the dustbin of history. Thank God.'

Jenny was surprised at herself. He had brought her here and involved her in his past life without warning and without her permission. She should have been angry. What did she have to do with his dead wife, his dead mother-in-law who hated him, the dead old man who went out well-meaningly with presents for the village? She should insist on leaving and after, well, perhaps after, lunch in Hartscombe (why was she always so inconveniently hungry?), she should make him drive her home and avoid seeing him again. Was he trying to stage a repeat of his past life with her, Jenny Sidonia, of all unlikely people? She ought to have been angry but the situation was so curious that she thought of hanging on to see what happened next.

'We're going to have a picnic in the kitchen.'

'Why?'

'You'd like that, wouldn't you?'

Unfortunately she supposed she would.

The driver brought in a cardboard box with sandwiches in plastic wrappers and tins of beer, the sort of lunch Leslie would have sent out for while he stayed working at his desk. They sat in the kitchen by a rusty cooker the size of a steam engine, installed to feed dinner parties which hadn't taken place for years, and families who had long stopped visiting. They sat under iron hooks from which hams had once been suspended, and well-populated fly-papers, beside tarnished saucepans and shelves which supported no more than a few pieces of broken china, beside the electric kettle and the two-ringed cooker which had been enough to provide Lady Fanner's light meals. Jenny ate gratefully, having decided to stop worrying for the moment – the sort of decision she came to easily.

'What I want to know is' – she chose something harmless to ask – 'are you going to get some embassy to buy one of Mark's dreadful pictures?'

'Of course.' He looked at her seriously. 'Did you think I'd deceive him?'

'I wouldn't put it past you.'

'Well, madam.' He changed the subject. 'Would you like the house?'

There was a long silence and then she said, 'Yes, I would. Very much. It's madness, of course.'

'Why is it madness?'

'How could I possibly buy it, or live here? It's quite impractical.'

'Nothing you want's impractical. It's people who don't know what the hell they want that are the impractical ones.' So that, she thought, was the Titmuss philosophy of life and no doubt simple enough.

'All right,' she laughed at him, 'I'll buy it.'

'You can't.'

'Why not?'

'It's already sold.'

'Who to?'

'Me.'

She unwrapped another sandwich, wondering where on earth they had got to now.

'I happen to be a good friend of my ex-mother-in-law's solicitor. He told me the whole damn thing had been pawned to the bank, oh, for years before she died. So I got the bank to sell it to me. Quite quietly, of course. They tried to get some fancy price on the ground that there might be a new development round here, a bloody great new town.'

'You mean they'd build over this valley?' Jenny was dismayed. 'That'd be sacrilege.'

'It won't happen,' Leslie assured her. 'Not if I have anything to do with it.'

'So you're going to live here?'

'That depends.'

'What on?'

He stood up, brushing crumbs off his dark suit. 'Would you like to see upstairs?' he asked her.

They inspected servants' bedrooms, with crumbling ceilings and peeling wallpaper. They saw guest bedrooms and the room where Charlotte Titmuss, when a young girl, had pinned up the rosettes she won at gymkhanas and her many photographs of horses. They went into her mother's bedroom, where the furniture had not yet been sold and the big bed was stripped to the mattress, and smelt the sour smell of old age and spilt wine and the sweet smell of death. It was there that, suddenly and with great authority, Leslie Titmuss kissed Jenny Sidonia for the first time. She was not, she supposed, surprised that it happened, but she was astonished by the result. Like a skier who had been standing nervously and then, without taking a breath, pushes off down the steepest part of the mountain, she felt elated, irresponsible and in extraordinary danger. Whatever the Titmuss kiss was like it was far from the comforting warmth and reassurance provided by Mr Sidonia.

The incident of the kiss was curiously isolated. When it was done they left the bedroom and continued their tour of inspection. They walked for a while in the overgrown and neglected garden and then drove into Rapstone village. Leslie, now acting as a tour guide of his past life, showed Jenny the church, starting with his father's grave, and then took her inside, where they found the Reverend Kevin Bulstrode pinning up notices about a vigil for Aids Week.

'Mr Titmuss! This is an honour.' Although he preached weekly sermons about the lack of compassion and true Christian principle of the government, Kev the Rev. became effusively respectful to the Cabinet Minister. His eyes sparkled and he blushed like a young girl in the unnerving presence of a pop star. 'I see your mother, of course, and she tells me all about your doings. We're very proud of you in Rapstone.'

'This is Mrs Sidonia. She's thinking of taking a place in the country.'

'Am I?' Jenny smiled, but the Rev. Kev ignored her, having eyes for Leslie alone. 'Terribly expensive here now, of course. For the smallest two-up, two-down. That is, unless you're like me and work for the C. of E. Then you get a tied cottage.'

'You mean that draughty great Rectory, falling to pieces?'

'I'm afraid so. In the church we have to accept draughts like the Thirty-nine Articles.'

'Your organization needs to slim down. Sell the Rectory to the highest bidder and put you in a decent bungalow. With double-glazing. I used to cut nettles for the old Rector,' Leslie told Jenny. 'Sixpence a day and a glass of ginger-beer. The Reverend Simcox was a Socialist. You're not a Socialist, are you, Rector?'

'Only' – Kev the Rev. blushed more deeply, horribly torn between good manners and his obligation to the truth – 'in so far as Our Lord was a Socialist.'

'How far was that? Paid-up member of the Nazareth Labour Party, was He?'

Now Jenny was torn. She thought what Leslie had said quite funny, but she hoped the Reverend Kevin wasn't being bullied.

She gave him one of her most glittering smiles and said, 'It's so lovely round here. Quite extraordinary.'

'Well, we think so. And we hope it'll stay that way. There have been rumours –'

'Never believe rumours,' Leslie advised him, 'until you hear them officially denied. By the way, Bulstrode. I wanted to thank you for what you did for my ex-mother-in-law. At the end. Apparently it was well beyond the call of duty.'

'I did what I took to be my pastoral job. She wasn't an entirely easy woman to visit.'

'She was impossible.' Leslie spoke with feeling. 'She must have been hell when she was doing anything as common as dying. You did very well. And I'm not going to forget it.'

What did he mean? As a member of the Cabinet, Leslie Titmuss obviously had considerable influence. Might it be Rural Dean? For a heady moment the vision of a mitre swam before Kevin's eyes. He accompanied his visitors down to the lychgate and saw them into their car, bowing like an old-fashioned Hartscombe shopkeeper who has been patronized by royalty.

They drove out of Rapstone into the next village. Jenny saw that it was in every way uglier and looked more down at heel than the cluster of old brick and flint cottages and half-timbered houses they had left. 'This is Skurfield,' Leslie told her. 'My village. That's ours – "The Spruces".'

'The birthplace?' she asked, and he didn't laugh. The small house, as neatly kept as his father's grave, was where his mother lived.

'Don't you want to call on her?' she asked politely.

'Another time, perhaps.'

'She'll be upset, won't she, if she finds you've been down here without calling?'

'If you don't mind, then.' He looked grateful.

They rang a bell which chimed and went into a strong smell of furniture polish and an array of gleaming china ornaments. Jenny was surprised at how pretty the old woman was, and how pleased she seemed to be to see her. They stayed only long enough for a cup of tea to be made and drunk. Jenny admired the house and Leslie's mother said, 'I told my son, I don't want him to move me from here. Not ever.'

'Don't worry,' Leslie laughed. 'I've given up that idea.'

When they left, Elsie Titmuss said to Jenny, 'I hope you're not the sort to go on demonstrations?'

'Not really,' Jenny smiled.

'And I hope to see you back in my house, dear. I really hope so.'

After that they drove back to London. When he dropped her at her flat Leslie said, 'See you next week,' and she said, 'Yes.' They met regularly but they didn't sleep together, nor did he kiss her seriously again for a long time. This puzzled her. She knew that there was about to be a great change in her life and she was eager to begin it.

'What on earth,' Sue Bramble said, 'can you possibly see in him?'

'He's like no one else.'

'Thank goodness.'

'And he knows exactly what he wants. That's quite an unusual thing to know.'

'What he wants is you, undoubtedly.'

'He comes from the country.' Jenny ignored Sue's remark. 'A most beautiful place. I think he really loves it there.'

'You mean, he's just a local yokel at heart?'

'Something like that.'

'Jenny. The man's a Cabinet Minister. In the government. He's always on the television. You don't get there with a straw in your mouth and a few rustic sayings, do you?'

'I don't know. I don't know anything at all about Cabinet Ministers.'

'Just watch him on the box. Especially when he's trying to be terribly sincere. Then you can tell how devious he is. And his suits! He looks like a man with his foot in the door who's trying to sell you encyclopaedias.'

'I don't think that's in the least bit fair.'

'Jenny Sidonia,' her friend told her, 'it was a bad day when you decided to be fair to Leslie Titmuss.'

Whether or not Leslie was as devious as Sue Bramble said, he hadn't told Jenny the whole truth about his purchase of Rapstone Manor. Certainly he had had several conversations with the manager of the caring West Country Bank in Hartscombe and it was true that they had discussed a deal. He had waited, however, until he had shown Jenny the house before he decided to buy. The day after their journey into the country he made his final offer. Then he strolled, in his shirt sleeves, into the office of his Minister of State.

'Ken,' he said. 'I could do with a word with you in private.'

Joyce gathered up some papers and left the room, confident that she would soon share in any secret the Secretary of State had to offer.

'Are you trying to be funny?' Leslie asked when the two men were alone.

Ken, also wearing a striped shirt, braces and no jacket, as was the working custom at H.E.A.P., looked up innocently from his desk. In his heart was the great hope that he had got his superior rattled.

'Funny about what exactly?'

'About the proposed Rapstone Valley development.'

So he knew. Ken thought that Leslie would find out sooner rather than later. 'Oh, that. Well. I didn't want to trouble you at this stage.'

'Trouble me, Ken. That's what I was put here for. And if you don't trouble me, my lad, I'm quite likely to trouble you.'

'It's very early days. I just happened to hear something in confidence.'

'From Kempenflatt and his construction company? When you were at the opera together?'

'Something like that. Yes.'

'In future, when you hear something in confidence, Ken, you share it with me. Otherwise I might lose confidence in you. There's a bit of a minor reshuffle in the wind, you know.'

He's threatening me, Ken thought. He really is rattled. 'I didn't think you'd be interested in every little development scheme that just might be applied for.'

'Or did you think I'd be particularly interested in this one? Did you decide not to tell me until it was all nicely sewn up?'

'I couldn't do that, could I? The final decision will be entirely up to you, of course.'

'Of course. I think, Ken, that's something you should bear in mind. That's my advice to you, my lad.'

'But Fallowfield Country Town, if it ever happens, is something I thought would be absolutely in line with your present thinking.'

'Is that your view of the matter?'

'It's yours, isn't it? You put it so well in that smashing speech you made at the U.C.D.A. dinner. The one about the whingers and belly-achers who don't want to share England's green and pleasant land with any upwardly mobile young couple who can save up enough to buy a house. You remember, when you talked about "not in our back gardens"?'

'I didn't realize' – Leslie sat down, half-despairing, half-amused, in the armchair from which Ken Cracken habitually held forth to particularly privileged journalists – 'that I'd got a Minister of State who was entirely wet behind the ears. Politically speaking.'

Politically speaking, Ken thought to himself, I think I'm doing rather well.

'What I say to one pressure group or another, Ken' – Leslie spoke quietly, patiently, as though instructing a child – 'doesn't pre-judge any decision I may have to make. At the end of the day. The whingers and belly-achers, as you called them –'

'As *you* called them.' Ken was confident enough of his own position to interrupt.

69

'I may call a good many people, including you, all sorts of names from time to time. But at least have the sense to remember that the whingers and belly-achers have votes. The green welly brigade is going to support us at the next election, unless we push them too bloody far.'

'The construction industry's likely to vote for us too.'

'Exactly. Maybe they've got enough to be grateful for already. They don't need any more favours. And it's not just the green wellies, Ken. It's not just the lot with converted barns you mix with at Glyndebourne Opera House or wherever you choose to spend your leisure hours. There are millions of little people, perfectly decent people in small businesses, up and down the country, who are deeply concerned about the environment.'

'You mean the Save the Whale nutters?' Cracken did his best to sound sceptical.

'Have you got something against whales, Ken?'

'Well, not personally.'

'Well, you'd better not knock them. They may not be very much use to anyone, swimming about the ocean and suckling their young, or whatever it is they do. They may not add much to our gross national product. But don't knock them, lad! There are plenty of votes in whales. People find them sympathetic. Just like they worry about rain forests and the ozone layer. I hope you're not going to call good folk who're concerned about the ozone layer belly-achers, are you, Ken?'

'Well, no, of course not,' said the Minister of State, who had been tempted to do so.

'In the same way there are plenty of people, decent, small people, who are concerned about our beautiful English country-side. They're not snobs, Ken. They're not down-at-heel country gents with stately homes. They're folk who were born there. Take my mother, for instance.'

I don't believe this, Ken thought, amazed at the effect he was having on the head of his department. He's going to go on television and start talking about his mother.

70

'What about your mother?'

'Well, her vote is just as good as Christopher Kempenflatt's, I should think.'

'Just as good,' Ken conceded.

'Concern for the environment' – the Secretary of State stood up, as he reached his peroration; he was no longer rebuking a Junior Minister but making a public pronouncement – 'is vitally important. What we are doing to this world of ours. Can we keep the place free of litter and pollution? That's the great political question of our time. And remember this, Ken. It's a *safe* political question. It's got damn all to do with socialism or public ownership, or the so-called welfare state or the politics of envy, as we knew them in the Winter of Discontent and the bad, sad old days of Harold Wilson, who didn't give a fart about whales, from all that I can remember. It's everyone's concern, from the chairman of the building society to the girl in the local hairdresser's who's prepared to give up aerosol sprays for the sake of her convictions. It's the way we can appeal to the whole country, including –'

'Including your mother?'

'I think you've got the message.' Leslie gave his subordinate an extra-long stare and then moved slowly to the door. 'Keep me informed on the Rapstone development, will you? Every inch of the way.'

When Joyce returned to the room she found Ken alone and barely able to contain his mirth. 'It's Leslie Titmuss,' he told her. 'He's gone green!'

Tomorrow

The best lack all conviction, while the worst
Are full of passionate intensity.

'The Second Coming'
W. B. Yeats

CHAPTER NINE

Kempenflatts, the builders, opened their attack on the Rapstone Valley, not with a salvo of bulldozers and a bombardment by concrete-mixer, but with a delicately understated exhibition which the public was graciously begged to attend in Hartscombe Town Hall. To the piped music of Purcell and Edward Elgar the citizens could see an artist's impressions of Fallowfield Country Town which made it look, not a blot, but a thing of beauty on the landscape. Fallowfield, it seemed, would be a tastefully conceived Camelot with pedestrian precincts and parking facilities, an up-to-date version of the lost Atlantis which had that mythical city's talent for disappearing tactfully from view. Just as Atlantis dived beneath the waves, Fallowfield Country Town was, it seemed, quite capable of vanishing between folds in the hills and behind newly planted municipal coppices, so that it would not, God forbid it ever should, give the slightest offence to the critical eye of the most dedicated rural conservationist.

So the water-colour paintings in the Town Hall showed ponies trotting, badgers building, birds nesting and fox cubs sporting in the foreground and, somewhere in the leafy distance, a vague impression of rose-red desirable homes, an occasional elegant church spire or a slimmed-down municipal clock-tower peeped shyly over the brow of some well-positioned hill. Nothing, it was stressed in the captions to the surrounding photographs, would be lost by the proposed development. Rapstone Nature Area, and here Hector Bolitho Jones was shown bottle-feeding a baby lamb on his patch of ancient chalk down-land, would be kept intact and carefully preserved as a public park for the delight of the fortunate citizens of Fallowfield. The public-spirited Kempenflatt was, out of the kindness of his heart, prepared to add many facilities to the Nature Area, including a children's play area, hand-rails for senior citizens who wished to climb the steep path to the woodlands, and the free supply of Walkmans to visitors so that they might stroll through an area of unspoiled countryside with rustic information plugged into their ears.

More photographs showed the enhanced quality of life in other Kempenflatt developments. There were carefully selected views of children laughing in school playgrounds, old people feeding ducks by municipal ponds and string quartets performing in shopping piazzas. Over this part of the exhibition ran the modest legend HOW KEMPENFLATTS BUILT JERUSALEM IN ENGLAND'S GREEN AND PLEASANT LAND.

The local inhabitants didn't, at first, react strongly to this exercise in gentle persuasion. The exhibition was mainly attended by old people who were not allowed to return to their bed and breakfast accommodation until nightfall, and children seeking free gifts of Genuine Old Rapstone Country Mint Humbugs and I LOVE FALLOWFIELD T-shirts to add to their collections. They showed little interest in the photographs and drawings on display and were unimpressed by the news that an application was in hand to twin the as yet non-existent Fallowfield with Siena.

An underground movement opposed to the Kempenflatt occupation was soon to find its voice, however, and freedom fighters were to hear a somewhat muted call to arms. The centre of the resistance was, at first and appropriately enough, centred on an isolated spot above the Rapstone Valley. There was a field, so high that it was sometimes obscured in low clouds, which on bright days commanded a view of no less than three counties. It should have been in itself an area of great natural beauty. To be honest, it wasn't. To be brutally honest, it bore a close resemblance to those make-believe shantytowns which privileged American students erect on their campuses as a protest against the intolerable conditions in Soweto.

There was a rickety fence round the field and two posts on each side of the gateway which supported, except on the frequent occasions when it blew down in the high winds sweeping the area, the ranch-style notice CURDLES RABBIT HACIENDA: ANGORAS OUR SPECIALITY — ALSO BRED FOR YOUR TABLE DELIGHT. Beneath it, in smaller letters, was the invitation *Come in and Take Your Pick of Rapstone Free-Range Lapin Dinners — Prepared for Your Freezer in Handy Packs.* Behind the fence, in a number of home-made buildings of various shapes and sizes, assembled from scraps of available corrugated-iron, hardboard, tea-chests, sheets of asbestos and the bodies of defunct pick-up trucks, the rabbits, destined to become Tasty Segments or Cuddly Sweaters, bred with enormous rapidity and little assistance. These buildings were also liable to collapse like card houses in the wind, sending the liberated occupants bounding off to ravage the carefully tended gardens of the neighbourhood. Further into the field, and under the shelter of the trees, three huge mobile homes, sunk up to their axles in foul weather, housed the members of the Curdle family who had been as fecund as their charges. These homes, which also served as the hacienda's offices, were connected by an elaborate system of outdoor wiring to a huge generator, for the Curdles went without no modern aid to living and were lavishly supplied with coffin-sized freezers, calculators, video machines, cordless telephones, microwave cookers and even a small but powerful electric organ which none of them could play. A large dish, also sunk perilously into the mud, picked up a flickering supply of soft porn and children's cartoons from satellites wandering above them in the heavens. Around these dwellings another shantytown provided sheds, workshops and an outside lavatory. Cropping the remains of the grass was a shaggy and under-exercised pony on which the Curdles offered to give riding lessons to anyone foolish enough to pay them for such a service.

The rabbit hacienda was a matriarchy. Dot Curdle, a huge, astute woman who had in her youth, and indeed in middle age, called on the amorous services of most of the personable young men, and many not so personable, in Hartscombe and the surrounding countryside, regulated the affairs of her family and her business down to the minutest detail. She was up before dawn, cobbling together hutches, skinning, dividing and freezing small corpses, cutting angora, sending out bills and concealing her excess profits in a number of biscuit tins under the flooring of the mobile homes. She supervised the lives of her children and grandchildren with a benevolent despotism and if any task didn't fit into her extended timetable (she rose at dawn and liked to wait up until Billy, at sixteen the youngest and least law-abiding Curdle, was safely home from the lager battles in Hartscombe) she would say, with an air of total confidence, 'Wilf will see to it,' and her diminutive husband Wilfred, a withered apple of a man who was always smiling, invariably did so.

Dot was the child of the long-deceased Tom Nowt, a well-known Rapstone poacher who had fallen foul of Lady Fanner long before the war and had found himself before the magistrates for the offence of snaring rabbits in the Fanner woods. He had been imprisoned for a noisy week in Worsfield gaol, which institution he left to the enormous relief of the staff; his habit of using his cell as though it were some dark corner of the Rapstone woods had not made him a popular prisoner. Neither he nor his family had ever forgiven the Fanners for this humiliation and it was perhaps in tribute to her father's memory that Dot had devoted her life to the proliferation of rabbits.

One day, taking a quick meal on a copy of the *Hartscombe Sentinel*, Dot saw, for the first time, the full details of the Fallowfield proposals. She discovered that the hacienda was due to become a suburban supermarket area, architecturally adjusted to a hilltop position, with abundant parking facilities. She guessed that the farmer from whom they had, for many years, rented their field was proposing, if the plans received official blessing, to sell their home and business from under them. The whole life of the Curdles would vanish under an area of parked cars, piled groceries and supermarket trolleys.

'Hang about, Wilf,' she said. 'This is not on!'

'What's not on?'

'Dumping a bloody great town on our rabbit farm.'

'Oh, that.' Wilfred, ever philosophic, seemed to regard the changes as inevitable and not worth discussing, like death or the weather. 'After we've gone, perhaps. This place'll see us out.'

'We're not going anywhere. We're going to stay here and stop their tricks.' Dot was reading voraciously every inch of print on the subject of Fallowfield Country Town: "The scheme presented by Kempenflatts the builders," she announced to Wilfred, "is likely to run into considerable opposition from rural pressure groups and other protesters."

'What's that mean?'

'It means,' Dot explained patiently but with considerable force, 'that's what we're going to be. Our family. A rural pressure group and other protesters.'

'What do we do then?'

'We protests.'

'How does it say we do that?'

'It doesn't say. Most likely because it doesn't want us to know. It's crafty.'

'So what do you reckon?'

'The old Rector would have known,' Dot remembered. 'The Reverend Simcox was one for protesting about most things.'

Simeon Simcox, Kevin Bulstrode's predecessor at the Rectory, had been a life-long Socialist to whom shares in the Simcox Brewery had given a secure vantage point from which to set right the evils of the world. Wearing his dog-collar, an old tweed jacket with leather patches and an expression of benign joy he had headed innumerable protests against the Bomb, against apartheid, against the war in Vietnam and in favour of low-rent accommodation in Worsfield. His younger son, Fred, had long worked as a doctor in Hartscombe, having taken over the practice of old Dr Salter who, diagnosing his own cancer, had sought death by attempting an impossible jump in the hunting field, had failed to find it and had lived on, paralysed, for several painful years. This was a practical joke of fate which he had been able, incredibly, to laugh at. Fred had been more attracted by the old Doctor's acceptance of the immutable facts of life and death than by his father's optimistic march towards a paradise which became ever more distant and unattainable. Unlike his elder brother, Henry, who had started out as an angry young novelist and had now become a crusty old blimp, writing articles for the newspapers denouncing as dangerous illusions their father's most dearly held beliefs, Fred had opted out of all political activity, being content with the quiet life of a general practitioner in the countryside where he had spent his childhood. Sometimes, but not often, he wondered how he had come to pass over half a century on earth and travelled so little distance from his home.

Fred had once, many years before, joined a march for nuclear disarmament, which he had deserted in order to meet a girl with whom he was in love. He didn't expect to be involved in any similar demonstration for the rest of his life. However his consulting room was invaded during one morning surgery by the huge and urgent presence of Dot Curdle. He was pleased to see her, for although he despaired, like most people, of the mess the hacienda made of the field above Rapstone, Dot's great bulk had long been a familiar feature of his landscape. As a small boy he had greatly admired her father, Tom Nowt, and he had watched the old poacher bait fish-hooks with raisins soaked in brandy to catch pheasants, and ridden with him at night when he shot deer dazzled in the headlamps of a car. Until his father suddenly forbade this friendship he had spent much of his school holidays in Tom Nowt's hut in the woods, listening to tall stories of drunken nights and unlikely seductions. He had heard the amorous cries of Tom's caged calling-bird, which lured the game from the Strove and Fanner woods into his traps. His predecessor in the practice, Dr Salter, had brought Dot Nowt into the world and had given her, as he always said, 'a slap on the bottom and told her to get on with it, which is the most you can do for anyone embarking on life'. On the whole, Dot had made the most of this encouraging start and Fred had seen her children and grandchildren born, treated them when they were ill, which was seldom, and tried, without any success, to worry her about her huge weight which seemed to have no adverse effect on her health whatsoever.

'I want to talk to you, Dr Fred. Urgent.'

'You're not ill?'

'Not me. No.'

'Or any of the family?'

Dot seemed, suddenly, shy of embarking on the non-medical subject of her visit.

'Well,' she said. 'There is my Evie.' She mentioned a pale, sullen thirty-year-old who was always known as the brightest of the family and who had supplied the foreign words used in the hacienda advertising. 'I think the girl's sick,' she added with undisguised contempt.

'What's the matter with her?'

'She says she can't fancy her sex.'

'Her own sex?' Fred Simcox speculated wildly.

'She says she can't abide doing it, Doctor.'

'And that's a worry to you?' Fred heard his doctor's voice and wanted to burst out laughing at its concerned pomposity.

'It's a worry to Len Bigwell, seeing as he's her intended. We've got a big wedding planned for the autumn time. What's the matter with young things today, Doctor?' Dot settled back in his creaky patient's chair and seemed prepared to enjoy a trip down memory lane. 'We never had any trouble not fancying it, from what I remember. Looked forward to it, more or less, as I still manages to this day.'

Fred tried to picture the diminutive Wilf climbing aboard this great old steamer and said, again in the doctor's voice with which he was becoming bored, 'You want me to speak to her?'

'Wouldn't do any good. She can't bear talking about it either. She reckons it's the rabbits what put her off.'

'A marriage guidance counsellor from Worsfield comes to the Town Hall once a week.' Fred said this with little conviction. Old Dr Salter had always taken the view that the only possible marriage guidance was contained in the sentence, 'If you like it, enjoy it; if you don't like it, piss off out of it.'

'Marriage guidance.' Dot appeared to think this over. 'That might bring her to her senses. To be honest, Dr Fred, and I've got to be honest, that's not the reason I dropped into the surgery.'

'I didn't think it was.'

'Your dad. He used to protest. Organized a few demos and that, didn't he?'

'Oh, all the time.'

'He knew how to stop things happening that didn't ought to happen.'

'He thought he did.'

'And he put a stop to them?'

'Well, not very often.'

'But he had a go?'

'Oh, yes. He had a go.'

'And he might have won the day, like. If he'd gone on persistent.'

'I suppose he might. About some things.'

'So you'll remember how he used to do it.'

'Oh, yes. I remember quite well.'

'You're the one that's got to undertake it then.'

'Undertake what, exactly?'

'Stop them dumping a bloody great town on my hacienda.'

Even Dot Curdle's call to arms might not have immediately

moved Fred into activity had it not been repeated by a number of his patients and fellow citizens after the full account of the Fallowfield plans appeared on the front page of the *Hartscombe Sentinel*. Crossing the road on his way to a lunchtime sandwich in the entirely rebuilt Olde Maypole Inn (it now had all the advantages of muzak, one-armed bandits and the Seafood Platter which had ousted Dr Salter's favourite beef and pickle sandwiches), he was hailed by a Mrs Virginia Beazley, the wife of Mr Vernon Beazley who took the long journey to London each day to work for a prosperous firm of charity organizers. Mrs Beazley called them the Two Vees and often said they worked as a team for the humane concerns which, in less enlightened times, an idle populace had left to its government. Virginia had taken on the Worsfield Drug Therapy Unit, the Safe Sex Advisory Service and a growing organization called Help the Homeless to Help Themselves. 'All I want to do,' she often said, 'is to get people off their backsides and into the tough old business of "love thy neighbour".' She often added that she and the other Vee 'got their kicks' from such work. She was a tall, handsome woman of great energy and a commanding presence, and Fred sometimes had the unnerving suspicion that she was in love with him.

'Hi there, Dr Fred!' she called to him from the pavement as he was trapped on a traffic island. 'Who's going to get Hartscombe up off its bottom now?'

'I don't know.' He did his best to make his answer inaudible.

'Well, you are, of course!' she shouted, and when a lull in the traffic forced him to her side she explained, 'Vee and I are forming the Save Rapstone Valley Society and I can't think who the hell else we should ask to be chairman.'

'Chairman? I've got my practice –'

'But you're here all the time! Not like poor old Vee, who has to travel a hundred and fifty miles backwards and forwards to work every day. Anyway, Vee says you're just the chap we ought to scrounge for the job. He thinks you'd look quite reassuring on local television if only you'd invest in a few new shirts and not cut your hair as though you'd just come home from National Service. Also he'd like to give you a bit of advice about your specs.' And she invited the Doctor to buy her a large Kir in the Olde Maypole Inn.

While there they met Daphne Jones, who had escaped from her husband, Hector Bolitho Jones, and the Nature Area on the pretext of her monthly visit to the Hartscombe Cash & Carry. She was drinking Fortissimo lager with Barry Harvester, the young proprietor of the herbal boutique in the pedestrian precinct, who had a witch's knowledge of country remedies for all ailments and smiled in a particularly embittered manner whenever he saw a registered medical practitioner.

'Hullo, Doctor,' he said. '*Still* poisoning people with penicillin?' Fred resisted the temptation to answer, 'Whenever I get them out of your clutches.' Instead he offered to buy them all a drink, thinking that the female Vee was safest when lost in a crowd.

'It's not as though it's going to provide any low-rent council houses,' Daphne Jones said, with justice. 'It'll just be more homes for well-heeled business people like your old man, Virginia, commuting up to London.'

'It's another battle in the class war' – the herbalist was a one-man cell in the Hartscombe Workers' Revolutionary Party – 'and this one we've got to win.'

'It's a matter of preserving our national heritage,' Mrs Vee said. 'I don't see why we have to drag politics into it.'

'You try dragging politics out of it.' Barry Harvester fixed her with his most unfriendly smile and bit noisily into a radish. 'I don't think you'll find we get very far.'

'It's Titmuss we're up against in the end.' Daphne Jones was a great deal better informed than her friend Barry on matters of political reality. 'He's the one who wants to concrete over the South of England. For yuppies to live in it.'

Fred said nothing, thinking of yet another stage in what felt like a lifetime's battle against Leslie Titmuss, the boy who had once come in on Saturdays to cut his father's nettles. Mrs Vee said, 'The important thing is we all have to pull together. Us and our little group of founding fathers. Now, who are we going to be? Apart from us four – and Vee, of course, to deal with the charitable aspect.'

'We ought to ask the Curdles,' Fred told her.

'Really?' Mrs Vee was unenthusiastic.

'They stand to lose their rabbit farm.'

'Best reason I heard yet for the new town.' The She Vee giggled and punched Fred lightly on the upper arm. 'No, pax! Don't slap me down. I suppose it'd be democratic to ask the Curdles, or a representative selection of them.'

'Yes! Try being democratic,' Daphne advised her quite sharply. 'It doesn't hurt much.'

'Oh, and I think we should invite the Mayor, as a matter of courtesy. And the Head of the Hartscombe Grammar.' Mrs Vee ignored Daphne's advice. 'And Colonel and Mrs Wilcox for the footpaths. And the Church ought to have a place.'

'The Church has got no place. Not in the world today,' the herbalist told her, but in the end they decided that Kev the Rev. would be invited to serve on the committee. 'For our first meeting' – Mrs Vee was in a generous mood – 'I don't see why Vee and I shouldn't lay on a buffet. That is, providing everyone is willing to chip in, of course.'

'And I hope you'll be serving out the Armalite rifles and the ammo with the quiche, Mrs Beazley.' The herbalist, who had nothing whatever to do with firearms and who was prominent in animal welfare, downed his Fortissimo. 'I reckon we're going to need them to stop this lot in the end.'

'I'm prepared to take that remark entirely as a joke,' Mrs Vee said. 'I think fifteen quid each would cover a reasonable selection of salads and, let's say, one glass per head of carafino rosé. After that I'll put Vee in charge of a small cash bar.'

So, at this historical moment, an organization was formed to deliver a small part of England from subjugation by the Kempenflatts and the dangerous domination of Leslie Titmuss.

CHAPTER TEN

Driving through the Rapstone Valley, along hedged lanes which he could have negotiated in his sleep, past the patches of bracken where he had hidden and built shelters when he was a child, the diminishing ponds in which he had squelched and hunted frogs, the common where, at night, he had found glow-worms and occasionally made love, and through the tall beech trees, thin and grey as elephants' trunks, where he had ridden shot-gun with Tom Nowt, Fred Simcox was filled with anger. What had his patients done, what offence had they committed that their small world should suddenly be taken from them? Death, he knew, would deprive him of the hills and woodlands which had been for so long a part of his existence; death was the great, the accepted, robber but he saw no reason in the world why he should be so deprived by Kempenflatts the builders or, and here his rage, an emotion to which he was usually a stranger, rose to a level which was almost as intoxicating as Fortissimo lager and perhaps as likely to lead to violence, by the shadowy but apparently infinite power of Leslie Titmuss.

Fred had read reports of the now famous Titmuss speech at the Construction and Developers Association dinner. The *Fortress* had welcomed it, as it welcomed all his utterances, as a refreshing blast of common sense and plain speaking. Henry Simcox, writing what he called one of his 'Why, oh why?' pieces, had said it was time country dwellers stopped regarding it as their inalienable right not to have to look at their fellow citizens and were dragged, green wellies and all, into the glories of Britain's new industrial revolution. People who lived in the country, together with farmers, school teachers, hospital nurses and social workers, formed that group of mendacious malcontents of which Fred's brother, Henry, especially disapproved; and the fact that he spent his life in the gentle confines of South Kensington and found his rustic pleasures in a villa in Tuscany meant that he didn't have to bump into many of them. 'Why, oh why,' he wrote in a much-quoted article, 'if these pampered people want to live so close to nature don't they move to the Outer Hebrides and leave us to our prosperity?'

And the Titmuss war, Fred reflected as he entered the stuffy bedrooms of the few remaining villagers, or tried to convince weekending television executives that there was no magic potion for avoiding death, could even be thought of as funny. It was comic, no doubt, that opposition to the best-laid schemes of Titmuss should have to come from a country doctor who wanted to be left alone, and from a Trotskyite shopping-precinct huckster who sold nettle tea as a cure for arthritis. No doubt it was entertaining for Titmuss to know that their forces were to be assembled at a buffet in the Hartscombe home of Mr and Mrs Vee, to which Colonel and Mrs Wilcox, representing the footpaths, and Kev the Rev. were also invited. What else, after all, could they possibly do? The more hopeless the battle against Titmuss seemed, the more intensely it had to be waged and the more completely did Fred feel he had to dedicate himself to it.

Much of his feeling about Titmuss went back, as did his devotion to the Rapstone landscape, to the days of his childhood. It was Leslie Titmuss who had seen the young Fred skiving away from the C.N.D. march and who had informed the old Rector of his son's lack of dedication to that, or probably any, cause. It was Leslie again who had figured so improbably as a beneficiary in the Reverend Simeon Simcox's will, a matter which had only been explained, as a result of the Doctor's painstaking investigation, by the discovery that Charlotte, Grace

Fanner's daughter and Leslie's wife, had been a child of the old Rector's passionate and unsuspected past. It was true that Simeon Simcox's legacy had turned out to be financially worthless; the affair had split the family and caused the Doctor's mother, a woman slow to show any feelings except dry amusement at the vulgarities of the world, a good deal of carefully concealed pain.

Fred always thought of Leslie Titmuss as he first knew him, an irrepressibly cocky small boy with an unnatural pallor, short trousers and socks which concertinaed round his ankles, who used his nettle-cutting to ask endless questions of the Rector's two sons and to worm his way into their father's favour. At the end of every corridor which led into Fred's past, on every pathway of that half-remembered landscape, that figure seemed to stand, causing unnecessary trouble. So, when the Doctor saw the Cabinet Minister's picture now, in newspapers or on television, he remembered him as an intolerable small boy and hoped against all reasonable hope that Titmuss's undoubted power would thereby be diminished.

'We need an acronym,' said Mr Vernon Beazley, who knew about such things, 'and a logo.'

'What's he talking about?' Wilf Curdle whispered to his wife, and was immediately told to keep his mouth shut.

'I thought we'd agreed to call ourselves the Save Rapstone Valley Society.' Fred was already beginning to find his duties as chairman (Chair, as Daphne Jones insisted on calling him) unacceptably absurd.

'S.R.V.S.? That doesn't do anything for us. What we need are initials that make up a word you can say,' the He Vee explained patiently to those unacquainted with the needs of charity organizations. 'Like U.N.E.S.C.O. and S.C.R.A.P.'

'Hands Off Our Valley?' Daphne Jones was anxious to help. 'H.O.O.V.'

'Sounds like a vacuum, doesn't it?' Mrs Wilcox of the footpaths piped up unexpectedly.

'What about Piss Off Out Of Our Valley?' said Dot, who was surprisingly quick at crossword puzzles. 'You could say that. P.O.O.V.'

'Please, Mum, don't be disgusting.' Evie Curdle, tight-lipped and disapproving, thought her mother had a one-track mind.

'P.O.O.V.?' the She Vee said. 'I'm not sure that's what we're looking for, is it?'

'It doesn't *absolutely* ring a bell,' the He Vee agreed. 'Hang about a bit. What about, Say No Over Fallowfield?'

'That makes S.N.O.F.,' Dot told them with quiet satisfaction, while Evie explained that the one thing she couldn't eat was salad, probably, Fred thought, because she'd seen so many rabbits at it.

'Save Our Valley,' Mrs Vee said suddenly, and added with the authority Fred appeared to lack, 'I think that has a quiet dignity. Don't you, Chair?'

'S.O.V.?' Mr Vee tried the word out. 'I rather like that. Well done, Vee!'

'S.O.V.? Sovereign. What's that meant to sound like?' Barry Harvester was suspicious. 'On Her Majesty's bloody Service?'

'When Dad shot hisself,' Dot told the world in general, 'we found five gold sovereigns sewed up in the lining of his best breeches. Worth a fortune today, they'd be. We got rid of them to some bloody Scotsman who kept a stall in Worsfield Market. Wet behind the ears, we was, in those days.'

'Save Our Valley. Save Our Souls. That has, to me, the right note of urgency about it.' Kev the Rev. spoke excitedly, a plate balanced on his knees, eating as though his life depended upon it.

'I propose S.O.V.,' Mrs Vee said, 'and the Reverend Kevin Bulstrode seconds me. Will you be kind enough to put the motion, Chair?'

Chair was kind enough, and after a short and heated debate, and despite Dot's insistence that their logo should be an artist's impression of 'our hacienda bunnies', it was decided that a drawing of one of the valley orchids should adorn all their communications.

Fred listened to this with half his attention, thinking that the suggestions for protests and fund-raising and publicity, the printing of leaflets and the approaches to the Great and the Good and, it was to be hoped, the Generous, would end in the inevitable contest with Leslie Titmuss. It was Titmuss they must be prepared to fight, Fred decided, and Titmuss who would have to be defeated before the valley was out of danger and he could resume his normal life without the necessity of further buffet do's with the Beazleys. Meanwhile the voices around him rose and fell, coming to no definite conclusion.

'They can't just do away with the footpaths,' Colonel Rudolph Wilcox said. 'They've been there since the Middle Ages.' He and his wife, fearless devotees of rights of way and wearing similar types of tweed trilby in winter and white cotton billycock hats – of the sort well-off children used to play in at the seaside – between May and September, would tramp uncompromisingly across lawns, even through french windows and across carpets, to keep open what they knew to be ancient rights of passage. They don't know Leslie Titmuss, Fred thought, if they believe he's going to pay the slightest attention to anything that happened in the Middle Ages.

'When Doughty Strove tried to put a grass court across the bridlepath at Picton,' Mrs Wilcox said, 'Rudolph and I threatened to get a couple of hacks and ride across it every tea-time. That put a stop to his tennis.'

Ten thousand houses, Fred thought, wouldn't be so easily moved by an elderly couple on horseback. In the respectful silence that followed, he saw Hector Bolitho Jones, still wearing his anorak as though he didn't mean to stay long, staring at him over his encroaching beard. 'Perhaps we should hear from Mr Jones,' he suggested, 'as the expert on the wildlife in the district.'

'I don't see all that harm,' Hector surprised them by saying. 'I read as how the Nature Area's going to be preserved. They've given their word about that.'

'But as a park! In the middle of a town?' Fred argued.

'If they keep people that come into the area in order, I'm not so concerned what they put around it. Perhaps it'll be all the better for a strict enforcement of the bye-laws. As it is, there are those who think they can take all sorts of liberties.' Hector turned his bright, hostile eyes on his wife and the herbalist, of whom he entertained well-justified suspicions.

'You mean, you don't want human beings to have the same rights as your badgers?' Daphne Jones challenged him, and the group felt uneasily that they were in the presence of private grief. Fred knew that they had all formed only an impermanent and uncertain alliance to defeat the stolid determination of his old enemy.

In spite of everything, S.O.V. acquired a good deal of support in the locality, although it was not universally welcomed. Some of the doctors looked forward to the influx of patients a new town would bring; many lawyers had, like Jackson Cantellow, clients anxious to invest in the development; many shopkeepers said they would profit, and the Mayor felt that his high office required him to remain neutral in the matter (he had managed to acquire a small patch of woodland in the Rapstone Valley and hoped, when Fallowfield was triumphant, to sell it and build himself a lavish retirement home on the Costa del Sol, to which he would retreat with his long-time mistress, the manageress of a local chemist's, and finally ditch the Mayoress). Some teachers in Hartscombe dreamed of promotion to a huge Fallowfield comprehensive and the local undertaker welcomed the idea of a steep increase in deaths.

On the whole, S.O.V. could count on the support of the remaining villagers, who knew that Fallowfield houses would be more than they could afford, and the recent immigrants who had paid up to half a million pounds for cottages they had assumed would be in the countryside. A Mr Peregrine Lanfranc, who had opened a ruinously expensive hotel in the old Strove country house at Picton Principal, became hysterical at the thought of his clientele compelled to consume their marinaded duck and Château Latour between Safeways and the Doner Kebab House in Fallowfield High Street. He offered to raffle a free weekend for two in aid of S.O.V., but when the prize was won by Evie Curdle's fiancé, Len, she rejected the opportunity with disgust. Many other well-wishers organized coffee mornings, Bring and Buy sales and recitals in local churches and from these small contributions Mr Vernon Beazley's charity organization company took 25 per cent. 'It's the name of the game in giving nowadays,' the He Vee explained. 'You can't just sit outside the Cash & Carry with a begging-bowl, you know. Appealing to people's better natures is part of the new technology.' Fred Simcox, becoming aware of the Beazley commission, created a row he found enjoyable until the She Vee, taking his part against her husband, kissed him clandestinely and moistly in the ear after a stormy meeting. The Beazley take was reduced to 10 per cent, only to be paid on the basis of work done, and Fred tried to avoid lonely moments with the She Vee.

And he became aware of a momentous event which seemed likely to alter the whole future of the Rapstone Valley. One of the numerous small Bulstrodes ran a soaring temperature and the Doctor was called out to the old Rectory that had once been his home. He passed through the familiar rooms full of unfamiliar clutter and sat on the bed of a little, feverish girl who seemed to be facing, with admirable courage, the difficulties of being a child of the clergy, an experience which Fred remembered as like a lifetime of uneventful but emotional Sunday evenings. When he had diagnosed the measles and prescribed for her, and as he was moving into the damp air of the churchyard, he asked Kev the Rev. about the builder's lorries he had noticed at the gates of Rapstone Manor.

'Haven't you heard?' Kevin Bulstrode, swollen with inside

94

information, shared it proudly. 'Leslie Titmuss has taken it over. He's coming to live. Isn't that marvellous news?'

'Is it?' Fred was doubtful.

'Well, he's hardly going to allow a new town to be built in his own back garden now, is he?'

'I don't know.' Fred thought this over. 'There's one thing I have learned, over the years. You can never trust Titmuss.'

'Oh, I do hope and pray that that's all over now. I don't know how I could face Mr Titmuss in church while I'm campaigning against him as an active member of S.O.V. That' – Kevin looked proud of his interesting dilemma – 'would be so very embarrassing.'

'I can't see why you'll have to face him in church. Titmuss hasn't taken to God, has he?'

'I can't think Mr Titmuss is an unbeliever. You see, and of course I tell you this in the strictest confidence, he's asked me to marry him.'

For an absurd and entertaining moment Fred supposed that the Right Honourable Leslie Titmuss had proposed to Kev the Rev. Then he said, 'He's marrying who?'

'Ah, that' – the Rector had run out of information – 'remains to be seen. But Rapstone Manor, no doubt about it, is going to see a bit of life again. Perhaps the old place will see children . . .'

A long line of Titmusses, stretching out into the future? It was a thought Fred found hard to tolerate.

CHAPTER ELEVEN

Jenny Sidonia had been going out with Leslie Titmuss for a long time before anything in particular happened. 'Going out' was the expression she and her friend Sue Bramble used for staying in, in particular for staying in bed with someone; but when it came to Mr Titmuss 'going out' meant exactly what it said. They met for dinner almost once a week in one or other of the small restaurants near her flat, places she supposed he liked because they never saw any of those he insisted on calling his 'colleagues' there. These colleagues, presumably other members of the government, were shadowy figures whom Leslie spoke of, if at all, with undisguised contempt. Jenny, who had little interest in politics and to whom the names of the colleagues meant little, listened to his revelations of life in government, which seemed to consist mainly of internecine strife, without any particular attention. Then she asked him, because she supposed it would be polite to do so, what had made him wish to enter so strange and unrewarding a world in which people never seemed to wish each other well.

'I got pushed into the river,' he said – something which he hadn't spoken about for decades.

She felt an irresistible urge to burst out laughing and then she looked at him and realized that he was about to make a painful and intimate revelation.

'At a Young Conservative dinner dance, in the old Swan's Nest at Hartscombe. It was a formal occasion!'

'Oh, yes,' she could hardly trust herself to say, 'I bet it was.'

'And this snotty little gang of old Etonians pushed me in. Because I was wearing a hired dinner-jacket. They said I smelt of mothballs. Oh, and I had a ready-made bow-tie. You ought to tie it yourself, but I didn't know that. Bastards!'

His look of hatred was so intense that she could no longer stop the laughter bubbling out of her. 'I'm sorry,' she made a breathless apology. 'I really am most terribly sorry.'

He looked for a moment as though he were going to strike her, as she felt she probably deserved, or at least rise up in fury and slam out of the restaurant. Instead he stared at her in bewilderment and then, very slowly, smiled. At last a low, rasping sound emerged from him, which she found difficult to identify as a laugh.

'I suppose,' he said, 'it is funny.'

'Not really,' she gasped. 'Not really, at all.'

'I never laughed at it before. Not ever.'

'You can now?' She was able then to become serious.

'Well, yes. I suppose I can.'

'So that's what made you take up politics?'

'Oh, I wanted to before that. But then, well, I knew just what I had to do.'

'What?'

'Take it away from those old school twits. That's what I set about then. If you want to know the truth.'

'You mean, make the world safe for people with rented dinner-jackets?' Now he seemed not to mind being mocked.

'Anyway, I wanted to prove it wasn't enough to be able to tie your own dicky-bow. That didn't entitle you to a seat in Cabinet.'

'But you got one.'

'Oh, yes. I knew I'd manage it. In the end.'

What an extraordinary thing to know, she thought, for anyone sinking into the mud and clinging rushes, with the water ruining his first rented tuxedo. And she became aware of Leslie Titmuss's determination as though it were a pungent smell.

'There's one thing I've been meaning to ask you.'

She was sure she knew what was coming, but she was wrong.

'Take me to the opera.'

'What?'

'You go there, don't you? I don't want them to enjoy any more little sniggers at my expense. Like that day at Oxford.'

These were the things that drove him on, she thought, being thrown into the river and being laughed at by a collection of elderly academics. They forced him to seek things that might have been thought unattainable to the young Titmuss – a Ministry and perhaps, well this was such an enormous perhaps that she hardly admitted the possibility to herself, the lonely widow of Tony Sidonia. 'All right,' she said, 'I'll take you, if you promise me one thing.'

'What's that?' He looked wary as he always did when asked for promises.

'That you'll wear a rented dinner-jacket.'

'What's on next week?' Jenny telephoned Sir Willoughby Blane, who was on the Board of the Opera House, as he was on many boards dealing with subjects as diverse as prawns and Puccini.

'Give me a minute, Jenny darling.' Sir Willoughby felt for his folder. '*Simon Boccanegra*. Rather a heavy evening. Do you fancy that?'

'I might do. Wasn't he a politician?'

'A pleb politician in Genoa. Of a rather ruthless variety.'

'That'll do fine, then.'

'Wonderful. You'll be my guest, of course? I'll see if I can scrounge the Royal Box. Anyone you'd like to sit next to, apart from me?'

'Sorry. But I'd love you to get me a couple of seats. Somewhere in the back of the Grand Circle'd do fine.'

'Don't tell me you're being taken by a young man?'

'He's not all that younger than you are. I'll pay for the tickets.'

'Won't he?'

'I won't let him. This is entirely my treat.'

A politician, Sir Willoughby thought to himself as he put down the telephone. The word led him to a wild speculation, which he dismissed as impossible after he had laughed out loud and for a considerable time.

'Go out and get me,' Leslie said to his secretary, 'a tape of Verdi's *Simon Boccanegra*. And the words in English. Oh, and for God's sake, make sure the bloody thing's not a ballet.'

Jenny Sidonia enjoyed taking Leslie Titmuss to Covent Garden. The marble staircase up which she could see them climbing in a welcoming mirror, the buzz in the Crush Bar where she ordered a bottle of champagne to be put ready for them, in the interval, under the bust of Sir Thomas Beecham, as Tony had always done when they could least afford it – these things excited her as they had before. What added to her entertainment was the fact that she was standing Leslie a treat; he clearly found this confusing. By now long accustomed to command, being under her orders as to where they were to go, where they should sit and when they should have their first drink didn't come easily to him, and he was confused by not being the one who paid.

'How the hell much did these tickets cost?'

'I'm not telling you.'

'Why not?'

'You're such a puritan. You wouldn't approve.'

'And our government's handing out tax-payers' money to help this lot go to the opera.' He looked round at the well-nourished faces in the Grand Tier.

'Well, at least that's one good thing about your government.'

'Jenny. Why don't you let me pay?'

'Because you asked me to take you and I'm very obedient. At least I hope you've kept your side of the bargain.'

'What was that?'

'You mean you've forgotten? Just another of your politician's promises.'

He looked at her, puzzled, and she had to remind him. 'Didn't you go to Moss Bros and hire that suit?'

'Well, no. I have to wear it rather often. At functions.' He looked, she was glad to see, guilty. So she pressed home her advantage.

'And the bow-tie? You're not going to tell me you tied it yourself?'

'I've got used to doing it,' he admitted. 'Over the years.'

The lights dimmed and she was able to rebuke him with 'Leslie Titmuss, you've let me down completely' before the conductor bobbed up like a distant jack-in-the-box, received his applause and the overture began.

'The champagne's there. Under Sir Thomas Beecham.'

'Follow me.' Leslie Titmuss felt he was of some use at last. 'I can elbow my way through this lot.' He went through the Crush Bar crowd like a knife through butter. Some opera-goers fell back and smiled nervously, recognizing a well-known face; others gazed in amazement, having always thought the Minister's idea of an evening out would have been all-in wrestling, or dinner overlooking the Wembley dog races.

'Are you enjoying it at all?'

'Good God, yes. A people's politician! Elected by public acclaim. No wonder all the toffee-nosed Italian aristocrats hated him.'

'He came to a bad end.'

'I know,' Titmuss conceded. 'Poisoned by an underling.'

Jenny was surprised at his grasp of the plot. 'What about the music?'

'Oh, that's all right. In fact it hardly gets in the way at all.'

'You're joking!' She was suspicious; surely that was a bit of Titmuss self-parody?

'Yes,' he agreed. 'Do you mind?'

'I never thought that the Opera House was your particular stamping-ground.' Ken Cracken was suddenly upon them, leading

Joyce Timberlake, Christopher Kempenflatt, a Mrs Armitage who was Kempenflatt's lady, and a large man called 'Jumbo' Plumstead, with his wife – he being the merchant banker who was placing large stakes on the proposed Fallowfield Country Town development.

'I don't think you know everything about my interests, do you?' Leslie was unwelcoming.

'I'm Ken Cracken,' the youngish man with a fair moustache told Jenny. 'Joyce Timberlake, Christopher Kempenflatt, Mrs Armitage, Sir Hugh Plumstead, Lady Plumstead.'

' "Jumbo" Plumstead.' The banker was proud of his nickname. 'This is one of the long ones, isn't it?' He seemed to be talking about the opera.

'Jenny Sidonia,' she had to say, as Mr Titmuss clearly had no intention of introducing her to these people, whom he was looking at with smouldering distaste. They had spotted the Secretary of State's unlikely presence from their box, whose privacy they had left, together with a large plate of smoked salmon sandwiches, to satisfy the greater hunger of their curiosity about his beautiful and mysterious companion.

'Such a wonderful place to unwind!' Mrs Armitage, a woman whose hair, skin and jewellery were all the same shade of burnished gold and from whose crustaceous dress her powdered breasts were in danger of being ejected, told Titmuss as though in confidence. 'Christopher always says he forgets all his business worries after the first two bars of the overture.'

'We usually bring the Japanese customers here.' Jumbo Plumstead still had his mind on commerce even at the end of the first act. 'Such a relief not to have the little fellows bowing at you all over the Crush Bar and downing whisky. At least this is a night out with the Brits!'

'We're all still talking about that absolutely super speech you made at the U.C.D.A. dinner, Leslie.' Christopher Kempenflatt's mind also seemed to have returned to business with the cessation of the music. 'It's given us a great deal of encouragement on the Fallowfield project.'

'Hear, hear!' Jumbo rumbled. 'A hundred and fifty years ago those Save Our Valley blighters would have objected to Manchester.'

'Live in Manchester, do you?' Leslie asked Jumbo in what Jenny realized was a tone of considerable menace.

'As a matter of fact we've got a place near Lewes. On the South Downs.'

'The South Downs, eh?' The Titmuss eyes were particularly cold. 'We ought to remember them next time we want to dump a new town somewhere.'

'Of course you're joking!'

But Leslie didn't smile. He turned on his one-time tormentor. 'You ought to take the lady's advice, Kempenflatt. Put business right out of your mind when you go to the opera. This is neither the time nor the place to discuss important matters of planning policy. But you'd be much mistaken if you thought that anything I happened to say at your little dinner party meant that I've even begun to make up my mind about the Rapstone development. One way or the other. Come along now.' And he took Jenny's arm as she had once, so long ago, taken his. 'I reckon this show's costing you about two quid a minute. We can't afford to miss any of it.'

'That Christopher Kempenflatt,' he told Jenny as they found their way back to their seats, 'is one of the bastards who pushed me into the river.'

'I wish you'd told me,' she said. 'I'd've spat in his champagne.'

Later Leslie and his car delivered Jenny to her flat, as he always did after their evenings out. She had never seen the inside of his mansion apartment, nor had she any wish to do so. Sue Bramble, who was her lodger, was away for the night and Jenny felt suddenly miserable at the thought of turning on lights in empty rooms and of going to sleep, once again, with no one to say goodnight to. As usual Leslie kissed her cheek while his driver stared politely at a lamp-post.

'Thank you,' he said. 'That was a treat. I enjoyed it.'

'Shall we go again?'

'I'll start saving up.' He smiled at her.

The strange thing was, she thought, looking back on it, that what happened then was entirely her responsibility. 'Why don't you come in?' she asked as quietly as she could.

'What shall I tell my driver?'

'You can tell him to go home.' And so it was decided.

Very early the next morning, just as it was starting to get light, Jenny Sidonia woke up next to a naked Leslie Titmuss. He was quite motionless and breathing regularly, but his eyes were open. She had heard somewhere that this was how horses slept.

When they had reached the flat they had gone, almost without a word, into the bedroom. There Leslie took off his custom-made dinner-jacket and hung it carefully over the back of a chair. Jenny said, 'I won't be a minute,' and went into the sitting-room where she looked, for a little, at her outstretched hand. Then she took off her wedding-ring and put it in the drawer of a writing-desk which had once been the property of Tony Sidonia. She went into the bathroom and spent a short while taking off her make-up and cleaning her teeth. When she came back to her bedroom Leslie Titmuss was already undressed and between the sheets. The room was in darkness which was apparently how he preferred it.

His eyes always seemed cold but she was surprised by the heat of his body and, although he was so much older than she, he behaved as though he were enjoying a youth long postponed. At the same time she was made to feel as though she, Jenny Sidonia, was the height of his ambition, long awaited, like his position in the Cabinet, the Right Honourable in front of his name and the black official motor car always in attendance.

When he lay motionless, asleep, she thought, with his eyes open, he spoke.

'You like Rapstone, then?'

'I told you. It's beautiful.'

'You like the house?'

'I told you I did.'

'They want to build a town there.'

'The man who pushed you in?'

'Yes. That's his idea.'

'He can, can't he?'

'I don't think you should worry.'

He had said planning policy shouldn't be discussed in the Crush Bar of the Opera House. To talk about it when they were in bed for the first time, just after five o'clock in the morning, seemed equally inappropriate. She closed her eyes and fell into a deep sleep and when she woke again he was still looking at her.

'My son, Nick,' he said, 'is a librarian.'

'Is he?'

'He's got himself a job. Somewhere in the North-East.' Leslie had travelled to the sprawling town in an area untouched by the prosperity his government had brought to the South of England. He had walked through the rooms which smelt of disinfectant and floor polish, where pensioners slumbered over the news-papers and schoolchildren giggled and searched vainly for rude bits in the *Encyclopaedia Britannica*. He was enraged because the fear that he had had in the college garden was realized. His son was calling himself Nicholas Fanner. 'Mr Fanner,' they had told him, 'is in cataloguing.'

'He doesn't want me to help him,' he told Jenny. 'I don't want your name because I want to do something on my own,' Nick had said. 'I don't want to be given jobs just because you're in the Cabinet.'

'Are you ashamed of me, then?' Leslie had covered his hurt with anger. 'Not ashamed. Of course not. But we're different, aren't we?' Nick had tried to explain. 'We're two entirely different people.'

'Surely it's understandable,' Jenny said. 'He wants to be independent.' She felt sorry for Leslie and liked him better because of this unhappiness.

'I don't know. I don't really know about Nick. Just as I didn't know about his mother.'

'The one who liked men who ate sauce sandwiches?'

'Yes. That's the one.'

'Well. How do you get on at understanding me?' Jenny wanted to cheer him up; he seemed a prey to such sad thoughts.

'I think we've got something in common.'

'What, for instance?'

Loneliness, that's what she thought he might be going to say. Instead he laughed at her, 'Opera!' Then they started to make love all over again.

Sue Bramble, who shared Jenny's flat, had been to visit her lover, a trainer of horses who lived near Newbury. They had argued for a great part of the night about his apparent inability to so arrange matters with the wife from whom he said he was separated, so that he might marry Sue. Finally he confessed what she had half suspected, that this wife of his was only staying with relations in America and he had not, in fact, plucked up courage to break the news of Sue's existence to her. Filled with rage and swearing never to bestride one of his horses or travel to the races with him again, she had got into her Triumph motor car at dawn and driven back to London, disillusioned with life, love and the reliability of husbands. She arrived at the flat early and there found a tall, pale man in a dinner-jacket making tea in the kitchen. Although unshaven he had taken the trouble to tie his black bow.

'Hullo,' she said. 'I'm Sue Bramble. I suppose you're Mr Titmuss.'

He looked at her as though he was considering the possibility of denying it, and then said, 'Yes.'

'If you're making that for Jenny, she likes Lapsang. I'd better show you where it is.' And she added, quite unnecessarily, 'It was Tony's favourite.'

After she had made the tea he thanked her and took it away in silence. She heard voices and then the front door open and shut.

Later she sat on the end of Jenny's bed. To her disappointment, her friend looked unreasonably contented.

'The things you get up to the moment my back's turned!'

'I thought you were away till tomorrow.'

'I don't think I'll ever be away again. Men are such *liars!*'

'I'm sorry.'

'And I'm sorry I scared your Mr Titmuss. I thought he was going to jump out of his skin.'

'I don't think he was scared, particularly.'

'Nonsense. He bolted out of here like a rabbit.'

'He had to get home and change.'

'Well, I imagine he didn't want to turn up at the Ministry in his tuxedo.' Sue Bramble lit a cigarette in some gloom. 'Is he terrified I'll talk and it'll be all over the *News of the World*?'

'He did mention that possibility.'

'What did you say?'

'I told him you were totally reliable.'

'Too bloody reliable. That's my trouble.'

'Oh, Sue.' Jenny looked at her friend with great concern. 'Teddy has let you down, hasn't he?'

'Don't worry about me. You're the one we've got to worry about. Promise me, Jenny. You will be careful, won't you?'

'I'm sorry.' Jenny Sidonia gave the matter some thought. 'I don't think I can promise that.'

Later that morning, when Jenny was sitting contemplating the unsold and quite probably unsaleable New British Abstracts, the telephone rang and a female secretarial voice said, 'Mrs Sidonia? I have the Secretary of State here for you.'

'Jenny.' Mr Titmuss came on the line immediately, sounding brisk. 'I meant to tell you. I have to go to Rome next month. Something to do with my opposite number in the Community.'

It was a one-night stand, she thought with unexpected despondency, and this is his way of saying goodbye. 'I hope you enjoy it,' she said.

'And I've been thinking . . .'

'About me?'

'Yes.'

'What exactly?' She was not, whatever happened to her, about to weep.

'Well. Wouldn't Rome be rather a good place for a honeymoon?'

'What on earth can you be talking about?' It was ridiculous, the great swing on which her spirits were rising.

'I've rung the Rector of Rapstone and suggested a date for him to pencil in. They're both dead, I told him, so there's no reason why we shouldn't be married in church, is there?'

After they had spoken, she sat still for a long time, then she telephoned Sue Bramble and offered to buy her lunch in Soho. She wanted to cool off, as soon as possible, in the icy waters of her best friend's disapproval.

CHAPTER TWELVE

'What on earth would Tony think?' Jenny found the question particularly irritating, partly because it assumed that Tony was still around somewhere and watching everything she did with puzzled disapproval, but mainly because it was what she had avoided asking herself. Now Sue Bramble had, with a true friend's lack of mercy, faced her with it.

'How on earth should I know?'

'Well, what do you *think*?' Sue wasn't going to let her off lightly.

'I think Tony always wanted me to be happy.' Jenny played for safety.

'Oh, yes. I'm sure he did. But would he have wanted you to be happy with *Leslie Titmuss*?'

'I think he'd've left it to me.'

'Chalk and cheese?'

'What?'

'Your extraordinary Leslie and Mr Sidonia. By the way, was he wearing a made-up tie?'

'What do you mean?'

'When I caught him in full evening-dress at seven o'clock in the morning. Was that a ready made-up bow he was wearing?'

'I can tell you without a doubt' – in this new and confusing world there was one thing Jenny was sure of – 'he tied it entirely himself.'

'A real bow-tie which managed to look phoney! Only your Mr Titmuss could do that.'

'If he were exactly like Tony. If he wore all the right clothes, only he looked as though he slept in them and didn't give a damn anyway. If he knew all the poetry and history I'd never heard of, and read all the books I've never even opened and could be quite serious, particularly when he was making jokes – Well, then, I suppose Tony might be upset because I'd found someone who could do all he could do and perhaps better. But my Mr Titmuss, as you insist on calling him, can't do any of those things. He's chalk and cheese, as you said. So why on earth should Tony be jealous of him?'

She was, she realized, being absurd. Where on earth was Tony, to be jealous or not? If not on earth, was he floating through space, dodging secret weapons and television satellites, deeply distressed by her new friendship? She could only think of him in his fraying basket-chair in the untidy garden of their house in North Oxford, holding a book too close to his eyes and laughing tolerantly at the nefarious connivings of some long-dead Pope. No doubt he would be laughing at her and Leslie's strange behaviour, and when she thought about it she decided he might be right and laughter was the only possible reaction.

'I'm not saying he'd be jealous. I'm just saying he might not be very happy about your prospects.'

'You think Mr Titmuss is going to ditch me?'

'I think he'd ditch his own mother, if it'd get him higher up in that awful Cabinet or whatever it is he belongs to.'

'I tell you, you're wrong.'

'Am I?'

'Oh, yes. Mr Titmuss and Mr Sidonia aren't as entirely different as you think. There's a sort of honesty about both of them.'

'You really believe that?'

'Oh, yes. I do.'

'All right, Jenny.' Sue Bramble smiled in her most irritating and grown-up way. 'I just hope you go on believing it. That's all.'

*

This question of honesty was an important one to Jenny. Her mother, from whom she had inherited her looks but not her character, moved naturally in a world of lies, where the climate suited her. When she was a child Jenny thought that lying was a sort of game her mother played in the car, like Animal, Vegetable, Mineral or I Spy. She gave, Jenny soon realized, totally inaccurate information about where she'd been, what she'd bought, where she'd left her handbag and who had telephoned. She lied, it seemed, out of pure high spirits or for the pleasure of exercising her undoubted talent for invention. She would tell her husband, who was something in engineering and travelled a lot, that she had been shopping in Tesco's where there was this extraordinary crowd of Japanese tourists holding them up at the check-out, when they had gone to Sainsbury's and hardly been kept waiting at all. Jenny had heard her mother say to her father, when she was meant to be asleep but could hear them talking in the next bedroom, that she had taken their daughter for lunch at the zoo when she had, in fact, been left to play with her friend Sheena Dalrymple. She even heard some of the comical things she was alleged to have said about the animals she never saw. For a moment she wondered if she had gone mad and had never been in Sheena's house playing tedious games of Mothers and Fathers but had actually been staring at a camel and saying brightly, 'A horse with a house on its back!' Then she supposed it was one of her mother's peculiar games. Not until she was older did Jenny deduce that these games had some connection with the constant sounds of her parents quarrelling, the slamming of doors, cars driving away and then returning to further shouted accusations, denials and footsteps on the stairs. Then her father's travels seemed to last longer and her mother often met her from school in a strange car, driven by a man in a fawn overcoat who smelt like the hairdresser's and offered Jenny, to her intense embarrassment, curiously strong mints which he kept in his waistcoat pocket.

This was also a time when her mother began to go on travels

and Jenny was sent to stay with her grandmother in St Leonards-on-Sea. Granny Paget was a small, bright-eyed woman who swam in the coldest weather, picking her way barefoot across the frosty beach to flop into the grey water, wearing a one-piece woollen bathing-suit and a pink plastic shower-cap, large as a tam o'shanter, propelling herself afloat by thrashing her arms in a sort of windmill motion which she called 'the crawl'. Then she and Jenny would walk home across the shingle, the wind blowing so strongly at them that they were hardly able to move and stood for a long time poised for the next step, with Jenny's hair and her school mac billowing out behind her. When they got home they always had what Granny Paget called a 'slap-up tea' to recover from the swim and Jenny was allowed as many scones and as much anchovy toast as the old lady, although she never entered the water because of her intense fear of the cold. At these teas they would sit together and Jenny would go through the events of the day to be sure that all she remembered had actually occurred.

Granny Paget would also give Jenny Sidonia details of life in Hong Kong, where her grandfather had been stationed when in the army. Jenny was glad to have it confirmed that her mother's general account of life in that city was accurate, although when she got down to details the evidence became more shaky. 'Mummy says her nurse took her out for a walk and then pulled her into this terrible low den where Chinamen were sitting round smoking opium and playing cards. She said you had to pay a lot of dollars to get her back.'

'Fairy tales!' Granny Paget said with impatient scorn as she brushed crumbs off her lap and smeared another scone with raspberry jam. 'The nurse took her to Sunday School and I didn't want her to go because she was far too gullible already. So far as I remember, your mother believed in Father Christmas until puberty! And I never paid a penny to get her back.'

Once they received a faint telephone call and Jenny's mother, sounding as though she were under water, announced that she had travelled to Tenerife but would be back on Thursday morning and come straight down to St Leonards. She said, 'I can't wait to see you, darling.' Although they laid on extra supplies of scones and Jenny had a new dress, her mother never came. A week later a postcard from Malaga told them, 'Stuck here longer than I expected, darling. Just can't wait to see you.' 'Fairy tales!' Granny Paget said, as though she had never expected anything different. From that time truth-telling seemed to be more important than ever to Jenny.

When her parents were divorced, Granny Paget said, 'Your mother never found out the importance of sticking to things.' Jenny's father travelled to Oakwood, California, where he sired a large new family. Photographs of new half-brothers and sisters dandled by a strapping blonde at some distant poolside were posted to Jenny almost annually, accompanied by the briefest of notes from her father: 'Peter (or Barbara Joy or Hepworth) begs to be introduced and can't wait to meet his/her big sister.' Like her mother, these siblings seemed able to contain their impatience and she spent more and more of her holidays in St Leonards watching the pale, blue-veined body of her grandmother sink into the water and walking home along the wind-torn promenade. As she had little else to do she worked very hard and got into Oxford.

There, as a student, she was at first lonely and then, when word of her beauty was put about, much sought after. She embarked on a few love affairs with young men she expected to prove unreliable and in this, at least, they didn't disappoint her. It wasn't until her last year at the university that she was taught by Tony Sidonia. 'History,' he told his students in his first lecture on the Roman Church during the Renaissance, 'is an account of the way our ancestors lied to each other because they were too evil, or ambitious, or manipulative, or simple-minded, or cowardly to face the facts. Our great advantage over them is that we are able to tell the truth and that's the justification of our existence.' These words appealed greatly to Jenny and she copied them carefully into the front of her notebook. She was surprised, as Tony continued his lecture, to discover that the Borgia Pope was even less truthful than her mother.

Tony Sidonia rented, at that time, a cottage about ten miles to the north of Oxford and, in the summer, he used to invite his friends for Sunday lunch. Jenny came out in a car with some other students and felt privileged. She lay in the sun on the long matted grass of a 'lawn' which apparently had never seen a mower. She helped wash up and peel vegetables and she thought she had been invited to make herself useful. Tony was clearly attached to Sue Bramble, who was always there, and Jenny thought they trusted each other far too much to get married in the sense in which she understood the word.

Towards the end of her last year she was seeing Tony Sidonia more often – at dinner parties or visits to the movies, or when opera companies came on tour – but they were always with other people, for Tony had a wide circle of friends, ranging from white-haired Euro-Communist scientists to old Etonians from Christ Church and their girlfriends. For one thing Jenny was grateful; she was always invited on her own and no attempts were made to pair her off, as happened after Mr Sidonia's death. One Sunday, just after she'd done her finals, Tony arranged to pick her up and drove her to his cottage where she found that they were alone together and that the table, with bread, cheese, wine and pâté, was laid with two places only.

'Where's Sue?' she asked as she went, as usual, to wash the lettuce.

'She's not coming here this weekend. I told her it had to be over.'

'You quarrelled?' Jenny couldn't believe it. 'You never quarrel.'

'We didn't quarrel. I just told her I had something to do, and I couldn't do it with any honesty while we were living together.'

Jenny was silent. She had no idea of what was to come.

'Anyway, she agreed it was much better we told each other

the truth. Saves an awful lot of mess. She said she hoped that you and she would stay friends. I said I hoped so too.'

'Friends? Why shouldn't we be friends?'

'That's exactly what Sue thinks.'

She was washing the lettuce now, keeping her hands in the cold water with the tap running. She discovered a slug sleeping in a pale-green bed and dislodged it with a fingernail. Then she imprisoned the lettuce in a wire censer and went to the door where she swung it briskly through the air, producing a fine rain which glittered in the last of the year's sunshine.

'So now you've done your finals,' he said. 'Now we're free.'

'Free of exams.'

'Well, free of having to behave ourselves, like a teacher and a pupil. It's no good getting that relationship tangled up with emotions. No good at all. It always leads to a complete mess. I've always made that a golden rule.'

'Have you?' It was true. He hadn't given her a hint of what she now knew he must be talking about.

'So now,' he said, 'I can do what I've wanted to do for such a long time.'

'What's that?'

'Proposition you. I suppose you'd call it that.' He laughed then, as she had discovered he always did at the things he took most seriously.

All that happened almost exactly fourteen years before she was propositioned again, this time by Leslie Titmuss.

As he had suggested they went to Rome for their honeymoon.

She felt, not as though she had embarked on a perilous future, but as though she were flying back to a familiar past when she had always been looked after. In fact the looking-after was even more efficient than it had been in the days of Tony Sidonia, who often missed buses, was late for meals or forgot about aeroplanes in his constant preoccupation with trying to point out the truth to long-dead and self-deceiving pontiffs. With Leslie Titmuss the small details of life were reliably looked after, the car was waiting at the airport and a man from the embassy was there to dispense with any tedious formalities at the hotel reception. As she opened the windows and looked down on to the Spanish Steps where she and Tony used to sit among the sleeping students and guitar-players and sellers of cheap belts and costume jewellery, and eat their lunch-time *paninis*, Leslie Titmuss said, 'There's only a day and a half of meetings and one lunch and a boring dinner we'll have to go to. For the rest of the time you can educate me. I've never been to Rome before. Have you ever been to Rome?'

'Oh, yes,' she told him. 'Rather often.' The last time had been when Tony came nearest to popular success. The B.B.C. had asked him to make a historical documentary called 'In the Shadow of the Triple Crown'. They had been here with a film unit and stayed in the unusual splendour of the Eden Hotel.

Now Leslie was eager to learn the Italian phrases Tony had taught her, which she still wasn't entirely sure how to spell when he insisted on writing them down in his Filofax. They stood with their faces upturned among the crowds that filled the Sistine Chapel as though it were an airport in high season, and Jenny took her husband down the familiar corridors to the Vatican Library. They walked among the plane trees and statues in the Borghese Gardens and he found the white naked figure of Napoleon's sister, Pauline, carved in marble to be alluring. 'It's you,' Leslie Titmuss told her. 'Absolutely. It makes me think of you.' And Jenny remembered that, although they were as different as chalk and cheese, Tony Sidonia had said almost the same thing.

Nor were the one formal lunch and the official dinner a particularly high price to pay for Rome. She sat beneath painted ceilings smiling enchantingly as German and Dutch representatives, delighted to be free for an hour from the appalling tediousness of their jobs, flirted with her ponderously. On their last night Leslie asked Jenny to suggest somewhere for dinner and she took him across the river to a place she remembered.

The streets leading to the square of Santa Maria in Trastevere were darker and dirtier than when she had last seen them. The young people lurking in doorways, astride parked Lambrettas or sitting on the bonnets of other people's cars were no doubt up to no good, dealing in noxious substances or worse. Leslie strode through them bravely and held on to her as tightly as if she had been his wallet. But the square, the fountain and the golden mosaic front of Santa Maria were unchanged. 'We'll go in here before we eat,' she said, and led him into the church built on the spot where a stream of pure olive oil flowed during the whole day of Christ's Nativity. 'Give me some lire,' she said. 'I'll buy us a couple of candles.' 'Why? Are you religious?' He looked at her suspiciously. 'Not at all, but you can't be too careful. Not when it comes to luck.' They lit their candles together and speared them on spikes next to the guttering flames lit by those in fear of death, or the police, or pregnancy, or failure in examinations, or the general nerve-racking anxiety of getting through the day.

They sat in front of Sabatini's, protected by dusty shrubs through which children peered and thrust hands clutching for lire or cigarettes. And when she tasted the pale white wine and the metallic flavour of the spaghetti vongole Jenny was overcome with a terrible longing for the husband she had lost and in whose honour she had just lit a candle.

'You're crying!'

'No, really.'

Leslie Titmuss touched her cheek with his knuckles, and then withdrew his hand as though her tears had scalded him.

'It's him, isn't it? You used to come here with *him*. You're crying for Tony Sidonia.'

'Of course I'm not. Honestly. It's just that I'm tired. That's all. Tired, after all the excitement. You do like this place, don't you?'

She dried her cheeks carefully with her table napkin and, for the first time since their marriage, she felt miserable. The question of honesty meant a great deal to her and she had just lied and, in lying, betrayed Tony.

CHAPTER THIRTEEN

When Leslie Titmuss met Jenny Sidonia at lunch in St Joseph's, Oxford, he had achieved all but two of his ambitions. He had reached high office in a government which had ruled the country for so long that most young people could not remember another. And he had survived some temporary embarrassments, such as the death of his wife in the anti-nuclear protest at Worsfield Heath, to become a national figure. He was respected, enjoyed, if not liked, as a sardonic wit, a card, a man who gave honest utterance to the feelings of all ordinary citizens and who didn't give a damn for what the liberal intellectuals thought of him. Liberal intellectuals were responsible, after all, for most of the ills of the modern world, from drug abuse to the B.B.C. Some of his phrases had become part of the language, as when he called the welfare state 'The Scroungers' Charter', or the opposition 'The Ageing Hippies' because their principal concern seemed to be free hip-replacements in a population annually growing older. 'One chap's plastic hip,' Leslie Titmuss had been fond of saying when he was at Health, 'is another chap's crippling taxation.' The man who promised the Archbishop that he'd guarantee not to preach in Canterbury Cathedral provided that cleric kept his nose out of politics, who referred to barristers as 'wallies in wigs, wrapped in the tattered gowns of class privilege' and who had called the unemployed 'ladies and gentlemen of leisure' was always sure of a headline or a place on any chat show. He was then at the height of his power and his popularity

– and the England that had grown up in the last decade had been born in the image of Leslie Titmuss.

At the time of the lunch at St Joseph's all this had been achieved. Leslie was like a climber who scrambles up, with bleeding hands and boots lodged in precarious toe-holds, to the top of the apparently unassailable mountain and then has nothing to do but sit down, eat his sandwiches and admire the view. Although the first flush of triumph may have gone and the excitement of the ascent is over, it is still far too early to think about the way down.

Looking about him he saw only two more peaks to conquer. He would, what politician wouldn't, have liked to be Prime Minister, but only death, it seemed, would part the present incumbent from that office. He also wanted, he positively longed, to obliterate the memory of a failed marriage; and the only way he could think of doing this was by a marriage which would be a resounding success. He was tired of the sympathy hostesses bestowed on him for his widowerhood, as though it were some sort of physical deformity. His loneliness, he felt, put him back among the underprivileged, the no-hopers he had devoted considerable energy and talent to leaving far behind him. He wanted to marry but none of the ambitious personal assistants or party workers who were granted, for an occasional night, the freedom of his mansion flat came near to the idea of the sort of wife he thought his position demanded. He wanted a wife who would make him the envy of his few friends and, more satisfactorily, his many enemies. He wanted to hear the likes of his Minister of State Ken Cracken whisper, 'My God, how did old Leslie manage it?' Even, 'What the hell can she see in him?' would have been music to his ears. In the pursuit of matrimony he wanted to bring off something as seemingly impossible as the young nettle-feller from Rapstone Rectory earning a place in the Cabinet. When he found himself next to Jenny Sidonia for the first time he was presented, he thought, with the ideal challenge. He could hear the voice of his long-dead father, George Titmuss, who had no ambitions beyond being an accounts clerk at Simcox Brewery, saying, 'She's got class, boy. Undoubtedly class. Girls like that are not for the likes of you.' To which Leslie, calling over the gulf of the years, would have answered, 'Get stuffed, Dad, and just watch me.'

No doubt he overestimated the difficulties of capturing Jenny; he never understood her loneliness and consequent vulnerability. She was never that glacial and unscaleable peak he imagined her to be when he first took up the challenge. He thought, and this was perhaps Leslie Titmuss's most serious weakness, that people would never do what he wished unless they were bribed or threatened. There could, of course, be no question of threatening Jenny Sidonia, so some sort of inducement had to be offered to her. He guessed, quite rightly, that his political success meant nothing to her for as soon as politics were mentioned her gaze would wander round the room as though seeking means of escape. She would never have dreamt of allying herself with a man simply because he was in charge of the Department of Housing, Ecological Affairs and Planning; indeed such a position might well have an offputting and anaphrodisiac effect upon her. But he must have something she wanted because Leslie Titmuss, for all his apparent confidence, couldn't bring himself to believe that such a girl as Jenny Sidonia would love him for himself alone. And the perfect bribe, he came to convince himself, was Rapstone Manor.

Leslie had persuaded himself of the justice of his claim to the Fanner house many years before. He felt it was his because the family owed it to him. He had married their only daughter, who had not only been consistently unfaithful but indulged in political activities which were anathema to his party. The fact that he had married Charlotte Fanner because her father was chairman of the local Conservatives represented a debt which he had long since paid off. So he planned to acquire the house, when Grace Fanner died insolvent, from the deeply caring West Country Bank. But if he bought it the question was, what should he do with it?

His mother didn't want it and his son, at any rate for the moment, seemed to regard the prospect of owning a large country house in an appalling state of disrepair, as akin to a sentence of death. Then Leslie met Jenny Sidonia and thought that, although she might find the idea of life with him a doubtful prospect, life with him in a house which had impressed her, in a place she found beautiful, would prove a temptation she could not resist. So he decided to go ahead and buy the place. It was while the sale was going through that he picked up the information that Ken Cracken, his Minister of State, had been careful to keep from him, that there were plans afoot to submerge the Rapstone Valley in Fallowfield Country Town. He thought of the pointlessness of offering the girl he hoped to make his bride a charming and historic country house situated within hailing distance of the municipal Leisure Complex and the bus centre, bang in the middle of the pedestrian precinct. From that moment Leslie Titmuss became a secret underground member of S.O.V.

Nipping in the bud such an expensively fertilized plant as Fallowfield presented him with a problem which even he felt was a challenge to his political skills. His speech to the construction industry had been a great success and he didn't intend to retract a single word of it. However, as he had said to Ken Cracken, in the encounter that led Ken to the astonishing conclusion that his boss had gone green, free scope for market forces and healthy commercial development must be balanced against the claims of the environment, and there was, surely, more environment round the Rapstone Valley than almost anywhere else in the British Isles. Moreover, there was another powerful reason against the erection of Fallowfield Country Town. Christopher Kempenflatt stood to make an extraordinarily large sum of money out of it and Kempenflatt, as the Secretary of State would remember until the day he died, had publicly humiliated Leslie Titmuss at the Young Conservative dinner dance.

The question was how to prevent Fallowfield without the

charge that he was doing it to provide a quiet and privileged home for his new family. The answer was, Leslie thought, perfectly simple. There would be a free and independent public inquiry, and the function of a free and independent public inquiry was, the Secretary of State had no doubt, to reflect his preferably unstated wishes. When the inquiry had reported that, after careful deliberation and having heard all sides, the Rapstone Valley was not, after all, a suitable site for urban development, he would have no alternative but to accept its recommendations. There might be a few snide comments in some discontented newspapers, jokes about his back garden, but his reputation would merely grow greener and thereby more attractive. Jenny and he, together with the deer and badgers and the Duke of Burgundy's fritillary butterfly, could enjoy the valley unmolested, and the best-laid schemes of Kempenflatts the builders would come to nothing.

It was a time for weddings in Rapstone. Dot Curdle, using her full authority as head and undisputed ruler of the Curdle family, ordered her daughter, Evie, to take Dr Simcox's unpalatable medicine, somewhat hastily prescribed, and 'have a go' at marriage guidance. It was a command that Evie felt she had to obey, so she presented herself, wearing an extremely sullen expression, at the office under the Town Hall in which the marriage guidance lady appeared once a week to give counsel. With Evie was her fiancé, Len Bigwell, a ginger-haired, plump and perpetually smiling young man who loved her tenderly and was deeply moved by her heroic efforts to adjust herself to the unpalatable business of loving him.

'Sit down, both of you, and do just relax.' Mrs Tippett, the marriage counsellor, was a substantial, dark-haired woman with tragic eyes who wore a knitted suit, boots and numerous bangles. Evie and Len sat, perched nervously on the edge of their chairs. 'Sex,' Mrs Tippett opened briskly, 'is really nothing to be afraid of, is it?'

'Isn't it?' Evie looked profoundly unconvinced. 'I don't know so much.'

'Now then, Miss Curdle.' Mrs Tippett's voice became softer, more cajoling. 'I'm sure you're very much in love with your Les.'

'No.' Evie's small mouth shut tight as a mousetrap.

'You mean, you *don't* love Les?'

'No.' Evie's mouth was only opened wide enough to admit the smallest morsel of cheese and then snapped shut again.

'And yet' – the counsellor's eyes moved imploringly towards heaven – 'you're going to become his wife.'

'No.' Evie felt she was winning.

'Oh, dear. Has something gone rather wrong? A lovers' tiff sort of thing? This is *marriage* guidance, you know. That's what we're here to help you with. Now tell me, dear. Why aren't you going to marry Les?'

'Because I don't know no Les.' Evie feared that she had let herself down and said too much.

There was a moment of real panic in the counsellor's large eyes. Seldom or never had she given marriage guidance to a couple who were not only not married but didn't even know each other. And then the smiling man broke his silence to say, 'I'm *Len*. Len Bigwell.' 'Oh, dear. Silly me!' Mrs Tippett laughed musically and her bangles rattled an accompaniment. 'Of course you are. Sorry, Miss Curdle. I'm sure you're very much in love with your chap, Len.'

Evie sat with her mouth shut, giving no more away.

'Len loves *you*. I'm sure about that. Don't you, Len?'

'No problem,' Len assured her. 'Never has been.' He looked at his fiancée and blinked away tears, apparently of happiness.

'And you love Len, I'm sure. Don't you love Len, Miss Curdle? And may I call you Evie?'

'I don't care.'

'You don't care for Len. Really?'

'I don't care if you calls me Evie.'

The bangles jingled again as the counsellor looked at her watch; so far the interview seemed to be getting nowhere. 'You do want Len to be happy, Evie, don't you?'

'I'm not worried.' Evie Curdle looked longingly at the door.

'What?' The counsellor looked deeply concerned.

'She's honestly not worried,' Len explained, still smiling proudly, 'if I'm happy or not. That's what she's trying to tell you.'

'That's Len's business, isn't it? If he's happy.' Evie agreed so far with her fiancé.

'Your business too, Evie. When you're married to him. And if you make Len happy, then perhaps you'll make yourself happy too.'

'Not by doing it I won't.'

'Evie. Can I ask you this? Have you ever tried?'

'I haven't.'

'I have,' Len admitted proudly. 'On numerous occasions.'

'Well . . . how did Evie react?' Mrs Tippett clearly felt as though she were getting somewhere at last.

'Told me to get lost.' Len still looked admiringly at his future bride.

'But Evie. Don't you think Len loves you?' Mrs Tippett seemed increasingly pained.

'He says he does.'

'And you believe him?'

'I suppose so.'

'Well, then . . .'

'If he loves me he can do without it. Loving me ought to be quite enough for him. Anyway, that's what I reckon.'

'Evie.' The counsellor got up and paced the room, her arms crossed on her bosom, her military-style boots clicking on the linoleum. 'Evie, my dear . . .' She was about to embark on an inquiry which she knew might prove long and painful and she feared it might be difficult to obtain a stream of recollection from a client who was addicted to monosyllables. 'I wonder if we could go on a little journey together. Into your past. Now, I want you to be a hundred per cent honest about this. Is there anything in your childhood, anything at all, which might account for your distaste for . . . the physical side of married life?'

'Yes.' Evie answered immediately and the counsellor felt she had been pushing at a door which opened far too quickly and overbalanced her.

'Reeaally? How . . . how interesting! Do you feel you might be able to tell me?'

'I was brought up with a lot of bloody rabbits.'

'Rabbits?' The counsellor was slow to take in the relevance of the answer.

'Angoras and eaters. And I works on her family's rabbit hacienda *with* Evie. We are fellow workers,' Len explained.

'The angoras is the worst,' Evie told her counsellor with disgust. 'Always at it.'

'I see. Yes, of course. I do see.' Mrs Tippett sat down and consulted her watch, causing another jangle of jewellery. 'I think we must have a long chat about this. A real heart-to-hearter. Do you think you'd be able to come regularly on Thursdays? And it would be a terrific help if Les, I mean Len, would come with you.'

'You mean for marriage guidance?'

'Well, yes.'

'How long'd we have to keep coming?' Len was prepared for anything.

'Until we've helped you sort out your little problem.'

'You mean, until I give him sex?'

'Well, I suppose you could put it like that. Yes.'

Evie thought it over. 'If I do it once a week, I won't have to come?'

'Well, no. I'm sure Len thinks that reasonable. In view of your rather unusual upbringing. Wouldn't you, Len?'

'I'd settle for that.' Len was his usual cheerful self. 'Thank you.'

'Then it's either sex or marriage guidance?' Evie looked at the door again.

'Well, I wouldn't put it exactly like that.'

'I'll do the sex,' Evie said with the grim air of a youthful offender opting for a short, sharp shock rather than a long period on probation. 'I'd rather do that than come here again.' And then she made for the door with Len hurrying eagerly after her.

Not long afterwards and influenced by her intense dislike of marriage guidance, Evie and Len made love in a darkened caravan on the rabbit farm. The effect on her was not noticeable, but Len became a changed man. He smiled less but his self-confidence increased hugely. He worked out new ideas for packaging the freezer joints and toured the countryside looking for more retail outlets. 'Health food is the name of the game nowadays,' he told Dot Curdle with his new-found enthusiasm. 'We've got to sell rabbit as nature's greatest health food. Country-fed rabbit. A genuine green dinner.'

'Green?' Dot was doubtful. 'Only if it's gone off.'

'And I bet rabbit cures a lot of illness.'

'Does wonders for your love life, anyway.' Dot laughed. 'You found that, didn't you, Evie?'

'Please, Mum. Don't be disgusting!'

All the same, Evie admired the new, entrepreneurial Len Bigwell and, by the time they walked down the aisle of Rapstone Church together, she felt able to tolerate his love-making, which was already having such a beneficial effect on the family business. As for Len, he was so overcome with emotion brought on by the day, the organ music, the smell of orange blossom and Evie's new compliance that he looked at his bride through another blur of devoted tears. Fred, who had been invited to attend the ceremony, wondered at the success of Mrs Tippett's marriage guidance as an aphrodisiac in which he had not, up to then, had a great deal of faith.

A few weeks later he was back in the same church for another wedding, that of the Right Honourable Leslie Titmuss, M.P. and Jenny, only daughter of Edward and Joanna Banks. Leslie, who had had the invitations printed, had not included the name Sidonia on them.

As he sat in the church crowded with the notable inhabitants of Rapstone and the surrounding countryside, Fred wondered why he had been invited and why he had accepted the invitation. More years ago than he cared to remember Leslie had asked him to be his best man when he married Charlotte Fanner, and Fred, a young medical student with a love affair in tatters, had welcomed an afternoon away from the study of the central nervous system. Over the years they had grown so apart that they now seemed like strangers from distant countries, brought up in alien cultures: the country doctor who despised politicians, and particularly politicians of the Titmuss variety, and the Secretary of State who found Dr Simcox's retreat from the world of great issues and tough decisions into the safety of a country practice merely pathetic. So why had Fred come? Curiosity, he supposed, and – he thought how little, on the whole, he had changed since his student days – on an impulse to break up the monotonous routine of his life. As for why Leslie had asked him, the reason was obvious as soon as Jenny, crowned with flowers and smiling as though still amazed at what she was getting up to, entered the church on the arm of a conveniently tall cousin she hardly knew. He was standing in for her father who couldn't get away from his considerable family in Oakwood, California. Leslie Titmuss clearly wanted to show her off and fill his few friends and many enemies with wonder and envy. Leslie had no doubt that Fred had patronized him from his childhood and had despised his ruthless pursuit of fame and fortune. And now, Leslie had wanted to say, what have you got for keeping your hands out of grubby politics? Nothing but the prospect of a lonely old age, whereas I am now standing in front of the altar, where your father once prayed in vain for the coming of a new Socialist Jerusalem, waiting for a slim and beautiful young woman to deliver herself to me, forsaking all others. This may not have been exactly how Leslie Titmuss would have put it, but Fred Simcox thought it was, and Fred was never able to attribute high motives to the man he looked on as a threat to England in general and to the Rapstone Valley in particular.

It was all done with considerable dispatch. Kev the Rev. gave a short address in which he managed to mention 'compassion' four times, 'values beyond the marketplace' three times and 'England's green and pleasant land' at least twice. He had nerved himself to give this homily, which he thought of as a daring attack on government policies, but Leslie sat smiling imperturbably and Jenny seemed lost in thoughts of her own. Then the organ played and the happy couple, together with Elsie Titmuss and Jenny's mother, a flustered and larger edition of her daughter, who had arrived late and spent most of the service whispering loudly about the present she had bought and forgotten to bring, or forgotten to buy and therefore hadn't brought, or meant to buy as soon as she got a moment, set off down the aisle. So Jennifer Sidonia, feeling that she had said goodbye to her name and so to much of her past, became Jennifer Titmuss.

When they came out of the church and into the rain they were met by a political demonstration. It seemed, at first sight, to consist mainly of members of the Curdle family, with Evie prominent and showing all the joy and vitality she had lacked at her own wedding ceremony and waving a S.O.V. poster tacked on to part of a disused rabbit hutch. HANDS OFF OUR VALLEY, TITMUSS, other placards read, and IT'S YOUR BACK GARDEN TOO, LESLIE. Dot Curdle grasped in one fist a threatening placard reading DON'T LET THE BASTARDS CONCRETE OVER OUR FURRY FRIENDS, whilst the other opened to hurl a cloud of confetti at the newly wed Titmuss. She shouted, 'God bless you, sir, and your lovely lady!' Colonel Wilcox and his wife, who had refused an invitation to the church on grounds of conscience, stood to attention in their cotton hats, it now being officially summer, holding up the only insignia of the Ramblers' Society they had been able to find readily, a cheerful drying-up cloth showing a well-marked footpath snaking across a green landscape. Mr and Mrs Vee were among the assorted demonstrators, having organized the occasion without reference to their Chairman, who now came out of the church and looked at them with considerable surprise. Dr Simcox, the Vees felt, was far too old-fashioned to take advantage of the magnificent photo-opportunities the Titmuss wedding would provide.

'Not much of a demo, Fred. I was disappointed. Couldn't your Friends of the Earth have done any better than that?' Leslie Titmuss spoke with smiling belligerence. 'I thought at least you'd have had a bit of manure thrown, or organized an attack with reaping hooks by outraged yokels in smocks. Bit of a damp squib, wasn't it?'

'I'm sorry.' Fred felt, as his champagne glass was refilled by an elderly waitress hired from the Hartscombe Rowing Club, that the least he could do was apologize. 'I really didn't know it was going to happen.'

'But aren't you Chairman of the Save Our Valley Society? That was certainly my information.'

'Well, yes. I suppose I am.' It was Fred's way to smile at the pomposity of the title.

'You mean you're the Commander-in-Chief and the troops don't tell you when they're going to attack?'

'Not on this occasion, no,' Fred admitted.

'I'd call that mutiny.' Leslie Titmuss laughed. 'I suppose you'd say it was democracy at work?'

'I think they should have stayed away from your wedding.'

'Oh, I didn't mind in the least. I don't mind anything now I've got Jenny.' Leslie looked across to where his wife was talking to the Lord Lieutenant of the county with wonderfully simulated animation. 'I'm going to make it work, you know. This time I'm honestly going to make it work.' And he said it with such intensity that Fred was even more uncomfortable than he had been when he spotted Colonel and Mrs Wilcox holding up a tea-towel in the rain.

'You ought to try marriage,' Leslie advised him. 'Give up politics. You've clearly got absolutely no talent for it.' Fred didn't answer. He was looking round at the newly decorated walls, the fresh plaster and restored chandelier of the Rapstone drawing-room. There was every sign that Titmuss in his new-found happiness was planning on a long stay and he thought that, even without the ill-timed S.O.V. demonstration, the threat of Fallowfield was receding.

'The trouble with you and your father before you —' Fred was now looking across the room at Jenny, the house's newest and most beautiful acquisition. He heard, as though from a great distance, yet another attack by Leslie on the late Rector of Rapstone, whose memory still seemed to haunt him. 'You think your consciences are so much more important than other people's. You think you've only got to parade your precious consciences in some sort of bedraggled procession, take them out for a walk as though they were relics of the One True Cross, and all sorts of miracles will occur. Isn't that what your old dad thought? He imagined the Bomb would go away if he went out marching with a few mums pushing prams and a handful of weirdos playing guitars.'

Is *that* what this beautiful woman had done it for? Fred asked himself in bewilderment. Had she dressed herself up in lace and decorated her hair with orange blossom to listen to this sort of thing from Titmuss over and over again for the rest of her life?

'Wankers of the world unite, you've got nothing to lose but your self-advertising liberal causes!' Leslie laughed and Fred became increasingly uncomfortable in the presence of such an obviously cheerful Titmuss. Then he felt the politician's hand on his arm and Leslie's voice sank to a conspiratorial murmur. 'If you really want to fight the Fallowfield development there're a lot of better ways of going about it. Oh, there's the folk from satellite T.V. I'd better go and give them a welcome.'

There were several groups in anoraks piling their plates at the buffet, representatives of the news programmes who had covered the Titmuss wedding. As Leslie went to talk to them Fred, whose view of his host's conduct was never generous, thought he was probably going to lean on the broadcasters to exclude the S.O.V. demonstration. On the contrary, and to the delight of the Curdle family, whose shouts of self-recognition echoed from their mobile homes that night, the demonstration was prominently featured. Dot Curdle, waving her poster and flinging her confetti, was bounced into space and back into millions of homes, and the protests seemed electronically multiplied to sound like a substantial popular uprising.

The Secretary of State for Housing, Ecological Affairs and Planning gave a brief interview to camera before he left with his bride for Rome. The following is an extract.

INTERVIEWER: Minister. Does your acquisition of this lovely home, Rampton Manor House –

TITMUSS: Rapstone. Get it right, young man.

INTERVIEWER: *Rapstone.* I'm sorry. Does it mean, sir, that plans for a new town here are unlikely to go ahead?

TITMUSS: It means nothing of the sort! If the inquiry decides that Fallowfield Country Town can be built, it will be a great experience for my wife and myself to live as part of such an exciting new development.

INTERVIEWER: And the value of your property will no doubt increase?

TITMUSS: We hope the value of everybody's property will increase. We're not in the business of seeing decent, hard-working householders lose money as they did in the days of the last Labour government.

INTERVIEWER: So it all depends on the public inquiry?

TITMUSS: Of course. That's the way we do things in a democracy.

INTERVIEWER: And if it happens you'd happily live next door to a new town?

TITMUSS: Of course we would. Just like any other young couple, starting out in life. Is that it? I've got a plane to catch . . .
INTERVIEWER: Thank you, Minister. And many congratulations on your marriage.
TITMUSS: Oh, yes. Marriage is a wonderful thing. You should try it some time.

Although the interviewer may have had a somewhat ambiguous appearance he was, in fact, the happy father of two and the Secretary of State's last remark was uncalled for. Most of his audience found it appealing, however, and a sure sign that their much appreciated Leslie Titmuss had lost none of his zip.

Leslie had been happy in Rome. He couldn't help noticing and enjoying the looks of envy and increased respect caused by having Jenny at his side. She spoke a little Italian and he encouraged this performance with pride, although so far as he was concerned an inability to speak any foreign language was an essential feature of the no-nonsense politics he embodied. Foreign languages, in Leslie's book, were for wets and international socialists, although from Jenny's lips the words sounded entrancing and musical to his ears. He assumed she would be interested in clothes and she agreed, after some argument, to let him buy her a dress and a pair of shoes, but a tiny part of the expensive wardrobe he offered her. Clothes shops, she said, bored her and she took him on short visits to picture galleries, insisting that no one could really take in more than a few paintings on any one visit. He was grateful for this wisdom and failed to wonder who had taught it to her. He found the religious subjects, the pale saints bristling with arrows and the agonized crucifixions, embarrassing. He was more interested in the portraits of Popes and Emperors, persons of authority at whom he looked with fascination and some understanding.

During these days he felt that he had his new wife's full attention. When they were together she looked at him in a way he found flattering and he was engrossed in watching her, so that her smallest movement, the doubtful way she frowned at herself in a mirror, her habit of running a long finger round the rim of a wine glass as she talked, delighted him. He assumed she had picked up her knowledge of the language and the pictures on other visits, but he didn't worry about that until their last evening when she said she knew somewhere for dinner. It was when they had come out of the narrow streets of the drug-dealers into the square with its fountain and its gold mosaic church, that he felt, for the first time, the presence of an intruder. As they crossed the square of Santa Maria in Trastevere he knew that she was concerned, not with him, but with whoever her last companion there had been. When she lit a candle in the church he knew that it was not in tribute to her future but to her past. And when they sat together outside the restaurant her sudden, unexpected tears seemed an act of infidelity to him. They were married and alone, she was wearing the dress and the shoes he had bought her, they were going back to the house she had wanted, in the countryside she found beautiful. He had been consistently kind and considerate and had taken the greatest care of her at all times. If she were weeping it wasn't because of him; her tears, like her candle, were a tribute to another man.

Leslie Titmuss's jealousy of Tony Sidonia began that evening.

CHAPTER FOURTEEN

In the place on the Rapstone Nature Area, once known, although the fact is forgotten except by Hector Bolitho Jones and a very few former villagers now lodged in the Hartscombe Old People's Home, as Hanging Wood, there were, when Hector was a boy, at least fifty badgers. Their numbers had considerably diminished over the years. Some had died, like operatic heroines, of tuberculosis. Some had been frightened by poachers' lights and killed by poachers' lurchers, long-legged, sharp-toothed dogs who could run faster than they. A few had even, so it was suspected, been flushed out by terriers and kidnapped by the likes of sixteen-year-old Billy Curdle, who organized furtive and illicit dog and badger fights in a remote corner of the rabbit hacienda to make money. In these prize fights the badgers, heavily built and with tight-locking jaws, were sometimes able to defeat and kill the smaller dogs. At the top of Hanging Wood, where the old and close beech trees abruptly gave way to a corn field, there was a sett which was no less than four hundred years old. Now it contained one family of four. The sow had the scar of a deep and inadequately healed dog-bite in her stomach, but she had given birth to two cubs, born blind and now, at two months, just about able to find their way into the open air. At nightfall this family left the sett and the complicated system of tunnels which surrounded it and ventured out to feast on roots, fruit, eggs, insects, young birds and small mammals.

When out foraging, the badgers, short-sighted but with a keen sense of smell, recognized their family by the musk which they sprayed from their bodies. They had sprayed some of this pungent odour on Hector Jones's boots, so he was always a welcome and recognized member of the group. As his relations with Daphne deteriorated he would spend more of his nights with the badgers.

One moonlit night towards the end of that summer Hector had gone out after a supper with Daphne noted for its prolonged silences and deliberate, resentful chewing. He had climbed to the top of the wood, carrying no light which might alarm nocturnal creatures. The moonlit hills were not silent. Dogs barked distantly, owls shrieked and whirled down on mice stirring among the fallen leaves. There was a sound of running in the ground cover of brambles, which Hector took to be a deer on the rampage. So he climbed steadily to the top of the wood and was there rewarded by the sight of the old sow badger tirelessly collecting bedding of dried grass, twigs and leaves to make her family comfortable.

Then, from a clump of bushes far down the wood, Hector saw a little light. It was a distant pin-point but its presence, and the addition it gave to a feeling of danger provided by the sharp calls of birds of prey and the sudden flutter of death, sent the sow scuttling into the safety of her sett, her carefully gathered bedding forgotten. Hector looked after her with regret and then up to stare at what was happening in the clearing half-way down the hill.

Three men had emerged from the shadows, running, crouching, bent almost double, carrying objects that had the undoubted appearance of guns. They were dressed in flak jackets and berets, their parti-coloured trousers tucked into huge boots and their faces daubed with camouflage paint. 'Christ!' said Hector Bolitho Jones, seeing that they were undoubtedly soldiers.

Soldiers, but whose? He tried to remember what little he'd read in the papers, or seen on the television when Daphne insisted on having it on. The Russians, surely, had become friendly. But could the Russians be trusted? He strained his ears to listen for commands in a foreign language as the men vanished into the shadows beside a great holly bush. If not Russian, were they Chinese or Arabs – the spearhead perhaps of an Islamic invasion, a terrifying crusade in reverse, set off to burn the church and rape the women? Hector's mind raced. His father had told him about the war, about the nights they had watched in Hanging Wood for Germans landing by parachute; how some of the Home Guard had laid hands on a man from the Electricity Board with a small toothbrush moustache and thought, for a single intoxicating moment, that they had 'got Hitler'. Well, the foreigners were obviously back, looking leaner, healthier, more determined and better armed. Alone in the wood he thought how he might raise the alarm and if he would be heard above the owls' shrieks and the distant barking, and the rattle of wind in the treetops. In his pocket he kept a whistle which he used to command the dogs who corralled sheep in the Nature Area. He raised it to his lips and blew a deafening blast.

Then he heard a charge and a thunder of boots. He turned and saw another platoon in uniform rushing towards him. They ran, grinning with triumph and excitement. He raised his whistle again, but as he did so the leader of the second platoon aimed his gun at Hector's face. Their eyes met and, in spite of the camouflage paint, Hector Jones had no difficulty in recognizing the fair moustache and heavily lidded eyes of Ken Cracken, the Minister at H.E.A.P. Whether Ken had been recognized seemed not to trouble him. He had seen an old enemy unexpectedly delivered into his hands. He pressed the spray-gun he held and the warden of the Rapstone Nature Area was struck dumb by the great spurt of yellow paint filling his mouth and dripping down his clothes towards the boots on which the badger sow had so sympathetically sprayed her musk.

'All in all, I think, one of our better exercises. Would you say that, Jumbo? As O.C. of the Yellows, old fellow. And, by the way, bad luck.'

Christopher Kempenflatt, still in his flak jacket but with his camouflage paint washed off, stuck his legs out towards the log fire in his country house, a listed mill which was in no danger at all of redevelopment. He held up his glass and the devoted Mrs Armitage refilled it. In the room a number of other men, still in bits and pieces of army uniform, were gathered. They included Ken Cracken and 'Jumbo' Plumstead, who looked as game as an old colonel. Joyce Timberlake was also of the party; there was still a spot of camouflage paint on her face, for she had been a fully combative W.R.A.C. girl for the Reds.

'I was commanding from our base,' Jumbo admitted, 'but from what came over my radio it sounded like a damn close-run thing.'

'Doesn't matter about being close run,' Kempenflatt told him. 'When it comes to war, you either win or lose. There's no half measures.'

'Much the same in politics,' Ken Cracken said. 'By the way, I think our battlefield got a bit extended. Weren't we meant to keep to your chum's woods, Christopher?'

Kempenflatt had got cooperation for his latest war game from the farmers who had sold him options to build Fallowfield on their land.

'We moved our operations to another wood. We'd organized a really great pincer movement but some old fart with a whistle tried to hold up our advance,' Ken Cracken told him.

'Oh, really? What did you do with him?' Christopher Kempenflatt was only moderately interested.

'Let him have it with my paint-gun. Full in the kisser! As a matter of fact, it's something I've been waiting to do for a long time.'

When he got home Hector Bolitho Jones cleaned the paint off his face and out of his hair and put his clothes aside for Daphne to take to the dry cleaners. He told her that he had been attacked by lager louts with a paint-gun, but he didn't think they'd dare to do it again. However, he wrote another report to his superiors at S.C.R.A.P. to say that the hooligan who had been about to make love on a possible site of stone curlews' nests had returned to Rapstone Nature Area with a party in military attire. He had been sprayed with paint by a man he was now in a position to identify positively as Kenneth Cracken, M.P., Minister of State at H.E.A.P.

A few days later Hector visited the attic of the converted cottage in which he still kept, neatly packed away, certain of old Jones the gamekeeper's possessions. There was a tea-chest which contained his father's boots, carefully cleaned and wrapped in newspaper, his much worn and leather-patched jacket and an assortment of caps, his clasp knife, his silver watch and some homemade snares. There was also the gamekeeper's shot-gun, oiled and packed away in its case, and a khaki shoulder-bag still full of cartridges. Hector had never used this weapon. Now he often took it out of its case, raised it to his shoulder and aimed it, unloaded, at an imaginary target. He had no intention of using the gun against any of the wild creatures under his care, but ever afterwards, on his night-time patrols, he went armed.

The war in Rapstone woods had one other result. Leslie Titmuss was invited to lunch at the Sheridan Club by Lord Skirmett, President of the Society for Conservation, Rural and Arboreal Protection (S.C.R.A.P.). It was not an invitation he welcomed. Skirmett was exactly the sort of silver-haired, well-meaning and tweedy old Tory who was inclined to give trouble in the House of Lords on such subjects as the closing of rural schools. Leslie distrusted clubs like the Sheridan where the food was adjusted to the tastes of those who had been brought up in nurseries. However, as soon as his apologetic Lordship had explained the reason for the invitation, Leslie was glad he'd come.

'Of course the fellows at S.C.R.A.P. don't want to embarrass the Ministry in any way. But we can't have members of the government running around spraying our wardens with paint! I mean, one can understand a bit of high spirits . . .'

'High spirits?' Leslie shook his head sadly. 'I'm afraid I take a far more serious view of Cracken's conduct.'

'I'm glad to hear it. I must say . . .'

'And I mean –' Leslie held up his hand to stop Lord Skirmett, who shuddered to a halt in mid sentence like an elderly motor car conking out on the road. 'I mean –' his voice sank to a low and menacing tone – 'to take this on board at once. I'm grateful to you for coming to me on this one, Lord Skirmett. I suppose I can rely on your organization to see that the whole matter remains absolutely confidential. I know you won't wish to embarrass the government, at the moment when we're considering leaving some of our best reserves in your control.'

'No privatization?' Lord Skirmett asked hopefully.

'Wait for the statement. That's the trouble with the House of Lords. You all panic so easily. I think I can say that the proper preservation of nature is something which comes very high on our list of priorities. And I'm sure you'll understand how green our thinking is.'

'Green thinking?' Skirmett looked vaguely up to the ceiling as though trying to imagine what thinking of such a colour might look like. 'I'm so glad we've had this chance to exchange views, Secretary of State. It's been extremely helpful.'

'Oh, I agree.' But Leslie Titmuss did nothing with the knowledge he had gained for some time. He had no doubt that it would, in his future dealings with Ken Cracken, prove very useful indeed.

The Next Day

As I was going up the stair
I met a man who wasn't there.
He wasn't there again today.
I wish, I wish he'd stay away.

'The Psychoed'
Hughes Mearns

CHAPTER FIFTEEN

At last the orchids and the foxes, the ancient beech woods and chalk downlands, the rare butterflies and the unusual snails were to be submitted to the processes of democracy, which would decide whether they should survive or be obliterated for ever. This was the judgement which Leslie Titmuss wanted to be pronounced by others in accordance with his secret and never-to-be expressed wishes.

The heart of Worsfield, the town hall built to resemble a gothic château, the railway station built to look like a cathedral, the old biscuit factory which was, in its way, more imposing than either, had been demolished. Now its centre was filled with toy-town architecture. Immensely tall office buildings, the colour of raw liver embellished with blue-painted iron-work and plate-glass windows, looked as though some giant child had been let loose in the ruins with an infinite number of huge building bricks. Around these buildings the traffic swirled. Beneath the four-lane highways, in a warren of shopping malls, among bouti-ques and record stores and hamburger havens where the light of day never penetrated, the citizens of Worsfield went about their business like the rabbits which scuttled through the complex system of tunnels under the Rapstone Nature Area.

High up in one of the Worsfield towers the twenty or so members of the planning committee of the District Council assembled under the energetic chairmanship of a Mrs Babcock-Syme. She was a tireless local politician with flashing eyes and a husky voice which could rise to sudden rage or sink to a tone of naked sensuality, even during the discussion of planning matters, which would startle and fascinate the male members of the committee to such an extent that many of them became clay in her hands. It was not, in fact, a hard committee to manage. The majority of those who had the time to stand for election and go to meetings were either local builders or farmers. The farmers, quietly spoken men in business suits, were longing to sell their land at a handsome profit to developers. The builders, dressed in old tweeds and corduroys and keen on rustic pursuits, were always on the look-out for somewhere new to build. Neither of these groups had any fundamental disagreements with the alluring 'Chair', who was inclined to give out permission for most things to be built in most places because, as she was fond of telling the admiring men by whom she was surrounded, 'The name of the game is consumer choice.'

'When I was a girl at Worsfield Grammar' – Mrs Babcock-Syme was a local – 'we could only get three sorts of yoghurt at the corner shop. At the last count Luxifoods in the Mall had twenty-three. I call that a smashing victory for consumer choice. Yes, Mr Parsloe?'

Ted Parsloe, a retired headmaster whom Mrs Babcock-Syme suspected of not taking her entirely seriously, had raised his pencil and now said, 'Thank you, Madam Chair. I must say, I've never cared for yoghurt.'

'It's the same principle, Mr Parsloe. Applied across the board. We're giving the consumer the choice of living in an old town like Worsfield or a new town like Fallowfield.'

'With respect, Madam Chair. What if I, as a consumer, don't want to live in a town at all?'

'Then I would suggest, Mr Parsloe' – the Babcock-Syme voice sank almost to a whisper of flagrant sexuality – 'you move to the North of England where I understand there are still lots of empty spaces.'

'With respect, Madam Chair –' Mr Parsloe was grateful for

the fact that his advanced age made him safe from the allure of Hermione Babcock-Syme. He plodded gamely on like the only surviving explorer in a group otherwise gone down with an exotic tropical disease. 'There are plenty of empty spaces in the old Worsfield station area and all the empty warehouses by the canal. Why not build there if we need new houses?'

'May I, Madam Chair?' A red-faced builder smiled at Hermione Babcock-Syme in a roguish sort of way.

'Oh, yes, Mr Entwhistle. Please do.'

'It's far cheaper and easier to build houses on green field sites. Cost a fortune to clear the old station and the warehouses.'

'I'm sure we're grateful,' Mrs Babcock-Syme purred to Mr Entwhistle, 'for that very practical contribution. Yes, Mrs Tippett?' Mrs Tippett, the marriage guidance counsellor who had done her best to make sense of the love life of Evie Curdle, rattled her bangles, sighed heavily and said they still needed more houses in the middle of Worsfield for one-parent families on Income Support. When Mrs Babcock-Syme said that Fallowfield Country Town would provide rows of houses for such unfortunates no one thought to remind her that low-income one-parent families would never be able to afford the delights of the new town.

The Chair was now ready to sum up the discussion: 'The Secretary of State has given us the lead in his super speech to the builders. We can't have No Go areas for the operation of market forces. A new town would make Rapstone England's Silicone Valley of prosperity.' The Chair grew more eloquent as she saw a wide thoroughfare, bejewelled with the neon signs of fast-food outlets, leading between Parkinson Close and Titmuss Gardens to an imposing civic centre. Its name, she had reason to hope, would be Babcock-Syme Boulevard and her immortality would be assured. 'What I think most of us see here, with a very few exceptions' – she flashed a lethal smile at the headmaster – 'is a tremendous opportunity to make – yes, what is it, Mr Plant?' This was the planning officer whose secretary had just come in with a message. Certain plans, it seemed, concerning road access and a new sewage system had still not been supplied. Certain questions still had to be answered. With considerable irritation the Chair announced that, although she had little doubt of what the majority would decide, the matter would be adjourned until the next meeting.

That night Eric Babcock-Syme, who owned a garage on the Hartscombe Road, a business he saw growing to supply the Fallowfield motorway-exit service area, told Vernon Beazley that S.O.V. might as well pack it in because, without a doubt, Hermione's committee would give the green light to the new town. On the same evening the Right Honourable Leslie Titmuss made a speech to the Nottingham Chamber of Commerce. He made, of course, no reference to Fallowfield, which was, he was anxious to give the impression, no concern of his, at any rate for the time being. However, dedicated Titmuss-watchers were surprised to see that he spoke with considerable respect for the tiger, the black rhino and the world's diminishing supply of elephants. He showed a new interest in the ozone layer and announced that all H.E.A.P.'s vehicles were now running on unleaded petrol. He made a number of jokes at the expense of the Greens, townees most of them he said, who probably thought a badger sett was something trendy you ordered at the hairdresser's. 'I wonder how many of them,' he told his delighted audience, 'earned sixpence a day cutting nettles, weeded a potato bed, scared off birds in an orchard or picked a big bunch of bluebells in the local woods on the two-mile walk home from school on Mothers' Day?' Unlike most of those who only noticed nature when they got bored with preaching socialism, Leslie Titmuss reminded his audience that he was 'a countryman born and bred. I was brought up sniffing country air, that potent mixture of new-cut grass, cherry blossom and farmyard muck. My message to all of you is have no fear. So long as I'm at H.E.A.P. our environment is safe for future generations.' It appeared that the greenish tinge, noticed by Ken Cracken with such amusement, had deepened and somewhere, although not necessarily in the Rapstone Valley, there would always be a wood where the small Titmusses of the future might disport themselves and gather bluebells. On the distant African plains the few remaining rhinos might also snort their relief that Titmuss, at least, was on their side.

Although the new town seemed set for an early victory, the opposition to it was growing in strength. From its small and unpromising beginnings S.O.V. advanced rapidly and, greatly to his surprise, Fred found himself at the head of a substantial and fairly well-financed army of protesters. The converted barn, extended cottage, jacuzzi and carport owners were entirely with him. Although Fred disliked their habit of decorating the commons with gothic-lettered signs announcing the close proximity of their houses, 'Badgers End', 'The Coppice', 'Nut Trees' or, in the case of an old chapel converted to house two youngish men in designer knitwear, 'Shrivings', he was glad of their support and their subscriptions. Going on his rounds he would come across old ladies in gaunt grey houses in the back streets of Hartscombe, or in the middle of villages, who had played in the Rapstone woods when they were children and gone there for long walks with husbands, now long dead, who knew the names of the orchids and the gentians. They opened attics and descended cellar stairs to return with three-pronged Georgian forks, wine coolers, tarnished candlesticks, old lamps, spotted mirrors, dusty glass candelabras, dim oil paintings of the river and Hartscombe Bridge, sabres once used in the Crimea and silver teapots carefully wrapped in newspaper and hardly used at all. They gave these treasures to Fred to sell so that the valley might be saved, although for years past it had been a place they only visited in memory. In addition to these small donations, S.O.V. received, from a firm of solicitors who said their client wished to remain anonymous, a cheque for five thousand pounds to 'help in the propaganda war against Fallowfield Country

Town'. Fred banked it gratefully and with no idea who their unknown benefactor might be.

So, with a growing membership and bank account, Fred felt saddled with something he had never been used to – power. Could he and his strange assortment of allies hold their ground against what he still thought of as the Titmuss invasion and defeat the advancing tide of concrete, commercialism and pedestrian precincts? In moments of depression it seemed absurd even to try. But one day Mrs Vee told him that she had spent the morning walking in the Rapstone Valley. 'You think it's all yours, don't you, Fred?' she accused him. 'Just because it's where you lived all your life. You think we only got here lately and we're nothing but trippers, the sort you see with their little folding-chairs and Tupperware spread out all over Rapstone Common any Bank Holiday.' 'Of course, I don't,' Fred protested, although if the truth were told this was very much what he had, uncharitably, thought of the Vees from the time he had first met them. Now he felt, guiltily, that he must devote himself more whole-heartedly to the cause. After all, Mrs Vee spent her days sitting on strange sofas, chattering with incessant brightness and achieving, either by charming or by boring her victims, cheques of a size he would never have dared ask for.

'It's all the fault of that ghastly woman.' Mrs Vee rang him during his morning surgery.

'What ghastly woman?'

'The appalling Babcock-Syme. She's about to bully the District Council into giving planning permission. For Fallowfield. Only one person that can do anything now.'

'Really? Who's that?'

'You know Titmuss, don't you? He asked you to his wedding. You know him well.'

'Extremely well. In a manner of speaking.'

'He's the only one who can stop Babcock-Syme killing our valley. You can do it, Fred. You don't know your own strength. You can charm Titmuss.'

Fred had been expected to pull off many medical miracles, most of which were quite beyond his power; but he had never before been called upon to perform such a Herculean task as charming Leslie Titmuss. In view of Mrs Vee's clear devotion to the cause and the trust of the old ladies who had ransacked their attics for him, he felt bound to try. He phoned the Ministry, penetrated to the Secretary of State's office and left a message in which he felt no confidence. Then, driving on his morning rounds, he turned into the driveway of Rapstone Manor. It was not that he thought his diminishing fund of charm could be better spent on the new Mrs rather than the old Mr Titmuss. He told himself he would do better to call as an old family acquaintance and so arrange to talk to the Secretary of State. He could remember his short meeting with Jenny at her wedding and how her beauty had astonished him for many reasons, not least because it had so unexpectedly surrendered to Leslie Titmuss.

Jenny came round the corner of the house when she heard a car scrunch the gravel of the drive and then a ring at the front doorbell. There was earth on her hands and under her fingernails and a mark on her forehead where she had brushed back her hair with dirty fingers. The knees of her jeans were damp and muddy.

She stood still for a moment, looking at the back of the tall man by the front door. She noticed that his elderly tweed jacket hung from his shoulders as though from a coat-hanger. Something about the way he was standing, his hands in his pockets, at ease but in no way assertive, reminded her painfully of the lost husband she had been made to think of more often than she would have wished.

CHAPTER SIXTEEN

It was not that Jenny was unhappy living at Rapstone with Leslie Titmuss. Her life contained almost all she hoped for and very little of what she feared. The house itself had more than fulfilled her expectations. She spent a lot of time alone in it, but was never in the least lonely. The soft greenish light that filled the rooms, the constantly changing views of the park and the garden that greeted her as she moved from room to room, her new obsession with growing things which, instead of taking years, as she had supposed, to come to fruition, seemed to shoot up and proliferate with magical rapidity, all these acted on her like a drug, so that during any prolonged time she had to spend away from Rapstone she suffered acute withdrawal symptoms. Old Bigwell, father of Len Bigwell who was now happily married to Evie Curdle, continued to do the garden, coming full-time instead of the few hours a week that Lady Fanner had been able to afford. Spurred on by Jenny's constant praise and encouragement he resurrected the fruit cage, discovering in the jungle which filled it loganberries and white raspberries, as well as giant gooseberries which Jenny liked to explode in her mouth as she helped with the weeding. Slowly, like archaeologists excavating for traces of a lost civilization, they uncovered rose beds, bits of herbaceous border, patches where the strawberry plants were hidden under brambles and, under a rubbish tip, what must have been a forgotten rockery. Mr Bigwell, although secretly pleased by Jenny's flattery, made it a rule, like most professional gardeners, never to do what she suggested. She was only occasionally able to outmanoeuvre him by telling him that one of her favourite plans was impossible and never to be attempted. She would then retire to the house and keep watch from an upstairs window in the hope, sometimes fulfilled, of seeing him start to demonstrate his independence by digging the bed, applying the manure or sowing the seeds she had suggested.

Now she had taken to cooking and was proudest when she prepared the vegetables, or flavoured the meat with the herbs she and Mr Bigwell had grown together. Tony Sidonia had been a dashing cook who often improvised and she had thought herself a dull performer. But now she gained confidence and was happy in the kitchen, opening a bottle of white wine, chopping vegetables, listening to music and waiting, often for a long time, until Leslie got home. When he came he was always appreciative and rewardingly hungry. He praised her as fulsomely as she praised the gardener, and she was both pleased and unconvinced by his praises.

One night Leslie, who had cleared his plate, pushed it away and said, 'That was very tasty.'

'What?' she laughed at him.

'That was what my father always said. Every bloody night of his life. After tea he said, "That was very tasty, Mother. Very tasty indeed." I promise I won't do it again.' He looked at her, almost beseechingly. 'Don't let me, will you?'

What was unexpected about him were the jokes. She and Tony Sidonia had ritually voted for the Labour Party and, between elections, just as ritually denounced and derided the government of which the Right Honourable Leslie Titmuss was a member. Tony Sidonia's derision, however, was gentle compared to the savagery with which Leslie, at home with his wife, spoke of those of his colleagues who filled the other great offices of state. One might just as well have sent his suit to Cabinet meetings as it was 'the only smart thing about him'. Another was thought to have been extremely intelligent 'when he was alive'. A third had less idea of how to present a Bill than 'a waitress in a teashop'. And so it went on, to such an extent that Jenny often felt, quite mistakenly, that her new husband shared at least some of the views she and Tony Sidonia had taken for granted. Leslie was careful never to discuss politics in general at home, nor did he ask Jenny to read his speeches. When they watched him on television and she raised her eyebrows at some of his more outrageous utterances, he assured her that he was only having 'a bit of fun' or 'tweaking a few tails' and she was inclined to share the general view that political life in England would have been a great deal duller without the tail-tweaking propensities of Leslie Titmuss.

What she got from him was constant protection. From the start of their marriage he seemed determined to submit her to nothing she might find objectionable or even boring. He didn't ask her to go to meetings or cocktail parties in London. If they were invited to dinner with the 'colleagues', he would get his secretary to ring up with a convincing excuse if she showed the slightest reluctance to go. She was convinced that he only wanted her to be happy. She was right about this, but his feelings had changed since their wedding. He had once thought he wanted Jenny as a new possession to show to the world. Now he was like a millionaire who buys a painting of rare beauty, perhaps from a dubious source, and wants it kept in his home, never to be lent out for an exhibition, for his eyes only. He treasured her in his private not his public world, but he wanted her to be happy. He was perceptive enough to understand that this would not be the case if she had to go on trips with him to Chambers of Commerce or to many dinner parties with other government wives. He suspected that the 'colleagues' laughed at him for keeping his much younger wife under wraps, but he didn't mind, and when it came to laughing at people he could always win on points.

So, contrary to all reasonable forecasts and to the amazement of her friend Sue Bramble to whom Jenny spoke on the telephone almost daily, the Titmuss marriage had every appearance of success. They got on well in bed, a fact Sue found impossible to accept. Leslie would return home with as sharp an appetite for making love as he had for his dinner and Jenny, intoxicated by the fresh air, the silence, the small dramas of the garden and the white wine she got through whilst cooking, received him gladly and as though in a continuing dream. Perhaps one of his attractions for her was that danger which Sue Bramble had assured her lurked somewhere in Leslie Titmuss but which she had seen no sign of so far.

It was Leslie who said they should have Sue to stay. Jenny was grateful to him for the suggestion, although nervous about the outcome. In the end she couldn't resist showing off the house and the garden to her friend. Sue Bramble drove herself from London on a bright, spring day when the daffodils and the cherry trees were out and the azaleas in bud.

'Well?'

Sue had walked round the house as silent and non-committal as a police officer inspecting the scene of the crime. Now, when she had opened a bottle of wine in the kitchen and started to get the lunch, Jenny could stand the suspense no longer and asked again, 'Well? What do you think of it?'

'Terrible.'

'This house, and the garden? Terrible?' Jenny was standing in front of a chopping-board holding a half-moon shaped blade, frozen into puzzled immobility.

'Terrible that it's all so beautiful. Mr Titmuss used it to seduce you.'

'You don't think I married him for the house, do you?'

'One day I suppose I shall understand what you did marry him for.'

Jenny didn't answer that but started to chop parsley energetically, producing a clean, grassy smell and getting rid of the irritation she felt at Sue's obstinate disapproval. Then she chopped more slowly, smiled and said, 'You won't be too hard on my Mr Titmuss, will you?'

'Is he so delicate?'

'I'm not sure. He got rather badly laughed at once. He's remembered it all his life.'

'Don't worry. I'll treat him like a rare china ornament. I mean, I'll try to take him seriously.'

'I ought to tell you this.' Jenny pushed the chopped parsley into a neat pile with her blade. 'Something quite extraordinary's happened.'

'You're not . . .?'

'What?'

'Well. Not up the spout, are you?' Sue knew that her friend had been told that she couldn't, that she never would, have children. Had this extraordinary marriage, she wondered, produced some sort of medical miracle?

'No. Nothing like that. It's just that, well, we seem to be sort of entirely happy together.'

'I'm glad.' Sue seemed to accept the fact. 'Of course I want you to be extremely happy. Always.' Sitting at the kitchen table Jenny's friend raised her glass and drank to that.

'What were the games we used to play?'

The first evening of Sue's stay was going well. Leslie got home early and was perfectly polite, listening to her with studied concentration, as though it were important for him to understand everything she said. He was proud rather than embarrassed that they had met under strange and compromising circumstances and reminded her, 'You remember me? I was the one in the dicky-bow making early morning tea.' During dinner he enjoyed the company of two women, the blonde and the dark, laughing together in the candlelight. He opened more wine, spared them news of his day at the Ministry and listened sympathetically to Sue's accounts of the deceptive nature of men in general and racing trainers in particular. After dinner she lay back in a chair by the big log fire and reminded Jenny of the games they used to play.

'Charades. Wink Murder. "In the Manner of . . ." Oh, and The Truth Game, of course.'

'The Truth Game?'

'Oh, yes.' Sue explained it to Leslie. 'If you did something wrong – I mean, failed to drink a glass of wine in one gulp, or let the ash fall off your cigarette – then you got asked a question and you had to answer truthfully.'

'How did anyone know if you were telling the truth?' Leslie was interested.

'Oh, we could tell. We all knew so much about each other. Of course' – Sue looked at Jenny – 'Tony never had any problems with that game.'

It was the first time Tony Sidonia's name had been mentioned since their honeymoon. Jenny was quiet, hoping it would not be said again. But Leslie, raising his eyebrows, asked, 'Why didn't Tony have any problems?'

'Oh, because he always told the truth. Quite naturally. All the time. Didn't he, Jenny?'

'Well, yes, as a matter of fact. Who's for more wine?' Jenny got the bottle off the table and refilled their glasses, wishing for a change of subject.

'Such a truthful person, Tony. It really wasn't any fun playing the game with him.'

'But how can you be sure it was always the truth?' Leslie seemed eager for information.

'Oh, because he just couldn't lie. He wouldn't have been the slightest good at it. Would he, Jenny?'

'What would you like to do tomorrow?' It was Jenny and not Leslie who wanted to stop the Tony reminiscences. 'Would you like to go out to lunch somewhere?'

'Sunday lunch in the country. You remember those ridiculous great parties in Tony's garden?'

'In the summer?' Leslie's interest was apparently undiminished.

'The summers seemed so much better then, and longer. There

were always such an extraordinary number of guests. All sorts of people, writers, painters. Tony's mother, who was once a ballet dancer.'

'Myra was wonderful,' Jenny explained. 'Huge dark eyes and this amazingly straight back. She was really quite old then, but she'd play the piano for us and even dance occasionally. She danced so beautifully. No wonder so many men fell in love with her.'

'All sorts of writers, and wasn't there a general or something?'

'Oh, yes. Definitely a general. She said she took his mind off the war.'

'Do you remember,' Sue started to laugh, 'Willoughby Blane's shorts?'

'You were *outrageous!*' Jenny couldn't help laughing at the memory.

'Sir Willoughby Blane.' Leslie was smiling. 'The old bore who can tell you all you never wanted to know about prawns?'

'The man who brought us together.' Jenny did her best to bring the story up to date, but Sue remained firmly in the past with Tony Sidonia. 'It was so hot that year,' she said. 'We were all wearing, well, not very much really. And Willoughby Blane turned up in these vast, voluminous shorts. Tony had a long table with oh, about twenty people round it, out in the garden. I was sitting opposite Willoughby and he was next to that dreadful ex-ambassador's wife. What was her name?'

'I always forget.' Jenny was trying to put the past behind her.

'Mrs Lessore?' Leslie, who never forgot a name, had met her at the Oxford lunch.

'Gudrun Lessore was next to Willoughby Blane. On his right, I think.' Sue was apparently blessed with total recall. 'And, as I say, I was sitting opposite. Now you've got to understand that Tony's garden was always in a hell of a mess. This was before he married Jenny. The grass was never cut and was full of old bones and bits and pieces the dogs couldn't eat. Well, I looked under the table and I saw, what do you think? A chicken's foot! I suppose we'd had chicken for lunch and this old claw had got out into the garden. I hadn't got any shoes on so I somehow got this awful old yellow chicken's foot between my toes. And I managed . . . Jenny saw me do this, didn't you, Jenny?'

'Yes,' Jenny had to admit, 'I saw you.'

'Well, I managed to lift up my leg under the table and insert this terrible dead claw up Willoughby's baggy shorts. And he thought Gudrun Lessore was making a most intimate pass at him. He became all giggly and flirtatious.'

When she finished there was silence. Jenny looked anxious. Sue, not in the least contrite, smiled down into her glass. Leslie sat forward in his chair, frowning as though seriously trying to assess the full significance of this story, and then he burst into loud laughter. Much relieved, Jenny then laughed with him, as though the incident were much funnier than it had seemed at the time.

That night in bed Leslie lay quiet again, apparently asleep with his eyes open. Jenny watched him for a long time and then he said, 'Was he really like that?'

'Who?'

'Tony Sidonia.'

'I'm sorry,' Jenny apologized for her friend. 'I don't know why Sue kept on about him. It was stupid of her.'

'How did you *know*?'

'What?'

'How did you know he was always telling the truth?'

'I'm not sure.' She tried to think of a reason which would convince him and failed. 'I just did know. That was all.'

'And that was important to you?'

'Oh, yes. The most important thing in the world.'

He seemed to think about that for a while, then he closed his eyes and was really asleep. The subject wasn't mentioned again that weekend and Jenny wasn't troubled by thoughts of Tony Sidonia until much later when she saw the back of Fred Simcox as she walked round the house.

*

'Of course, I remember you at the wedding.'

Now that she was facing Fred in the sitting-room she could see that he didn't really look in the least like her late husband. All the same Tony Sidonia felt nearer to her at that moment than he had been since he died. Jenny thought again of Tony when Fred said, with a kind of self-confident modesty, 'I've become the sort of pest who dumps leaflets on people.' Indeed, he had a glossy folder in his hand, decorated very much like the developers' propaganda, with a picture of sheep grazing. This document had been prepared for S.O.V. by an advertising agency well known to Mr Vee.

'Why?' she asked. 'What's it all about?'

'The new town we're threatened with.'

Jenny took the folder politely, feeling he was glad to be rid of it. 'I mean,' he said, 'I'm sure you're attached to the valley.'

'I've come to love it. Of course, you know it much better than I do.'

'Since I was a child. Your husband and I were boys together. My father was the Rector.'

'And Leslie used to cut his nettles.'

'He's told you that?'

'Oh, yes. Quite often.' He smiled when she said that and she felt she had been disloyal to her husband. 'I don't think you need worry too much,' she said. 'Leslie doesn't want this valley spoiled, either.' So she established Leslie's credentials as a responsible and caring politician.

'I just hope' – Fred looked at her, smiling – 'he's going to tell the District Council that.'

'What've they got to do with it?'

'Quite a lot. If they say "yes" no one can appeal. And it seems they're all ready to give the green light to Fallowfield.'

'Does Leslie know that?'

'I'm sure he knows most things. But it wouldn't do any harm to remind him. I'll give him a ring, if I can, over the weekend.'

'I'm sure he'll be glad to hear from you.'

Fred wasn't so sure. All the same he felt he'd gone as far as he could with the beautiful and apparently receptive Mrs Titmuss. 'Well,' he said, 'I won't bore you any longer.'

'Your patients'll be waiting.'

'Not many round here. They're terribly healthy in this valley and seem to live forever.'

'Like Lady Fanner?'

'She was well over eighty when she died,' he told her. 'A pretty good advertisement for a diet of gossip, champagne and cigarettes.' He was looking out of the tall windows. 'You've tidied up the garden.'

'If you've got time I could show you what we've done.'

'I'd like to see.' And when they were walking down the long border she'd planted and he was admiring the white cloud of narcissi in the rough grass of the orchard, she wondered what old Lady Fanner had been like. 'Extremely malicious. She had a bad word to say of everyone. I must admit, I miss her dreadfully. The Rapstone Valley's a much duller place without her.'

As she walked him to his car she said, 'I'm glad you're fighting for the valley.'

'I don't know about fighting. I seem to spend my time asking people for money. Oh, and organizing strange sorts of events. I want to get some jazz evening going in aid of S.O.V., but the people I used to play with are knocking on a bit.'

'*You* play?' Tony Sidonia didn't perform on any instrument but she remembered the piles of old records he listened to, Bix Beiderbecke, Coleman Hawkins, Dizzy Gillespie, Django Reinhardt and Le Hot Club de France.

'On drums with the Riverside Stompers. That's what we used to call ourselves. We might try the pub at Skurfield again. If we manage it I'll send you a ticket. And your husband, of course.'

Jenny tried to imagine Leslie at a jazz evening in a pub and failed. As Fred opened the car door she said, 'I'm sure they'll come in droves to hear you drumming for the valley. Everyone'll want to help.'

'Including you?'

'Of course. I told you.'

'You mean you'll join S.O.V.? You get all sorts of treats.' He laughed, inviting her to laugh at his organization also. 'Not only me on drums. Car-boot sales. Sponsored footpath walks with Colonel Wilcox. Wine, cheese and poetry reading in the Hartscombe Town Hall. How can you possibly resist it?'

'I don't suppose I can.'

'Good. I'll send your membership card.'

And he drove away, leaving her alone and wondering, only for a moment, whether she had done the wrong thing. What she had done, in fact, was to kick away the small stone which would start an avalanche.

CHAPTER SEVENTEEN

Fred drove back to Hartscombe in a distinct glow of triumph. He told himself that by enlisting the support of the Secretary of State's wife he had struck a powerful blow for the salvation of his native countryside. He also allowed himself to feel that he had scored a victory over Leslie Titmuss, undermining that hitherto undented self-confidence which assumed that everyone connected with him would always do exactly what he wanted.

So, when he walked into the bar of the Olde Maypole Inn at lunch-time and found Mrs Vee running through the agenda of the next S.O.V. meeting with Daphne Jones, Fred couldn't resist taking his beer over to them and raising his voice above the muzak and the squeals of computer games to say, 'What do you think? Jenny Titmuss has joined the group.'

'You invited her?'

'Well, yes I was up in the valley, so I called.'

'Mr Chairman!' Mrs Vee spoke in a tone of vibrant admiration which filled Fred with immediate foreboding. 'You're a political genius!'

'It wasn't at all hard. She's very sympathetic.'

'God!' Hector Bolitho Jones's wife was also awestruck. 'Think of the publicity we're going to get.'

'Front-page stuff. No doubt about it,' Mrs Vee agreed. 'PLAN-NING MINISTER'S WIFE JOINS ANTI-PLANNERS. S.O.V.'s really going to be put on the map. Thanks to our Chairman. We ought to give an exclusive to the *Fortress*,' she suggested, 'and then they'll be sure to make a big thing of it. I'll ring Vee and get him to take it on board.'

'No.'

'What?'

'No announcement in the papers.' Fred had decided.

'Why ever not?'

'Because that's just what they'd do.'

'What who'd do?'

'The opposition. If something like that happened to us they'd get the newspapers full of it. We've got to show them we're different. So let's keep quiet and treat Jenny Titmuss just like any other member.' To his surprise his words came out with authority. But he was thinking, Why am I tangling with a world I was never cut out for? All I shall succeed in doing is making trouble for a woman I found myself liking very much.

Mrs Vee looked at him in a penetrating and deeply understanding way. 'Is that your decision, Mr Chairman?' she said in the solemn tones she might have used if he had just announced that he was terminally ill.

'Yes,' he said. 'That's what I've decided.'

'For God's sake.' Daphne Jones had no doubts on the matter. 'I don't agree with that. If I catch my enemy with his balls hanging out and I happen to have an axe in my hand, I strike!' This was a political precept which she had heard enunciated by the President of the Worsfield Students' Union and she had been much impressed by it.

'No, Daphne!' Mrs Vee was prepared to behave with nobility. 'Fred has his principles. We've got to respect them. That's why we chose him to be our Chairman. All right, Mr Chairman. Sir.' She put a proprietorial hand on his knee where it remained visiting. 'No publicity from us, although God knows what the gentlemen of the press are going to find out for themselves.' So Fred finished his lunch and went about his business visiting the sick, feeling that he had, in some way, betrayed both Jenny and Mrs Vee and he hoped, so far as Jenny was concerned at least, that he had done his best to repair the damage.

It goes without saying that as soon as she was left alone, Mrs Vee telephoned her husband with the news and he then put through a call to the *Fortress* into whose Mr Chatterbox column he often dropped hints about clients who employed him in their charitable concerns. The name Mr Chatterbox did not, as might be expected, mask the identity of an elderly, grey-haired gossip but a languid, comparatively young, untidy and dissolute old Etonian called Tim Warboys who, although he found anyone who hadn't been to Eton, and many who had, totally absurd, had a strong sense of self-preservation. He was about to be promoted to the Whispers from the Gallery parliamentary column and he knew that writing stories hostile to Leslie Titmuss in the columns of the *Fortress* was the journalistic equivalent of searching for a gas leak with a lighted match.

So, after getting the news from Mr Vee, Tim Warboys rang the press officer at H.E.A.P. and was told that any suggestion that Mrs Titmuss had joined a group at war with her husband was totally untrue, that any hint of such news would be met with a writ and that the Secretary of State would no doubt be speaking to the *Fortress*'s proprietor Lord Dowdswell, who, as Tim well knew, was a close personal friend. As all this was relayed after a pause for consultation with the Secretary of State himself, Mr Chatterbox said that he had never believed the story anyway and had thought it only right to alert the press officer to so scurrilous a rumour. He then went to the first of four cocktail parties persuaded that it was true but that his column had much better concentrate on the ludicrous attempts of an allegedly socialist M.P. to get himself elected to White's Club. So, in the course of one day, Jenny's membership of S.O.V. was pushed towards centre stage and then back into the wings to become a matter of concern for no more than three people.

'What did you think you were doing to me? Or did you just not think at all?'

'I told him what I felt. That's all.'

'What a luxury! That's perfectly all right for you, of course. You can go round the world saying exactly what you feel. That's the privilege enjoyed by people who have no responsibility for anything.'

'Of course I'm responsible. I have to be responsible for what I say.'

'And what about me? Did you think about me for one single moment, during the Doctor's visit?'

Elsie Titmuss had come to dinner that night and had helped Jenny in the kitchen, talking a lot about her distant past, taking little swallows of gin and tonic and revealing old scandals about people in big houses of whom Jenny had never heard. As always they got on well and were ready to receive Leslie with interest and excitement. When he came home he was in a black mood which Jenny did her best to ignore. He waited until Elsie had gone and the dinner cleared away before launching his attack and Jenny, who thought it must have been one of the 'colleagues' that had infuriated him, was surprised to find the cannonade directed at her. At first she wasn't alarmed by his fury; she was busy trying to follow an argument which seemed to involve people she hadn't met, in a world she hardly understood.

'Did you?' he repeated, staring at her like some cold lawyer cross-examining a hostile witness. 'Did you think about me at all?'

'Of course I thought about you, Leslie. I knew exactly how you felt.'

'Oh. How did you know that?'

'Because you told me.'

'What did I tell you?'

'You told me they'd never build a new town in the valley. Not if you knew anything about it. You told me that the first day we came here.'

'I don't mean . . .' Leslie sighed and looked at his wife with exaggerated patience. 'I don't mean how I felt about the new town. I meant how I felt about people *knowing* how I felt.'

'I'm sorry.' She looked back at him in genuine confusion. 'I don't know what you're talking about.'

'Of course you don't. I'm talking about politics. That's a dirty word to you, isn't it?'

'Not necessarily.'

'It's another world to you, beneath your notice. A world where you have to say what you don't mean in order to get what you want. It's a world where you may have to tell lies. That wouldn't have suited your precious Tony Sidonia, would it? He could sit in some old library somewhere and feel cosy and contemptuous of squalid politicians who have to practise a few deceptions to get anything decent done in the world. Well, I have news for you. The time has come to forget Mr Sidonia!'

There was a silence and then Jenny seemed to crumple at Tony's name, which had never been thrown at her with such violence before. Now Leslie looked down at her as she sat crouched in a corner of the sofa, her hands hugging her elbows and her knees bent sharply. He seemed surprised at the result of what he had said because he lowered his voice and made an effort to sound reasonable.

'All right . . .' And he repeated 'All right' as if trying to get the attention of the House of Commons at Question Time, although what he had to say would never be heard in Parliament. 'I don't want the town. You don't want the town. The bloody interfering doctor doesn't want the town. You know I don't want it. But Jo Public mustn't know that!'

She looked up at him. He assumed an unspoken question and was encouraged to answer it.

'Why mustn't they? Because I'm the man of the free market. The patron saint of the builder and the upwardly mobile property investor. That's why they elected me and why I got my job. If I come out against the new town they'll say it's for one reason and one reason only. Because I live here. Because I want new houses everywhere except in my own bloody back garden. You understand that, don't you?'

167

He waited for an answer but she didn't give it to him. On the other hand she looked at him constantly and didn't turn her face away. He took that for encouragement and went on being reasonable.

'So let's spell it out, my darling. I have to keep absolutely quiet. Not take sides in any sort of way, you understand? There's going to be a full public inquiry, a judicial proceeding with arguments from all sides. Evidence taken. All the trimmings. Plenty of money for the lawyers. And at the end of that, you want to know my own, personal, entirely private prediction? This is not for publication, just between you and me, strictly off the record. I promise you that Fallowfield Country Town will be dead as mutton! So we'll be able to go on living here in peace. That's what you want to know, isn't it?'

'Yes,' she said. 'Yes, I suppose so.'

'But none of that can happen if I'm seen to be personally involved. That's why I had to wake up old Dickie Dowdswell in Palm Springs and get him to kill the story in the *Fortress*.' Confident now that he had won the debate and that the final vote would be in his favour, Leslie went to a table between the two tall windows and poured himself a drink.

'What story?' Jenny frowned, no longer understanding.

'The story about your joining Dr Fred's tin-pot resistance movement. The Doctor's no doubt a specialist in hopeless protests. He learnt the art from his father who was a pacifist vicar.'

'My joining?' Jenny was puzzled. 'They were going to put *that* in the paper?'

'Of course they were. It's news because you're my wife.' And why on earth, Leslie wondered as he drank whisky, did he find himself involved with women who insisted on joining inconvenient organizations? He remembered the trouble he'd had convincing the world that the undoubted fact that his first wife had signed on with the Campaign for Nuclear Disarmament was a pure invention. 'Don't worry your pretty head,' he told Jenny. 'The story's killed. And now all you have to do is tell the Doctor you never meant to join in the first place.'

168

She was looking at him, without understanding. He brought his glass and sat down beside her, and then he remembered to ask her if she wanted a drink. She shook her head.

'Tell him he must have misunderstood. You talk quietly, so he probably didn't hear what you were saying. He wanted you to join, so he seems to have assumed you agreed when all you were doing was being politely interested.' He drank. 'You'll know how to get out of it, I'm sure.'

'You mean,' she had found a voice now and spoke quite loudly, 'you want me to lie about it?'

'We all have to from time to time. I bet even Tony wasn't busy being George Washington every day, was he? It wouldn't surprise me at all to discover that he found a use for a good thumping lie occasionally.'

Then she said that she was going to bed and left him.

Leslie finished his drink slowly, determined not to hurry after her. He felt he had nothing to reproach himself with. His argument, he thought, had been moderate, sensibly put and unanswerable. He had, he hoped, done something to shake Jenny out of an unreasonable obsession with her departed husband. He climbed the staircase slowly and when he reached the bedroom he saw a small shape under the covers. Her face was turned to the wall and her dark hair spread over the pillow. He smiled at her and made a final concession.

'I'll do the dirty work for you, if you like. I'll explain to Dr Fred that it was all a misunderstanding. Would *that* make you feel better?'

But, it seemed, it wouldn't. That night Jenny moved away from him in bed, a rejection he had never suffered before. He lay in the darkness and his feeling of having been unfairly treated hardened into a deep hatred, not of Jenny or even of Fred Simcox, but of the late Tony Sidonia.

The next morning the storm between them seemed to have passed. Leslie got up when Jenny was still asleep and went to bath and dress. When he came back to the bedroom to say goodbye, he was as friendly as before their quarrel and seemed to bear her no ill will. The last thing he said was, 'I'll look after everything. No need for you to worry.' When he had gone she reviewed their quarrel with the fairness which, she sometimes worried, might have been her way of avoiding trouble. Perhaps, after all, his embarrassment was understandable. If she'd known there was a danger of it getting into the papers would she have joined S.O.V.? As she wandered into her natural home, the kitchen, in her dressing-gown, put the kettle on the Aga and listened to the comforting sound of Mrs Bigwell's Hoover, she was about to give Leslie Titmuss the benefit of the doubt. Then she remembered what he had said about Tony, the unexpected attack on a dead man which had unbalanced her like a blow. Was that forgivable? And could it be forgotten? As she had been used to doing for so many years she consulted her friend Sue Bramble.

'Well, I've never been absolutely crazy about your Mr Titmuss, as you well know, although he was perfectly civil to me that weekend. Much to my surprise, I must say. But what's he done that's so terrible? He just didn't want you to join this Save the Badger Club, or whatever it is.'

'He wanted me to tell a lie.'

'Well, he might have wanted you to do much nastier things. Like climb into a rubber suit and squirt soda-water at him. Men have such unfortunate wants sometimes.'

'He did want me to lie,' Jenny repeated.

'And then he told you you needn't. And he'd do it for you.'

'That's right. Yes.'

'Well, it's so rare to get a chap to do anything for you nowadays. My bloody trainer wouldn't even change the wheel on my car, let alone put himself to the trouble of getting a divorce. If you've found a man who'll do things for you, I say be grateful. Even if he does have a row of pens in the breast pocket of his business suiting.'

'He doesn't.'

'Not do things for you?'

'No. Have a row of pens.'

'Oh, well. He looks the sort who would.'

'It's the way he attacked Tony.'

'What did he say again?'

'He more or less called Tony a liar.'

'Well, he didn't know Tony, did he?'

'Of course not.'

'Then he's talking nonsense. He's just jealous.'

'Of Tony?' Jenny couldn't believe it. 'I mean, Tony's not here to be jealous of.'

'I bet your Mr Titmuss wants to think he's got you all to himself. No memories. Nothing. He probably longs for you to have been a virgin when he married you.'

'Do you think so, honestly?'

'Don't worry, darling. Absolutely nothing you can do about that.'

So Jenny was surprised by her friend's lenient attitude towards Leslie Titmuss and she felt she had been unnecessarily upset. This suited her very well because she wanted, above all things, to avoid another quarrel.

Fred Simcox sat in his consulting room faced, once again, with the immense bulk of Dot Curdle. When he asked her why she had come to see him, she muttered a word which sounded to him like 'perdition', so that he was inclined to say that she needed the services of Kev the Rev. rather than his. 'Perdition?' he asked, and she nodded her head in a meaningful manner and withdrew a bundle of papers fom a Tesco's bag. 'It's a perdition which I wants everyone to sign, but you should sign it particular as a doctor who knows about things.' Then she read out a preamble which she had composed and Evie had typed out in rough.

'"Science has taught us,"' Dot thundered, as though

announcing the end of civilization, '"that eating of chicken produces salmonella and the gastric. It's dicing with death to eat beef, lamb and pork meat, or tinned tongue, as these fatty substances gives you heart attacks. For a healthy diet keep to regular meals of pure, local raised, free-range rabbit meat, low in fat or starch which raises the blood pressure. Rabbit will cure heart disease. It can be cooked in a variety of ways ranging from haut cuisine to peasant. We the undersigned being consumers, producers and experts in the field are gravely concerned" – Len Bigwell told us to put that "gravely concerned". He says as how everyone's gravely concerned on the news nowadays – "are gravely blah, blah . . . at the prospect of our locality losing a huge natural source of this vital food by the closure of the Rapstone Valley Rabbit Hacienda."' Here Mrs Curdle paused and looked at Fred triumphantly. 'So will you put your name on the dotted?'

Fred was tempted to sign any document, however misleading, which was designed to protect the valley. Then common sense prevailed and he said, 'Perhaps I could have that and tidy up the scientific side a bit.'

'You do that, Doctor. I'll trust you to get it right, after all you done for Evie.'

'Marriage guidance worked, did it?'

'Puts me in mind of old Dr Salter as was here before you. If ever us children got ill he'd come round with a big black bottle of medicine and say, "This tastes like liquid cow-pat and if you don't get better at once you'll have to drink it all up." Well, we was well again before he left the house. You got the same idea, didn't you? 'Course she'd rather have the sex than that nasty old marriage guidance.' Then the telephone rang and Fred's panic-stricken receptionist announced a person of great importance who insisted on coming in to see him. Before he could ask for further details his door was pushed open to admit Leslie Titmuss.

'Mr Titmuss.' Dot Curdle heaved herself to her feet. 'We'd like your signature to my perdition too, sir. Save the Rabbit Farm. I'll leave it with you.'

When she had gone Leslie looked at the document, dropped it on to Fred's desk and said, 'Are you going to sign this rubbish?'

'I'll have to edit the medical bits. But, yes. I want to help her keep her rabbit farm.'

'Poor old Fred!' Leslie looked at him with pity. 'Why don't you give up politics?'

'It is my morning surgery. Could we make a time to talk?'

'You're even more ridiculous than your old father was when he went on marches all over the place. Neither of you had the faintest hope of achieving anything. Why don't you just give up?'

'I suppose I could ask you the same question.'

Leslie looked at Fred with particular coldness and didn't bother to ask him to explain.

'If you hadn't taken up politics, if you didn't go around making speeches about market forces and consumer choice, we might have had a bit of peace in the Rapstone Valley.'

'So you and your well-heeled friends can enjoy the rural life?' Leslie was, in fact, far better heeled than Fred would ever be but the Simcox family had, since childhood, represented his idea of wealth plagued by guilt and a half-hearted hankering for socialism in order to ease their consciences.

'So long as there's any countryside left for everyone to enjoy.'

'It's not going to be saved by you having a few jumble sales and coffee mornings. You know that. It'll be decided by people who've got power, and that hasn't been your lot for a long time and it may never be again.'

'You mean it's going to be decided by you?'

'It'll be judged in due course by a proper, fair, public inquiry.' Leslie repeated the words which he was going to use again and again to distance himself from the future of his new home.

'In the end you'll have to decide whether to accept the inquiry's decision. If there is an inquiry. As of now the District Council seems about to condemn the valley to death without an inquiry.'

'Please, Fred.' Leslie smiled at him tolerantly, as though he were a child. 'You may be the world's greatest expert on prescribing the pills my government has to pay for when you can't think of how else to treat your patients, but please, don't try to teach me my job.'

'Doesn't everyone have a right to teach politicians their jobs?'

'Oh, Fred.' Leslie now managed a look of genuine pity. 'You used to have a bit of life in you once. You used to chase girls, although as far as I can remember most of them got away. You used to play mournful jazz numbers rather badly on the drums. Now you're growing old with nothing better to do than chatter about democracy.'

'I notice you chatter about it quite a lot.'

'I know what it means.'

'Look, I've got a whole line of patients waiting.'

'It means handing over power to whoever's got a majority in Parliament and then forgetting about it for the next four years. And it doesn't mean calling on people when they're out and trapping their wives into joining their funny little pressure groups.'

'Did you say, trapping?' Fred was genuinely puzzled.

'Jenny was reasonably polite, as she always is. And then you ran away and claimed she'd joined your Save Our Back Gardens Group, or whatever you call yourselves. Very pleased with yourself, weren't you? You even had to ring up and tell the bloody newspapers.'

'I didn't do that.'

'Oh, no? And you didn't make my wife a member, without her consent?'

What was going on? Fred thought that Jenny must have lied in the face of her husband's anger. Clearly she needed help.

'Did she tell you that?'

'Of course she told me that. Why do you think I'm here? I'd be a great deal too busy to waste my time in National Health surgeries if you hadn't involved Jenny.'

'Then I must have been mistaken.'

'Or shall we say pushing your luck?' Fred noticed that Leslie Titmuss had come very close to him, so that their faces were almost touching. It was an unnerving way he had, Fred remembered, when he was a perpetually obtrusive small boy.

'Say what you like.'

'Then will you kindly remove my wife's name from your list of members?'

'Of course,' Fred told him. 'If that's what she wants.'

Leslie left then, feeling, with some contempt, that his victory had been far too easy. Fred spent the next two hours listening to long stories of vague complaints, wishing he could threaten his patients with Dr Salter's horrible black bottle, and being sorry for Jenny Titmuss.

CHAPTER EIGHTEEN

It was now early autumn, the sunniest time of the year, with the leaves only just on the point of changing, a smell of damp earth in the woods and heavy dew on the bracken fronds or sparkling in spiders' webs among the ripe blackberries. There were mushrooms and toadstools scattered like lost golf balls on the Rapstone downland as the District Council postponed its decision. Leslie Titmuss got into his car to drive to his Ministry each morning before the day warmed up and he would shiver a little at the hint of frost soon to come. It was in those days, when Kev the Rev. filled his church with giant marrows, ripe apples and bunches of corn, which were duly prayed over by a congregation of stockbrokers and P.R. men kneeling in rustic ritual, that the marriage of Hector and Daphne Jones suffered an irretrievable breakdown.

Their daughter Joan Baez Jones had grown into a large, awkward thirteen-year-old whose passage through the Nature Area was noisy and destructive. She often disturbed nesting birds, broke hospital cages and, on one never-to-be-forgotten occasion, rode her bicycle over a nest of curlew's eggs. When Hector lost his temper with her daughter, Daphne accused him of preferring the young of animals, who proliferated thoughtlessly and with no idea of schooling or career prospects, to that of their own child. Thinking over what she said, in the quietness of the woods, Hector had to admit that his wife had a point. The fury which he had directed at the thoughtless Joan Baez would have turned into gentle and loving concern if she had only been born a badger cub. It was when he was out watching badgers that it happened. He came home a little before dawn, put his gun in the shed where he always hid it, and was surprised to find the house lit up and unlocked. He went upstairs to find the beds unslept in and the suitcases gone from the top of the wardrobe.

In the sitting-room he found a note written on a page torn from one of his daughter's school exercise books.

Dear Hector [he read with mounting excitement] I have rung Barry and he's coming up at once to fetch us in his car. It's obvious you prefer anything that has four legs on it to your wife and daughter. Often I think you haven't noticed how many legs I've got for a long time and I've had about enough of it. I don't think you give a damn about Joannie and her school problems. She complains that all you've told her about nature study her teacher disagrees with, particularly when it comes to the intelligence of such things as foxes which everyone knows fully deserve to be treated as vermin. Anyway, Barry has a couple of rooms over his shop which he says we can use till the Council finds us something. I'm going to try and get back into the Social Services. I'll put nothing in the way of your seeing Joannie, not that I suppose you'll bother. But if you have her out I'm not letting you take her into the woods. She's a young woman now, though I don't suppose you've noticed that either.

Hector read the note over again, and a third time, savouring its news to the full. In such a way do punters read telegrams telling them they've won the pools, applicants enjoy the good news of their selection for important jobs or actors relish favourable notices. The silence, the luxury of his new-found, hard-won solitude lapped around him like the water in a warm and comforting bath. He climbed the stairs, undressed as far as his shirt, vest and underpants, a comfortable form of night attire of which his wife disapproved, and fell asleep breathing gratitude on Barry Harvester, the Hartscombe herbalist, who had brought him the peace he had longed for.

The next morning he rose early and enjoyed his silent breakfast and his walk into the Nature Area. Now all he had to fear was the time when the schoolchildren came filing along the nature trails. They had to be watched for flower picking and wandering from the marked footpaths, just as the senior citizens on their organized rambles had to be prevented from picnicking or sitting on the grass. He wondered, as he often did, what the flowers and the animals had to do with these forked radishes, dressed in bobble hats and anoraks, who did nothing but destroy their peace.

With his wife and daughter gone, Hector Bolitho Jones hoped that, in time, other human intruders would go also. In his new-found happiness he had forgotten the prospect of a great sea of human faces surrounding the Nature Area with the coming of Fallowfield Country Town. This was the concern of politicians in distant offices, whose days were spent far from the cry of curlews or the late fluttering of fritillary butterflies.

'We have got him,' Ken Cracken said, 'on toast.' He spoke with his mouth half full of the sausage sandwich Joyce had got him from the Ministry canteen. It was their habit to arrive at work with the cleaners and, although their nights had been devoted to love, at dawn their talk was all of politics.

'You're very sure of yourself.' Joyce Timberlake spoke in admiration.

'I'm sure of the Worsfield District Council. They're about to put a new town in Leslie's back garden. He won't just have to go green. He'll have to become a wet. Can't you see the headlines: TITMUSS TO ACT AGAINST FREE MARKET ECONOMY. And at that moment' – Ken Cracken refreshed himself from a plastic mug full of strong, sweet, instant coffee – 'he's going to lose the Prime Minister's love. It'll really be quite heartbreaking.'

At which moment the telephone rang. Leslie Titmuss had got in earlier than the earliest cleaner and wanted to see his second-in-command without delay. 'On toast,' Ken said as he moved triumphantly towards the door, 'with a nice dollop of sauce on the side.' The image seemed to fuel his hunger and he returned to his desk and took a final mouthful of sausage sandwich to sustain him on the journey upstairs.

'I wanted to talk to you about the Rapstone development.' Leslie sat very still and spoke quietly. The room was as impersonal as the top of his desk, where a framed photograph of Jenny stood alone and out of place on the bleak stretch of mahogany. Ken Cracken smiled, invited himself to a chair and sat with his legs stretched out, still thoughtfully chewing. 'I thought you might,' he said.

'I'm told the District Council's inclined to say yes.'

'Well, no wonder. After your smashing speech to the builders.'

'As I tried to explain to you, Kenneth. A new town's going to upset a lot of ordinary voters.'

'Ordinary voters, eh?' Ken Cracken was relishing the moment. 'Well, we mustn't upset *them*. As I always say, we ought to have abolished local government long ago. It's always been a pain in the bum. Still, if that's their thinking . . .'

'I'm assured it is.'

'And you don't want the damn thing built . . .'

'I never said that.'

'I mean, if their decision is likely to be contrary to the present high priority the government's giving to the preservation of wild life, wilderness areas and broad-leafed woodlands . . .' Ken spoke with a kind of brutal cynicism which was almost a parody of the way in which his Secretary of State used to mock the ideas of the green welly brigade.

'Advise me, Kenneth. I'd be very grateful.' Leslie's voice had become gentle, almost caressing, a dangerous signal which Ken Cracken was unwise to ignore.

'Well, if you really don't want it to happen, just say the

building of a new town is too important a matter to be decided at local level and you're calling in the papers and ordering a full public inquiry. You could say that, couldn't you?'

'No.'

'Of course' – Ken Cracken smiled with delighted understanding – 'now you've gone and bought yourself a house in the place, I do see the difficulty.'

'I couldn't say it. You'll have to say it.'

'Me? But you're the boss . . .'

'Exactly. That's why I'm telling you what to do.'

Ken felt a moment of uncertainty as he watched Leslie get up and go to the window.

'You can say that as I've bought a house in Rapstone it would be inappropriate for me to make the decision. Go on to say that you have advised me to order a public inquiry as the matter is too important to be settled at local level. Not a brilliant phrase, Ken. Not headline stuff. You'll never make a first-class speech. But it'll do. You'll say that you recommended putting the question to a full public inquiry so all the objectors could have their say. You'll make it clear that was your advice. You can ring Tim Warboys on the *Fortress* and start leaking the story now.' Leslie looked down into the street below. The workers at H.E.A.P., self-important and anxious men in mackintoshes, bright chattering girls, older women loitering to exchange gossip, postponing for as long as possible the start of another day in the typing-pool, were arriving, stepping off buses or emerging from the Underground. They would initial files, stamp orders, copy letters, photostat plans and slowly but surely England would change. Old buildings, streets filled with memories, would tumble to make way for office blocks, desirable apartments or shopping centres. Fields once sensitive to the seasons would freeze into commuter towns, drive-in supermarkets or eight-lane motorways. Often such changes occurred after the flicker of a word processor and initials scrawled by someone who would never see the results of their decision. Leslie looked down as his staff hurried up the big stone steps into the Ministry and, in the silence, Ken Cracken so far forgot himself as to say, 'You can't expect me to do that.'

'What's the matter, Ken, my lad? Are you hoping to embarrass me?' Leslie looked from the window to his Junior Minister.

'No. Why should I?'

'I don't know. Perhaps you want to take over my job. You like living dangerously, don't you?'

'I don't know what you mean.'

'Trouble with you, Ken, is that you missed the war. Oh dear, oh dear, what a pity we can't organize a nice little bit of fighting so you could work off some of your high spirits. I might persuade the Prime Minister to invade the Scilly Isles. You'd appreciate that, wouldn't you?' Leslie sat behind his desk now and looked like an indulgent headmaster half-amused by an inadequate pupil's tiresome habit of letting off stinkbombs in the lavatory. 'I can imagine you jumping off the landing craft, shrieking with excitement. Until they started chucking live bullets at you, of course.'

'Well, if that's all for the moment . . .' Ken sat forward but didn't get up as there was more to come.

'You were even too young for National Service, weren't you?' Leslie, who had done his time in the Pay Corps, spoke like a veteran of World War Two. 'What a shame. You might've enjoyed the square-bashing. The spit and polish would've turned you on. It might, I say it just might, have saved you from making a rare idiot of yourself in other people's woods at night.'

'Leslie' – Ken tried a friendly smile which came out a little crooked, hoisting his moustache up on one side only – 'I honestly have no idea what you're talking about.'

'Have you not? War games. That's what I'm talking about.'

'War . . .?'

'Don't look so bloody innocent. I gather it's the latest craze among hooray bankers, building tycoons and upwardly mobile politicians. Provided they're young enough to have missed the real war, of course. It's taken over from pushing people into rivers.'

There was another silence. Leslie looked down at the naked wood on top of his desk and seemed to sink into deep thought. Ken, wondering if it were all over now, got up as quietly as possible, but stood still when his superior looked at him again. 'You leak what I told you to leak, my lad,' he said. 'And stand by it, or I might leak the news of the daring commando raid with paint-guns in the Rapstone Nature Area. What are the ordinary voters going to think of that, eh? A so-called responsible Minister playing silly games of soldiers.'

'I'll give Warboys the story.' Ken now needed no more time to make up his mind. 'From a government source. That do?'

'Perfectly. Oh, and you can say I'll stick by the finding of the public inquiry. Whichever way it goes.'

'Of course.' Ken was on his way to the door. 'Is there anything else?'

'Only one thing. Don't eat the canteen sausages for breakfast. They spurt grease all over your tie.' And here Leslie Titmuss did a parody of Christopher Kempenflatt's old Etonian accent. 'Rather lets the Ministry down, that sort of thing. Wouldn't you agree, old chap?'

Joyce looked at her scowling Minister of State when he got back to his room and decided that, in one way or another, Titmuss must have slid off the toast.

'There's going to be an inquiry,' Ken told her. 'Leslie must have a lot of faith in it. He's going to accept the result, whatever it is.'

'So he'll get away with it.'

'What?'

'No town in his back garden, and no political fall-out. I always told you. It doesn't do to underestimate Leslie.'

'We'll have to wait and see about that, won't we? Just for now, I've been given a job.'

'In Northern Ireland?' Joyce looked at him with pity.

'Oh, very funny! No. I've got to ring Tim Warboys at the *Fortress.*' Beneath his moustache, Ken's lips pursed as though he were about to take some peculiarly nasty medicine. 'I'm going to square the press for Titmuss.'

IN MY BACK GARDEN IF YOU LIKE. That was the headline of Tim Warboys' Whispers from the Gallery column and it went on:

Leslie Titmuss might have been put in an embarrassing position by the proposal to build a new town next to his lately acquired home, Rapstone Manor. Opposition hopes that Titmuss would block the development for selfish reasons were dashed by the Secretary of State's decision to leave the question to the high-flying Ken Cracken, Titmuss's Number Two. Cracken has decided that there should be a full public inquiry and Titmuss has told friends and Cabinet colleagues that he'll accept its findings. Once again the man who the Prime Minister calls 'our Leslie' has shown he is a Minister who accepts democratic decisions and the changing face of England. What a contrast to such out-dated snobs as the Labour Member for Smoketown South who's burnt his cloth cap and is trying to oil his way into White's Club in the faint hope of being bought a small dry sherry by a Duke.

Once evening not long after he'd read this paragraph, designed to preserve its author's position as the government's favourite journalist, Fred got a telephone call which astonished him and led him to turn down the volume of his Charlie 'Bird' Parker record. His caller was Mr Chatterbox of the *Fortress.*

'We've got a story about you, Dr Simcox. Rather an odd one.' Tim Warboys, calling from his bed which contained an insatiable married lady from the Home Maker section of his paper, sounded exhausted. 'Do you really think that eating rabbits is the way to avoid heart disease?'

'Absolutely not. I've never said that.'

'Apparently it was in some sort of manifesto you signed.'

'Whoever told you that?'

'Come on, Dr Simcox. You know we don't reveal our sources. But this one couldn't be more reliable. Was it in this document of yours?'

'Well, yes. But I didn't sign it –'

'Do *you* eat a lot of rabbit, Dr Simcox?'

'Not since I was a small boy and my mother made rabbit pie.'

'Delicious, was it?'

'Not very. My mother wasn't much of a cook.'

Tim eluded another sticky embrace from his partner to make a note on his bedside pad. Then he said, 'Well, thank you, Dr Simcox. I think we can get a paragraph out of that. Oh, by the way, wasn't your father a pinko vicar? Always marching for peace and stuff like that?'

'Well, yes. But look. I want to make it absolutely clear that I don't think there's the slightest connection between heart disease and eating rabbits.' But the telephone was buzzing nonchalantly and Tim Warboys had turned, in a desultory way, to satisfy his partner once again.

This strange conversation produced the following paragraph written by Tim Warboys under the headline COUNTRY G.P. BASHES BUNNIES:

It's a case of 'run rabbit run' in the Rapstone Valley. Harts-combe doctor Fred Simcox says other varieties of meat are responsible for all sorts of ills, including heart attacks. The bunny-bashing doctor lives, it seems, on rabbit pie as his mother made it. 'Delicious,' he says, 'and twice as tasty as chicken.' Older readers may recall the name Simcox. Fred's father, the Rev. Simeon Simcox, was always popping up in the Swinging Sixties when he led marches for the C.N.D., the A.N.C. and any other set of letters that took his fancy. Has Fred inherited his father's quirky love of lost causes? He has admitted he is desperate to help the owners of the local 'rabbit hacienda' which is in danger of being swallowed up by a new town. And the Rapstone rabbits are in danger of being swallowed up by the Doctor's health-conscious patients!

As a result of this story Fred wrote a number of letters to the *Fortress* and left messages for Tim Warboys, who never returned his calls. Finally he was rewarded by a short piece in the Healthy Living section of the paper headed IS BUNNY DOCTOR RIGHT? EXPERT SPEAKS OUT. It continued:

Bernard Wheatkins, Professor of Dietetics and Longevity at the University of Worsfield, has backed rabbit-eating G.P., Fred Simcox. Professor Wheatkins, who first established the connection between arthritis and fried fish, told our medical correspondent, 'Rabbit meat may help keep many people free of heart failure. Research has shown that poachers in the early years of this century, who fed mainly on rabbit, lived to an extraordinary age.' The Professor, who has made a close study of the psychology of illness, says, 'Rabbits are life-loving and active little blighters. Think of how they breed. Who knows if this positive attitude may not derive from the chemical make-up of the food product?' He foresees a day when bunny may take the place of beef at the British Sunday lunch table.

The result of these events was a further extraordinary increase in business at the Curdles' hacienda and, as a sign of their new prosperity, Len Bigwell was seen driving a second-hand Porsche. He asked a Worsfield advertising agency to plan a new 'promotion' for the hacienda's products and appointed Jackson Cantellow his solicitor with a view to forming a company which might, at some date, be floated on the Stock Exchange. Fred wondered how on earth this nonsense had started, and remembered that the only person who had seen Dot Curdle's 'perdition' in his consulting room was Leslie Titmuss.

CHAPTER NINETEEN

Fred Simcox had only been in love twice in his life before he met Jenny and both times it was with the same woman.

He had known his old partner's daughter, Agnes Salter, since they were children. When he was a young man they had made love, passionately and often, in an old hut Dot Curdle's father, Tom Nowt, the poacher, had built in the woods and which he made available to them in exchange for a few pints of beer in the Baptist's Head in Rapstone. There, under the skulls of poached deer, among the shot-guns and snares and the skins of foxes and squirrels, under an army blanket on an iron bedstead which squeaked and rattled its complaints, warmed by a wood-burning stove which belched acrid smoke when the wind was in the wrong direction, Fred had made love with a white-skinned, red-headed girl in ways which he had the privilege of remembering all his life.

When Agnes, in those days before the pill, became pregnant, Fred, then a medical student, had failed either to marry her or find the money for the abortion she subsequently had. She had married his brother Henry who finally went off with a young lady in television. Fred, of course, forgave Agnes but never himself. At last, when Henry was safely married to Lonnie, the television researcher, Agnes and Fred came together and he fell in love with her once again.

Their second love was entirely different from their first. Although they didn't live together it was much more of a marriage. Agnes had a flat in London and made her living cooking other people's dinners. Fred had the house which went with his practice in Hartscombe. They stayed often in each other's homes and, because they had inflicted such wounds on each other, they now behaved with almost too much consideration. Lacking any element of danger, their relationship finally lost its passion. It was as though they were so determined to be friends that friends, in the course of time, was all that they became. They still visited each other, confided in each other and, very occasionally, went to bed together to try and rediscover that ridiculous excitement they had known in a hut on a blanket that smelled of wet dog. Although it was never found again, Fred had loved Agnes for the second time. Because she was undoubtedly an original spirit, a woman who enjoyed the awfulness of life, laughed at loneliness and detested things like summer holidays and Christmas, he had found it hard to love anyone else better.

Of course he had tried. He had taken girls driving across Europe; girls had stayed in the room over the surgery and listened to his old jazz records or even more devotedly sat at the bar while he played the drums with his old friends in the Riverside Stompers. He had liked many of them and thought there was no reason why they shouldn't have become excellent wives for a local G.P., but the memory of Agnes as she had been somehow made them seem tame and colourless, and the duty he felt he owed to Agnes as she was made him reluctant to take on another life-long commitment. In his forties the turnover had been quite rapid; something, a toss of the head, a way of lighting a cigarette, a smile of derision at some pomposity, would prick his desire and set him off, believing he felt all the wild and breathless excitement he had known when he bicycled off to meet Agnes at Tom Nowt's hut in the woods. But finally, when it became clear to him that he wasn't going to meet Agnes or anyone like her, and when whichever partner it was felt her attention wandering because the Doctor's was wandering also, they would part, usually without rancour. So Fred went to the weddings and looked after the children of old lovers who rarely thought about him now and he, with his mind still full of Agnes, found it hard to remember exactly when, or in one case even if, he had made love to them.

Then he fell in love for the third time in his life, with Jenny Titmuss.

Although he felt no older, and certainly no wiser, than he had been when he was first sent away to school, or when he disappointed his father by defecting from a C.N.D. march to meet Agnes, Fred had reached that time in his life when he knew where he had got to and was prepared to settle for it. He still went to London and had dinner with Agnes, enjoying her hilarious denunciation of all the things women of her age were meant to value most; but now he rarely sought out new companions. Most of the time he felt he would have liked to have been left in peace, without the demands of the Rapstone Valley protest or the lure of a slim back, a narrow waist, a cascade of red hair pushed back, swaying in front of him in the street. Now, if such a vision turned towards him he felt a sense of relief if the face didn't touch him. He would be spared, at least, the long process of getting to know someone new, the dinners in country house hotels, the repetition of his old stories which had come to sound to him like the words of an actor whose play has run too long. But just as S.O.V. came to involve him in the affairs of the district and in the making of protests, however absurd, his sudden love for Jenny Titmuss shook him out of his contentment, bringing him an excitement which he had hoped never to feel again.

He didn't fall in love when he saw her at her wedding, although he knew there was nothing in her face to save him from that predicament. He didn't even fall in love with her when he called on her at Rapstone Manor and she had, he was sure she had, promised to join his organization. He only fell in love, suddenly and hopelessly, on the morning that Leslie Titmuss called on him in his surgery. This event occurred after Leslie had left and he felt sorry for Jenny. He thought she must be in distress and had been forced to change her mind about her membership by the domineering Titmuss. He found it hard to imagine anyone married to Leslie not being in distress and that, as well as her beauty, moved him almost unbearably. So his love for Jenny was, although he didn't admit as much to himself, brought about by his lifelong dislike of Leslie Titmuss.

As soon as Leslie had gone about his business, Fred had explained to Mrs Vee that there had been some confusion and Jenny Titmuss wasn't a member and had never agreed to become one. When he had arranged this matter Fred telephoned Jenny to set, as he told himself, her mind at rest. He chose to ring in the morning, when she was likely to be alone, but the voice that answered him was that of Leslie Titmuss in a hurry.

'Oh, it's you.'

'Of course it's me. You sound disappointed.'

'Not at all. I just wanted to tell your wife I 've made it clear to everyone here that she never agreed to be a member.'

'You mean you told the truth? I hope it wasn't too great an effort. I'll let her know.' The telephone clicked and then buzzed angrily. Fred put it down and set off on his rounds. He thought that ringing Jenny again might make life difficult for her and he didn't want to encounter Titmuss. For their next meeting he would have to rely on chance. Until that happened he thought more often about Jenny and less about many years ago when he went to meet Agnes Salter in a hut in the woods.

A few weeks later in the Badger in Skurfield, Fred sat behind the old drum set, got down from the attic, and in remembrance of things past underlined the deep, mournful and persistent beat of 'St James Infirmary'. The Riverside Stompers had got together again. The group consisted of Joe Sneeping from the off-licence in Hartscombe on trumpet (he also supplied the vocals and tried to confine the band strictly to music played in New Orleans during the prohibition era), Terry Fawcett from Marmaduke's garage on clarinet, and Den Kitson from the Brewery who performed no better on the banjo than he did on the guitar or bass. They hadn't played together for a number of years and now they had blown the dust off their instruments in the hope of blasting the developers out of the Rapstone Valley. Once, in the heyday of rock 'n' roll, they had been shouted down by teenage tearaways in this same pub and had Coca-Cola cans thrown at them for singing that very blues number. Now the belligerent teenagers, filled to the brim with Fortissimo lager, were busy fighting more dangerous battles in the pedestrian walkways of Hartscombe and Worsfield. The audience for the Stompers' jazz were elderly and respectable, the sort that, when Fred was young, had sat respectfully through Gilbert and Sullivan operas. They wore anoraks and Fair Isle sweaters and the girlfriends they had once taken to hear Humphrey Lyttelton or Chris Barber were now grandmothers who in some cases brought their grandchildren. This newer generation sat wide-eyed at music as remote from their times as Byrd or Monteverdi, amazed that its sadness should give such obvious pleasure to those who played it.

And then, finishing a complex riff on the drums, Fred looked up and saw Jenny standing by the bar, ferreting in the depths of her handbag to pay for the half pint of bitter she had ordered. Looking dizzily down a precipice of years he saw himself sitting behind the drums in the garage where the Stompers used to rehearse, on the night when Agnes Salter walked in and stood, listening quietly until she announced her need for money because she was pregnant, a situation which he then proceeded to mismanage. Now, when Joe Sneeping, in the New Orleans accent he had learnt off countless records, told them they could take ten, Fred stepped off the platform and made his way towards Jenny. In her way, it seemed to him, she was in trouble and he didn't mean to fail again.

'It was good of you to come.'

Jenny and Elsie Titmuss, in their new-found friendship, sometimes shared pub lunches. Jenny had seen a notice pinned up advertising the Stompers concert on a night when Leslie was the guest of the Euro M.P.s in the Midlands, an event which he had considerately spared her.

'You like jazz?'

'I'm not exactly an expert. My husband used to listen to it all the time.'

'That's odd' – Fred turned from her for a moment to order himself a pint of the family bitter – 'I can't remember Leslie being so ecstatic about the brothel music of the Deep South. I mean, we were never offered Titmuss on tenor sax. Not so far as I can remember'.

'Not Leslie!' Jenny smiled. 'My first husband. Who died.' She was surprised by how easy it had become to say it.

'I'm sorry.'

'It was a long time ago.' She lifted the mug of beer which her wrist looked too thin to keep steady. 'I ought to say I'm sorry. That silly muddle about me joining your group of protesters.'

'I hope that didn't get you into trouble?'

'Not really.' She was looking at him across the surface of her beer. Then she drank, put her mug down on the bar and said, 'Of course, Leslie's got his politics to look after.'

'That's what he told me.'

'Did he? When?'

'When he came to see me. To tell me you didn't mean that about joining us.'

'Is that what he said?'

'I'm sorry. I must have misunderstood . . .'

'No.' Although she was looking away from him now and down at the bar, and though her face was hidden from him by a veil of dark hair, her voice was clear and determined. 'You didn't misunderstand. I told you I wanted to join.'

'And now you can't?' It was as far as he could safely go in trying to form an alliance against the deviousness of Titmuss.

'I suppose not. What a ridiculous position to be in. I just didn't want you to think I'd, well, lied about anything.'

'Of course I didn't think that.' But he had thought that she had, or had been forced to do so by her husband. That moment, when she looked up at him and seemed to be on his side, was the most splendid that the Save Our Valley Society had yet produced. Then he heard Joe Sneeping call him from the platform and he had to go back to open the second half with 'St Louis Blues'. He played with a new vigour and, it seemed to him, a return of youth. In the middle of 'Slow Boat to China', introduced into the Stompers' repertoire despite the purist protests of Joe Sneeping, Jenny left quietly to go back to her house and wait for her husband. She lifted her hand to Fred on her way out and he felt that, in returning her salute, he was waving goodbye to a small soldier off to the front line of battle.

CHAPTER TWENTY

Leslie Titmuss couldn't find a photograph of Tony Sidonia.

What he now felt about Jenny's first husband was something different from the vague and jealous unease which had come over him in a Roman square during their honeymoon. Now it was as though Sidonia had entered their marriage, deliberately challenged him and made him look mean and dishonest. When he had dealt with the matter of Jenny's sudden adherence to S.O.V., and had arranged it in the way he was accustomed to settle countless small difficulties in the course of his working life, Leslie felt that Sidonia was observing him, looking down with amused contempt at the way he rearranged the facts to suit his own purposes. And in this conflict between two men, one of whom was dead, he was afraid that he knew which side his wife was on.

Thinking about it, as he found himself doing a lot of the time, Leslie came to the conclusion that he couldn't believe in Tony Sidonia and the thought brought him much comfort. On the whole, and in spite of the comfort and reassurance of power, Leslie still held a simple view of human nature. Mankind, it was his considered opinion, was motivated by greed. The carrot was money, the stick failure, bankruptcy, 'jobloss' (as he liked to call unemployment) or, in the most obstinate cases, a cardboard box to sleep in by the Worsfield canal. This was the simple mechanism by which people moved forward, obtained a larger share of the market, built tunnels and motorways, erected new cities and gutted and rebuilt old ones. Money was to be found, not in building ships, tilling the land or mining for coal but in countless 'service industries', selling computers to revolve money, peddling insurance policies, advertising more and more different varieties of indistinguishable washing powder, lager or cigarettes. By and large, it might be said, and even was said by Leslie when in a more than usually caustic mood, England had become a nation of hairdressers. But if they were happy hairdressers, well supplied with cars and videos and a large variety of undemanding television channels, if, above all, they were hairdressers who were content to go on voting for Leslie and the 'colleagues', he had no particular objection to them. What he couldn't stand, what enraged him and made him mutter 'Humbug!' and 'Hypocrite!', although not at present in the hearing of his wife, were people who suggested that human behaviour could be attributed to motives other than a laudable desire to 'do well' and provide a decent home for the children. Such a one, he saw quite clearly, was Sidonia.

And yet, in spite of his high moral attitudes, his unreasoning addiction to telling the truth, his bloody air of uncalled-for superiority, what had Sidonia done in the world? He had died leaving nothing but a still mortgaged house in Oxford. He had devoted his life to digging up unsavoury details about the lives of long-dead Princes of the Church, work which created no jobs and trained no one to survive in the harsh world of the marketplace. Sidonia, for all his pretensions, had achieved nothing. And then he remembered that his rival had achieved something which was very precious to Leslie, he had achieved Jenny.

'I have absolutely no idea what he looked like.'
  'Who?'
  'Sidonia.'
  'Why should you want to know?'
  'Curiosity.'
  'I see.'

But Sue Bramble didn't see. Neither did she have any idea why Leslie had asked her to lunch. Having seen him with Jenny, and been startled by his obvious pride in her, and the intensity with which he seemed to look only at her, it never occurred to Sue that there was anything even mildly flirtatious about the invitation. And yet she believed that Leslie, like God, did nothing without a purpose, however obscure his aims might be to ordinary mortals. So they sat together in the restaurant where he had once dined with Jenny, near the flat which Sue now had to herself, and she was nervous, not knowing what precisely was going on, and afraid for her friend. She said, 'You will look after Jenny, won't you?'

'Of course. Don't you know that's all I want to do?'

'Yes. I do know that.' Although she couldn't bring herself to trust him entirely, she was prepared to take his word about looking after her friend. She also, in spite of herself, felt flattered to have been chosen to receive the politician's confidence.

'The odd thing is that Jenny hasn't got a picture of him at home. Absolutely nothing.'

'You've asked her?'

'No. I've looked.'

'I see.' Sue felt a chill at the idea of him choosing some moment when Jenny was out shopping, or in the garden, to quietly open drawers and peer into possible hiding-places, putting things back so that his search shouldn't be discovered. And then the head waiter interrupted them to ask Leslie to sign a menu for some admirers at the next table. Men in suits and grey-haired women were smiling at them and Sue couldn't help feeling important in the politician's company.

'I've looked and I can't find any trace of him at all,' he said when he had signed with a flourish.

'She left behind all the traces when she moved in with you. You should be flattered.'

'Should I?'

'Of course. So you don't have to think about it really, do you? Just go on as if Tony Sidonia never existed.'

'But he did, didn't he?'

'Oh, yes. And I don't suppose anyone who knew him will forget him.'

'Why?' Leslie looked hard at her and spoke with sudden bitterness. 'Was he a perfect person?'

'Of course not.' She laughed at him, but was not unfriendly. 'No one is. But somehow he seemed to know what was right. And if you had Tony on your side you knew you couldn't be so bad after all. Now, why don't you forget about him?'

'Because he's dead.' He frowned when he said that and looked, Sue thought, tormented. She began to get the vaguest idea, a mere glimmer of his troubles. 'And you're afraid he isn't?' she suggested. 'Not in Jenny's mind, anyway.'

'I do want to understand her. Completely. That's the way I feel I can do most for her. Of course I only want Jenny to be happy with me.' Leslie spoke with the sudden unexpected sincerity which had won him, many years ago, his party's nomination for the Hartscombe seat and had convinced the House of Commons at a few dangerous moments since then. It wasn't wasted on Sue Bramble. 'I just feel I could make her happier if I really knew about her life. I mean, I haven't kept any secrets from her.'

'I don't think she's kept any secrets from you, either. She probably just didn't want to trouble you with a lot of old photographs.'

'So she burnt them?'

'Well, not exactly.'

'What exactly?'

'She left them in the flat.'

'You've still got them?'

Sue was silent for a little and then she told him, 'Yes.'

'If I could only see him. See them together.'

'You think you'd know what you're up against?'

'I do want to feel close to Jenny. As close as you are.' He gave Sue Bramble the sincere look again.

'Because you're really not up against anything,' she tried to reassure him. 'Quite honestly you're not. Tony Sidonia's lost and gone forever.'

But, in the end, she was persuaded to let him come back to the flat with her and there, in a bottom drawer where sheets and blankets had been put away, were two photograph albums and Jenny's old wedding ring. It was the ring she had taken off on the first night she spent with Leslie, wrapped in cotton wool and put into an envelope. Sue handed the books to Leslie, telling herself that it was somehow touching that he should want to know as much as possible about Jenny and also feeling some pride at having information to impart.

He stood impassively, turning the pages without any particular expression of interest. At first she tried to give him a bright running commentary. 'That was Tony's cottage. Oh, there's Willoughby Blane in his famous shorts. Their house in Oxford. Jenny's birthday party. That was the Christmas when we did charades. Tony as Marlene Dietrich. That was them in Rome. Tony standing in front of St Peter's and Jenny kissing his ring. Shocking, really. Tony with a crowd of students. Of course they all adored him.' The picture showed him in a big basket-chair in a garden with girls and young men sitting on the grass, listening to him talking. 'Tony's old mum. Myra Sidonia.' And then, as he said nothing, she stopped guiding him round the photographs and went out to make the tea he had asked for.

When she came back with it he said, 'I put them back. I think I remember them well enough.'

'I hope it's made you feel better.'

'You've been an enormous help.' He stirred the tea into which he'd asked her to put two spoonfuls of sugar.

'It was another world. But like I told you, it's gone forever. I'm not even sure she still thinks about it.'

'Just one thing.' He looked at her solemnly. 'It would be better if you didn't tell Jenny you'd shown me these things. Could you promise me that?'

'I suppose so . . .' She felt involved in a conspiracy, a sensation she didn't particularly like.

The day after his lunch with Sue Bramble, Leslie Titmuss directed his ministerial Rover towards a turning off Fetter Lane, a jammed little thoroughfare handy for the Law Courts, barristers' chambers and similar resorts for persons in trouble. He got out in front of a narrow and gloomy building, went up in a lift which sighed with the hoarse complaints of worn-out machinery and entered the offices of the Neverest Detective Agency: 'All Inquiries Undertaken. Complete Confidentiality Guaranteed'. He was ushered without delay into the office of the head of the agency, a man called Arthur Nubble, of whom he had some previous knowledge.

It was not the first time that Mr Nubble had been concerned in the affairs of the Cabinet Minister. He had been a small, fat boy at a boarding-school with Fred Simcox and his brother, and a faded school photograph now hung above his desk beside his certificate of affiliation to the Private Inquiry Agents Association. Since his school days Arthur Nubble had gone into various service industries fashionable from time to time: coffee bars, boutiques, gossip columns and, finally, detection. With a recent increase in divorce and industrial espionage he had prospered, although it suited his romantic view of his trade to keep his premises as squalid and down-at-heel as they would have been in fiction. He had been engaged by Leslie Titmuss on a previous occasion in proceedings concerning the Reverend Simeon Simcox's will and, although he had done his best to serve both sides in that case, Leslie had not learned the full extent of Nubble's duplicity and was prepared to engage him again in a matter which was unlikely ever to surface in a court of law.

'Leslie' – Arthur Nubble liked to call all his clients, especially criminals and Cabinet Ministers, by their Christian names – 'I was delighted when I heard you'd called. Thank you for having faith in us.' His soft brown eyes pleaded for a compliment as urgently as a spaniel begs for a tin of dog food.

'I was brought up to trust nobody,' Leslie told him. 'Especially a professional peeper into other people's bedroom windows. All the same, this is something pretty simple. You can't really mess it up.'

'It's good of you to say so.' Arthur Nubble smiled with delight, as though he had got the praise he was asking for. He also mopped his forehead with his handkerchief, as he always seemed to be suffering from over-heating, however chilly the weather.

'It's this man.' Leslie felt in an inside pocket and brought out a photograph. 'I want you to find out everything you can about him.'

'Is it a divorce matter?' Nubble picked up the photograph and saw a tall man in a garden talking to some admiring young people who sat before him on the grass.

'No. It's a private matter. There's no question of divorce. The chap's name is Anthony Sidonia. He's the one in the chair, holding forth.'

'And where do I find him, Leslie?'

'In some North Oxford cemetery, I imagine. He's dead.'

'Then what do you want me to find out about him?' Nubble always tried not to seem surprised by any instruction. On this occasion he didn't succeed.

'Everything you can. Especially . . .' Leslie was silent for a long time, as though he found the next words hard to say. 'Especially if he always told the truth.'

CHAPTER TWENTY-ONE

It's no sort of comment, favourable or otherwise, on the general
integrity of planning inspectors, to say that Gregory Boland was
a peculiarly honest man. His honesty wasn't anything he could
help. It had been with him all his life, like a birthmark or a
stammer. Some of those who knew him found it faintly ridiculous, some inconvenient. His wife felt sure this unfortunate
defect was what had caused Greg's failure as an architect in
private practice. That, she told him, and his resolute refusal to
join the Freemasons. Building developers, it was well known,
always gave jobs to the architects they met whilst swearing
strange oaths in the banqueting rooms of provincial hotels. Greg
had smiled and announced in his soft Scottish accent that if he
couldn't get the contract for the new bacon factory without
putting on an apron and pressing the point of a pair of compasses
to his naked bosom he'd rather stay at home and build kitchen
cupboards. His home was well furnished with fitted cupboards,
but Sir Joseph Buddle, F.R.I.B.A., whose membership of the
ancient order of Masons in no way improved his brutal style of
architecture, got the bacon factory with the geriatric ward of a
local hospital thrown in.

Gregory Boland was also rare among architects as he lived in a
house he had built himself. Jo Buddle, who had dumped the pile
of vast building-bricks on the centre of Worsfield, who wrote
regularly in the *Architectural Review* saying that we must forget
the past and stamp the culture of the 1990s on our towns and

villages, lived in a Georgian rectory with a walled garden, a place he furnished with Chippendale and English water-colours. Gregory, who also built in the modern manner, was prevented by the handicap of honesty from living in a house any more or less beautiful than those he was able to design for his customers. Accordingly he and his family inhabited a smallish concrete block in an area to the south-east of London where planning permission was not too hard to come by. This home which looked, in a poor light, like a small bunker built to withstand the onslaught of World War Three, was a source of derision and complaint from the neighbours and of regret to Mrs Boland and the children, who pined for a thatched cottage beside an old mill stream. Living with cheerful determination in this unsympathetic residence, Gregory Boland found his practice fading away and so, looking for a regular source of income, became an inspector with the Ministry of Housing, Ecological Affairs and Planning.

As such he presided over inquiries where his height and his flaming red hair made him an imposing figure. Having been brought up by a father who had been a postman, lay preacher and an elder of his church, and having fought his way up without losing his faith in a punitive God, Gregory Boland was quick to smell a whiff of corruption in any planning application or council proceeding. His clear blue eyes behind gold-rimmed spectacles were always on the look-out for builders who gave councillors peculiar and talismanic handshakes before the proceedings began. Such was the upright judge who was to hear the application for permission to build Fallowfield Country Town. In due course his recommendations would be laid on the desk of Leslie Titmuss, who had, in the particular case of Fallowfield and the Rapstone Valley, agreed to accept them, however inconvenient they might be to his own life and happiness.

'The Inspector's Greg Boland.'

'What's he like?'

'Scottish Wee Free. Straight as a die. Slightest touch of

pressure being put on him and he'll be off like a shot in the opposite direction. I've made the fullest inquiries.'

Ken Cracken and Christopher Kempenflatt were in a corner of Bettina's, an upper-crust disco tucked away in a Mayfair mews. The music overlaid their voices, as the shadows in the corner where they sat drinking a late-night bottle of champagne almost concealed their presence. Their companions for the evening, Joyce Timberlake and the gold-burnished Mrs Armitage, had gone off to exchange confidences in the Ladies, leaving the two men to discuss business.

'He doesn't sound quite the right chap for us.' Kempenflatt was doubtful.

'He's absolutely the right chap for us. Anyway, if he hadn't been straight Leslie Titmuss wouldn't have let them appoint him.'

'I thought you said that Titmuss was leaving the whole Fallowfield business to you.'

'That's what he *said*.' And Ken Cracken laid his finger along the side of his nose in a gesture used by generations of the Cracken family to mean 'pull the other one, it's got bells on'. 'Leslie's got to make sure this business is done strictly on the level. If anyone thought he was swinging it in favour of his country house he'd be finished.'

'I thought that was rather what you wanted.'

'There are more ways than one of skinning a dead cat.' Ken Cracken again used a phrase which had been a great favourite with his grandfather when the old man was in the fur trade. 'But you're right. I wouldn't mind Leslie retiring gracefully to the back benches, after years of valuable service to the country and the Party. All that sort of rubbish. Perhaps the time has come for the old boy to take things easy.'

'And let you pinch his job?' Christopher Kempenflatt had never, since the day when he pushed the great servant of his country into the river, favoured the subtle approach.

'Of course, although that'll be entirely up to the Prime

Minister. And you need to build Fallowfield. With a bit of luck we may both get what we want.'

'How're we going to manage that?'

'Politics, Christopher. Some of us were born with a bit of a talent for it. We might as well finish the bottle, before the girls get back.'

Dancing with minimal movement in the company of the wildly gyrating editor of the Home Maker pages, Tim Warboys noticed the Minister at H.E.A.P. drinking in a corner with the Chairman of Kempenflatts building consortium. Any story about Leslie's Ministry, he felt instinctively, might result in his own immediate transfer to the obituary column, so he averted his eyes. In another corner he saw the much-pilloried Labour M.P. who had tried to get into White's, doing his best to present a swinging image to his research assistant. The absurd hypocrisy of such a fellow behaving like a conservative started an avalanche of column inches in Warboys' mind. His dancing became minimally more animated as he shaped his first sentence: 'A Bettina's Bolshevik takes the floor, but not in the House of Commons. Who is the unknown blonde with whom Labour leftie Dudley Dumpton seems anxious to form a liberal alliance?' Exhausting though it undoubtedly was, and however absurd he felt swaying slightly and clicking his fingers in time to the music, Tim Warboys thought there was nowhere like Bettina's for getting an insight into politics.

Ken Cracken was right. Leslie Titmuss had discovered the name and character of the Inspector who would hear the Fallowfield inquiry. Leslie had no rooted objection to honesty, provided it was not used, as in the case of Jenny's previous husband, to make wounding comparisons with himself. The honesty of Gregory Boland could only underline his own incorruptibility. He had agreed to abide by the result of the inquiry, and the inquiry was to be conducted by an inspector who was above suspicion. How could he conceivably be criticized for that?

It might be thought that Leslie was taking a risk, but having examined the case with the iciest impartiality he came to the conclusion that he was betting on a certainty. Apart from Christopher Kempenflatt and two or three farmers who hoped to make millions, there seemed to be few people who could see any good reason for building over the Rapstone Valley. The number of new houses could easily be fitted into many villages and on the outskirts of Worsfield. A new town would block the roads, pollute the rivers, lay waste the countryside and provide a permanent blot on a much-loved landscape. Given the fact that Gregory Boland was clearly closed to any dubious approach by the Kempenflatt consortium, Leslie Titmuss didn't see how he could possibly decide in favour of Fallowfield Country Town.

He had only one worry. Could the opposition to Fallowfield get its act together? His plan depended on a well-organized outcry by the public, to whose demands, after judgement had been pronounced in its favour, he would bow graciously. He would have every opportunity of showing the human heart beneath the rugged Titmuss exterior. Could Fred Simcox, never to be classed among nature's politicians, get the outcry going effectively? Leslie thought back to the ease with which he had won the skirmish over Jenny's membership of S.O.V. and didn't feel encouraged. At least he could see that the protesters had a decent Q.C. to argue their case. He arranged for his solicitors to send another cheque from an anonymous benefactor to help with the legal expenses of the protest group. 'Send it to Dr Simcox,' he told them. 'It'll be a rare treat for him to get a glimpse of so much money.'

Leslie and his wife also discussed Gregory Boland's character.

'He'll say exactly what he thinks and the hell with the consequences.'

'Well, that's good, isn't it?' Jenny, stretched in front of the fire that autumn evening, flicking through a catalogue full of hopelessly optimistic pictures of a herbaceous border, had almost forgotten they had ever quarrelled.

'He won't try to guess what I want and do it. He'll come to a perfectly honest decision.'

'Isn't that what we want?'

'Just the sort of chap your ex would have approved of.'

'My ex?' She was genuinely confused. 'Exes' to her were living husbands of the sort constantly complained about because of their failure to provide for the children's school fees or the awful hairdo's of their new wives. Death was not, surely, a similar act of infidelity, a ground for divorce, and it was only slowly, and with a distinct feeling of unease, that she realized who he was talking about. 'I don't know what you mean, exactly.'

'Only that Sidonia put such a high value on honesty. Never told a lie, all that sort of thing.'

Jenny stopped turning the pages, apparently engrossed in a portrait of lupins. She didn't know what to say.

'Isn't that what he said?'

'No. He didn't say it much. It was the way he behaved.'

'Admirable, of course. What did he talk about?'

Not to answer him seemed likely to prolong an inquisition of which she felt no good would come. 'He made jokes a lot of the time. About the things he did. The people we met. You can't expect me to remember everything.'

'No. No, of course not.' He sounded understanding and fell silent for a while. Then he said, 'I wish I could've met him.'

'Why?' She could imagine no two men less likely to understand each other than those she had married. Their meeting would, no doubt, have been a disaster, but it was also an impossibility. So why did she feel in such a panic?

'He must have been enormously entertaining.'

'Yes,' she said. 'He was that.'

'Judging by what Sue said about him.'

'You mean, when she was staying here?'

'Yes, of course. She talked about him then. And his wonderful old mother. What was her name . . .?'

'Myra.' Jenny smiled, feeling they'd moved to safer ground. 'She was tremendous value.'

'You said she'd been a ballet dancer.'

'With Sadler's Wells, I think it was. Oh, before the war. And she was with the Russians too. The Monte Carlo company. I can't remember who else.'

'I was never a great one for ballet.'

'I wouldn't think you were.' Jenny smiled at the thought of Leslie watching grimly as young men pranced about in revealing tights. 'Have you ever seen one?'

'Well, not so far as I can remember.'

'I didn't think so.'

'And she danced under her own name?'

'No. She called herself something else. What was it? Myra Zirkin. She said that was the name Fokine gave her because it sounded vaguely Russian. It seemed a bit pointless when her own name was so . . . impressive.'

'Is she alive?'

'Oh, no. She died before Tony. That was a good thing in a way. It would have been a terrible blow to her.'

'Pity. It might have been fun to ask her down.' Leslie opened his red dispatch-box and sat with it on his knees. He began reading documents with great rapidity, scribbling comments which were mostly dismissive and sarcastic. It was late, the fire was dying and Jenny got up to put on another log.

'What would you like? Tea, a drink or something?'

Leslie didn't answer but looked at the flaring wood and said, 'What about Tony's father?'

'Oh, he was killed in the war. When Tony was very young. Why do you want to know that?'

'I thought the dancer might have married an exiled prince or something romantic. She must have had a hard time getting Tony educated. I mean getting him so very educated.'

'I think his father left some money. A pension perhaps. He went away to boarding-school. Nothing else you want to know?'

She felt that Tony should be allowed to rest in peace and not be summoned to answer some sort of interrogation. She was prepared to say as much in answer to Leslie's next question.

But now he smiled at her and said, 'Did you say tea? That would be very nice.'

It was Arthur Nubble's practice to travel by bus and charge for a taxi, and it was only a short bus ride from his office to the narrow passage leading into the Charing Cross Road where he walked into the Entrechat bookshop. He pushed open a door, the bell pinged and a young man in a bow-tie uncurled himself from behind a pile of books, programmes, posters and other souvenirs of the dance to look at him with an expression of considerable hauteur. 'Yes,' he said. 'And what can we do for *you?*'

Arthur Nubble explained he was a solicitor wishing to trace the whereabouts or family of a certain Myra Zirkin in order that she might hear something to her advantage. The young man registered increasing distaste until he heard that Nubble's clients would pay generously for information. Then he burrowed into pre-war programmes, searched indexes and finally unearthed a Zirkin who danced minor roles at Sadler's Wells, in the Ballet Russe de Monte Carlo and, above all, in Dame Felicity Capet's Empire Ballet which, before the war, occupied a now defunct theatre in High Holborn.

'Zirkin? Of course I remember Zirkin. I knew all the secrets of all my girls. They used to confide in me. I insisted on that.'

This time Nubble had gone on a long bus ride to the furthest reaches of Putney and there, in a small flat at the top of a dull grey block, he had found Dame Felicity, a very old lady with huge, saucer eyes who had known Pavlova and who now sat among photographs of fauns, firebirds and sylphides in a cluttered room which smelt overpoweringly of cats. There was a black tom on Nubble's lap, marching round in search of the most comfortable position to sleep, its open claws pricking him through his trousers. 'Do push Dr Coppélius off if he's being a bore. You did say you loved cats, though?' Her long, white fingers were wrapped round the handle of the walking-stick she used to rap on the rehearsal room floor to stop the music so that she might abuse the dancers. 'And you say you're writing about the Empire Ballet?'

'With special reference, Dame Felicity, to your own career.' Nubble liked to vary his cover stories to add interest to his work.

'I don't know why you bother with Zirkin. She had very little discipline and, as I remember, particularly unfortunate knees. Only one good point,' Dame Felicity allowed grudgingly. 'She had a face like a magnolia.'

'She also had a son?' Nubble asked.

'Not as far as I was concerned she hadn't.' The old woman seemed to have no doubts. 'And I'd certainly've known about it if she had.'

'Really?' The cat had gone to sleep now, a hot, dead weight on his groin. 'I think I met her at Oxford after the war. She used to come and stay with her son who was a friend of mine.'

'I don't know what you're talking about!' In the old Empire Ballet she had never suffered fools gladly. 'After the war Zirkin wasn't in Oxford, or anywhere else in this world, for that matter.'

'I'm sorry, Dame Felicity. I don't quite understand what you're telling me.'

'I'm simply telling you, my dear man, that she went out to Germany with a concert party to entertain the troops during the war. She danced the Dying Swan as one of the turns, something she was quite unqualified to do. Anyway, the concert party's train was bombed, apparently by mistake. I suppose you could say' – the old lady was smiling gently – 'she died in action. Of course' – she forced the smile off her face – 'it was extremely sad. An amusing girl but hardly a genius.'

So Zirkin, the dancer, died during the war, a time as he knew from his briefing before the second Mrs Titmuss had been born. Nubble felt relieved that the interview was over and he could get out into the fresh air, away from this old woman who treated him as though he were some sort of idiot. Before he went he tried a final question.

'Dame Felicity. Does the name Myra Sidonia mean anything to you?'

'Myra Sidonia?' The huge, disapproving eyes were turned on him; the voice rose as though he'd tripped over the prima ballerina in the finale. 'Why ever should you bother me with questions about her?'

CHAPTER TWENTY-TWO

Pale sunshine continued until December and then withdrew, discouraged, as north winds and heavy skies promised snow. At midnight mass Kev the Rev. prayed, 'Oh Lord, guide the hands of Thy ministers and officials at Housing and Ecological Affairs to spare, if it be Thy will, this valley from falling victim to a materialistic society.' As his congregation shook his hand and came out into the cold, the doors of their Range Rovers were glued with ice and their children woke to a snowy morning which seemed intent on preserving the traditions of rural England. How God the Great Planning Officer would conduct Himself when the inquiry opened the following month remained a subject of endless speculation. In the Baptist's Head Len Bigwell was offering two to one against Fallowfield Country Town ever being built now the protesters had suddenly found themselves able to engage a Q.C. reputed to be the best planning lawyer in England.

After Christmas the snow lay fresh on the Rapstone Nature Area, marked with the hierographics of many pads and claws. In Worsfield it turned as grey as dirty washing, clogged the gutters and made the steps of the District Council offices a peril. Inside, in an atmosphere made soporific by central heating and legal argument, Gregory Boland, the Inspector, sat high over a sea of plans and towers of documents. The lawyers whispered, made jokes and passed each other notes. Young men and girls from Kempenflatt's office dozed, then woke with a start and tried to look interested. In the public benches sat the members of S.O.V., who did their best during long hours of anaesthetizing boredom to preserve their high mood of concerned outrage. The Curdles had arrived in force, dressed as for a wedding, and passed round tubes of wine gums and Polos. They then sat with their jaws working in a threatening manner. The Vees took copious notes of the proceedings which would later be fed into the computer in Mr Vee's office and circulated to many people who would never read them. At the press table the elderly man from the *Worsfield Echo*, who lived in an area so entirely bereft of natural beauty that the issue didn't concern him one way or the other, filled in his football pools and waited for something dramatic to happen. Such was the scene in the council chamber when Dr Frederick Simcox was called into the witness-box.

Every group throws up its own leader but Fred wondered, as he swore to tell the truth and tried to look as though he were taking the whole thing seriously, if S.O.V. hadn't thrown up the wrong one. Dot Curdle would have overflowed the witness-box, dominated the room and given everyone a piece of her mind. Mrs Vee would have had the facts at her fingers' ends and Mr Vee would have been able to lower his voice to that tone of quiet urgency which was so effective in gathering money which would go, after the payment of his considerable percentage, to feed children in remote parts of Africa.

The expensive barrister hired with Leslie Titmuss's secret contribution was a Mr Alistair Fernhill, who was about to become a judge. So he would go, after a lifetime in town planning, to a new world of murder, mayhem and indecent assault, of which he had no experience whatever. In that moment in a barrister's life, before being enveloped in scarlet and ermine and whisked into a position above the battle, Mr Fernhill had come to do his cases in a detached and world-weary manner, as though already remote from the struggles of lesser men. This aloof Alistair Fernhill, Q.C., revealed that Fred was a doctor who had been in practice locally for over a quarter of a century, and who, as Chairman of the Save Our Valley society, was one of the principal objectors. What would the new town do to the amenities of the countryside, the beauty of the landscape, the safety of the roads and the health of the population? Fred was taken through his evidence rather as an unwelcome visitor is led through the corridors of some grand house by a superior butler. His answers, he felt, lacked conviction.

It was as though all the talent for belief in his family had been taken up by his dead father. The old Rector of Rapstone had believed passionately in everything: Socialism, pacifism, Ban the Bomb and some essential good in human nature. After such an immense outpouring of faith the Simcox stock, it seemed, had been exhausted. If Fred believed in anything it was the countryside he had grown up in, the dark woods and secret hiding-places in the bracken, the memories of afternoons of love in Tom Nowt's old hut and moonlit swims in the muddy water of the river. And yet, as he tried to find words for these feelings which would be acceptable in a court of law, he thought of other arguments, different points of view. Might not childhood be as vivid in a Worsfield housing estate? Might not love be equally memorable if it were crammed into the back seat of a Ford Cortina behind the multi-storey car park? It was Fred's curse to see two sides to every question; it was freedom from this unfortunate character defect which had brought Leslie Titmuss his considerable success.

'You're a medical doctor, aren't you?'

The superior butler and embryo judge had sat down, to be replaced by another learned friend. This one had a voice like a hacksaw blade, gold half-glasses three quarters of the way down his nose and an expression of puzzled incredulity. This was Carus-Atkins, Q.C., Counsel for Kempenflatts, the builders.

'Not a doctor of botany, or forestry, or other rural mysteries?'

'Not at all.'

'So you are not an expert on the countryside?'

'No. I have just known it all my life. Perhaps I have a special feeling for the Rapstone Valley –'

'As a doctor you will be paid by the number of patients you attend.' The barrister interrupted the answer.

'I understand that's the intention of the present government, yes.'

'Then won't a new town suit you very well? You'll have a great many more people to provide pills for. You might make a great deal more money, might you not, Doctor?' There was some obedient laughter from the staff of Kempenflatt's office.

'I'd rather have less money, fewer patients and no new town.'

'Some people might think that rather an eccentric view.' Carus-Atkins peered over his spectacles at his supporters in the Kempenflatt camp. 'But then you are a somewhat eccentric doctor, aren't you?'

'I don't think so.'

'Given to acting as a drummer in a local public house?'

'I'm a member of a jazz group. Yes.'

'Enlighten me, Doctor.' The builders' Q.C. dug his hands deeply into his pockets and leant forward, his head on one side, his ear cocked as though he were eager to receive knowledge. 'Do you think eating rabbits an excellent cure for heart failure?'

Gregory Boland, the Inspector, pursed his lips and looked as though someone had just burst into song or started to undress in the course of the proceedings. The Curdle family nodded wisely, in total agreement with the proposition, and Mrs Vee hid her face in her hands and whispered, 'Oh Christ, here it comes!'

'No,' Fred answered without hesitation.

'How very strange.' Carus-Atkins received a newspaper cutting from an attentive junior and took it with the delicacy of a great surgeon about to employ a scalpel. 'Did you not say as much to a journalist working on the *Fortress*?'

'No, I didn't. That report was totally inaccurate.'

'Where do you suggest the journalist got the idea from?'

'From someone who came into my surgery and might have seen a document containing that piece of information.'

Looking round the council chamber Fred noticed Jenny for

the first time. Had she been there long or had she wandered in late, as she had done when he played with the Riverside Stompers? Seeing her brought the whole room into sharper focus. He felt suddenly younger, more energetic and, for a moment, mercifully unable to tolerate the opposition. At least there was no possible doubt about his dislike of Mr Carus-Atkins.

'Are you prepared to tell us who that person was?'

Fred looked at Jenny and was not prepared to supply the information.

'Dr Simcox. Are you really here to *help* this inquiry?' the Inspector intervened.

'So far as I can.'

'Then perhaps we could ask you to deal with the matter in hand.' Gregory Boland looked at him with a severity which Fred felt should have been reserved for his inquisitor. 'That matter is about building houses. It's got nothing to do with the medical properties of rabbit meat. May I ask you to remember that, Doctor?'

'Exactly my view, sir.' The Carus-Atkins effrontery astounded Fred. 'Now, Doctor. Please direct your mind to the issues in this case. You have told me you have a special feeling for this countryside, around Rapstone.'

'That's perfectly true. Yes.' Fred was looking at Jenny and the sound of the hacksaw voice seemed to grow faint as she gave him a small smile of approval.

'Are you a selfish man, Doctor?'

'Not particularly.'

'Isn't it rather selfish of you, if you love it so much, not to want to share it with other people?'

'If it's all built over, there won't be anything to share with anyone.'

'He's improving,' Mrs Vee whispered.

'Slightly,' Mr Vee whispered back.

'Dr Simcox. I understand your father, the Reverend Simeon Simcox, was a clergyman who indulged himself in a large number of anti-government protests.'

'He had strong beliefs, yes.'

'And he used to march all over the place. Organize demonstrations.' Carus-Atkins waved his spectacles aimlessly to suggest mental confusion in the old Rector. 'And the like.'

'Certainly.'

'Is that a characteristic you have inherited?'

'I hope I have inherited some of his concern for social justice. Yes.' In the ordinary course of events these were words which would have made Fred squirm with embarrassment. With Jenny looking at him from her seat among the protesters, he felt a certain pride in his answer.

'You have also inherited his dislike of Conservative governments.'

'My complaint against this Conservative government is that it's failing to conserve anything.'

Fred was rewarded now, not only by Jenny's interest but also by some laughter and a clearly audible 'Doctor got you there, then, didn't he?' from Dot Curdle.

'And I'm bound to suggest' – Carus-Atkins was leaning back on his heels now, looking at the witness with an indulgent expression such as might be used to a tiresome child – 'that your Save Our Valley society simply exists to satisfy your family craving to protest against the government. However much employment and wealth and prosperity it brings, you'll never be satisfied, will you, Doctor? You'll just . . . carry on marching.'

'I don't think it's necessary to involve this inquiry in a political argument.' Again the soft Scottish rebuke from the red-haired Inspector seemed directed at Fred rather than at his assailant.

'I think it's entirely necessary for me to answer the question.' Fred raised his voice and felt he was speaking directly to Jenny. 'As a matter of fact I've got no particular interest in politics. I don't want to spend my time organizing protests or going on marches. Protests and marches make me feel ridiculous. I'd like to be left alone to look after my patients and go drumming in public houses, as you put it so charmingly. But you won't leave us alone, will you? Your clients want to buy up the farmland and make money out of us. The government wants to change our lives and wreck our valley forever. Nobody who lives around Rapstone wants that to happen. Nobody! But it seems we're all at the mercy of strangers –'

'Dr Simcox!' The Scottish protest rose suddenly to a bleat, but Fred carried on.

'Do you think I enjoy spending an afternoon standing here answering your ridiculous questions about rabbits? I'd rather be treating carbuncles and changing dressings. But you don't give us any choice. When you come down here, hired by people trying to make money out of us, what else can you expect us to do?'

Fred had listened to himself in some surprise. He was further surprised to see Mr Carus-Atkins sit down and look triumphantly about the court, his cross-examination over. Perhaps he thinks he's proved I'm a total nut-case, Fred thought, and then the red-haired Inspector said, 'Thank you, Dr Simcox,' and he left the witness-box.

'You were splendid!' Jenny told him.

'I sounded like a diehard old Tory, didn't I? Keep the world safe for peasants and game birds. That sort of thing. That's the trouble with these people. We used to feel like young revolutionaries, now they seem to have turned us into the last defenders of the old regime.'

'Which people?'

'What?'

'Which people is it the trouble with?'

'Oh. I mean the new radical, tear it all down and start again, Conservative party . . .'

'You mean people like Leslie?'

'Well . . .' Fred hadn't wanted to say that, not knowing how Jenny might take an attack on her husband.

'That's who you mean.' They were in a pub, cosy as an aircraft hangar and only a little smaller, opposite the council offices. Jenny took a gulp of the white wine she had asked for and pulled a face.

'Is it all right?' Fred was concerned.

'Fine. Except that it tastes of slightly chilled, watered-down paraffin with a touch of vanilla essence.'

He laughed at the accuracy of her description. 'I'll get you a beer. It's probably safer.'

'I don't know what Leslie wants, quite honestly,' she said when he came back from the bar. He looked at her with excitement, feeling that she was about to confide in him. Indeed, she was. She felt at home with Fred, as she had with Tony, and that she could tell him anything and he wouldn't laugh at her, or make her feel an idiot, and probably, in nine cases out of ten at least, tell her something which would be a help. She was on the point of saying, I don't know what Leslie wants. He's started to ask me all sorts of questions about my first husband, a man who has been dead for six years now, who was as different from Leslie as chalk from cheese, who I couldn't explain to Leslie if I sat down and talked from now to September but who, in some ways, which I feel is slightly unnerving, was a little like you, Dr Simcox. She might have said all that but she knew she would have regretted it. It would, after all, have been disloyal to Leslie. So she said, 'I'm still sure he doesn't want the new town.'

'That's encouraging. Let's drink to that.' So they raised two glasses of Simcox's lager and clinked them together.

CHAPTER TWENTY-THREE

'Mr Sidonia? He's been dead a long time.'

'Of course I know that. But he was one of your most famous dons, after all, at St Joseph's. I just wondered if you remember him?'

'Remember him? Of course we remember him. Everyone except my colleague, that is, who was no doubt still in his rompers when Mr Sidonia passed on.' The square-faced porter peered out of his cubby-hole at the college entrance; somewhere in the background his colleague, who wore a single discreet ear-ring, was fitting letters into pigeon-holes. Girls and young men surrounded Nubble, reading notices and holding hands or embracing so flagrantly, despite the freezing weather, that he felt soured by jealousy. He was also tired and out of breath, having walked from Oxford station so that he could make a small profit on the cab fare. 'Mr Sidonia,' the porter said, as though to close the conversation, 'was a very nice gentleman. Very nice indeed.'

'Popular with the students?'

'I expect so.'

'You had girl students when he was here, didn't you?'

'If you've got an appointment with Sir Willoughby, he doesn't like to be kept waiting. Through the arch and in the far left-hand corner. That's the door to the lodgings.' So Arthur Nubble was sent about his business and he crossed the quad, whipped by the icy wind from the cloisters which had frozen generations of undergraduates on their way to the bathroom. When the secretary showed him into the Master's presence, Nubble reminded Sir Willoughby that he was writing a series on famous heads of colleges for the *Fortress* colour magazine, which was the cover story it had amused him to adopt. The Master, who knew the value of publicity in these tough, fund-raising times, received him with an effusive handshake and a small glass of the sherry he kept aside for students. He then talked persuasively about his own career, his remarkable insight into the life-cycle of the prawn and the essential part the Blane Biology Library would play in Britain's future. The government had been amazingly short-sighted about it and he wondered if some great philanthropist, such as the proprietor of the *Fortress*, might perhaps be interested.

'He might well be.' Arthur Nubble considered the matter seriously. 'Particularly in view of the distinguished scholars you've had at St Joseph's. I was thinking of Anthony Sidonia, on history.' This journalist said it, Sir Willoughby thought, rather as though history were a musical instrument in a jazz band. 'He was very popular, wasn't he, among the students?'

'Tony?' Sir Willoughby looked suitably distressed. 'Tragic early death, of course. So many of our older dons wouldn't have been missed *half* as much. Yes. Of course he was popular with the students. Not quite so popular with other history teachers.'

'Oh, really?' Nubble opened his notebook for the first time during the interview. 'Why was that?'

'Well, he spoke about his subject on television. He did it rather well and *looked* quite attractive. A lot of less photogenic historians felt rather sour about it. Touch of the showman, they said, about Tony Sidonia.'

'Jealous?'

'Oh, yes, I think so.' The Master liked nothing better than to relay old gossip. 'They suggested he only got the job because his then girlfriend worked in television. But she was only a researcher, I believe, and I don't think that had anything to do with it. Anyway, the programmes were very popular. Academics hate that.'

'Of course they were extremely interesting,' said Nubble, who hadn't seen them.

'Indeed, yes.' Sir Willoughby hadn't seen them either. 'I'm sure the criticism wasn't justified. Although I believe Tony never really got to grips with Savonarola. Not that I'd know. I'm only a poor biologist.'

'I think I might have met the girl who worked on those programmes. What was her name again?'

'Briar, was it? Something decidedly prickly. No. Bramble. Sarah, or perhaps Susan, Bramble. She turned up at a secretarial college here and then she found her way into the B.B.C. Most girls seem to, in the end.'

'I suppose he met her before he married.'

'Oh, yes. He knew La Bramble long before he met Jenny. Moved her out, I believe, before he proposed anything so outrageous as matrimony. Not that Jenny isn't an absolutely *super* girl. You've spoken to her, I suppose?'

'No. Not yet.'

'I've never known what mental aberration led her to take up with that appallingly common Cabinet Minister. We had a sweet, gentle fellow here who taught Anglo-Saxon, and he fell passionately in love with a most disagreeable Detective Inspector who used to treat the poor old dear just like a criminal, interrogate him and so on . . . By the way, that's not for publication.'

Nubble, scribbling energetically, looked up sharply at the Master's description of his employer. Sir Willoughby wondered if he had gone too far; the *Fortress*, after all, was not a paper to look sympathetically on critics of the government.

'Who was the chap you say Tony never got to grips with?' Nubble was frowning at his notebook. 'Savannah something?'

'Savonarola.'

'I wouldn't mind meeting him, if he's still around.' History had never been Nubble's strongest suit and he had soon left the public school he attended with the Simcox brothers to open an espresso coffee bar.

'I'm afraid not. They burnt him in Florence quite early in the sixteenth century.' The Master tried to be fair and tell himself that no doubt persons with no particular claim to education now wrote on academic matters for the quality papers. He decided to give the dubious candidate one more chance.

'Tony wasn't the only distinguished St Joseph's man. You know, we did have Isaac Newton.'

'Of course.' Nubble, who had heard of Isaac Newton, nodded wisely. 'I'll remind my readers of that, Sir Willoughby.' But the Master, feeling that every schoolboy should know that Newton went to Trinity, Cambridge, fled to his secretary's room where he telephoned Tim Warboys, another St Joseph's man who had achieved stardom, and discovered that nothing was known of Arthur Nubble in the *Fortress* features department or, indeed, of any article on famous heads of colleges. He didn't reappear but the secretary told Nubble that a crisis in the marine biology lab had brought the interview to a premature end.

Despite this sudden conclusion the sleuth felt reasonably satisfied with his morning's work. He was getting closer to Tony Sidonia and although he had as yet learned little to his subject's disadvantage he felt that his employer would admire his persistence and the ingenuity of his various disguises. When he got back to London he started to make inquiries of the B.B.C., becoming an independent film and television producer interested in a reissue of Tony Sidonia's brilliant programme 'In the Shadow of the Triple Crown', and perhaps speaking to some of the people who had worked on it.

Sue Bramble was in low spirits. She felt something she had not experienced before. She was lonely. Naturally high-spirited and gregarious she thrived on variety, changing her jobs as frequently as she changed her lovers, and greeting each new arrival with the enthusiastic certainty that she had hit upon the perfect answer to her problems. She had not found work or love difficult to come by. When she was doing her secretarial course at Oxford she had been a constant figure at undergraduate and indeed graduate parties. She'd worked in bookshops, as a waitress in a succession of restaurants and in a shop full of exotic second-hand dresses in the covered market. When she parted from Tony and he married, she moved to London and got her job at the B.B.C. She progressed rapidly from secretary to researcher to the director's assistant during Tony's programme on the Renaissance Popes. Later, working on a documentary about the turf, she met her trainer, helped out in his office for a while and made many new friends. When her situation with him grew complicated she came back to Oxford and wrote stories for various racing papers. When Tony Sidonia died she and Jenny seemed to be drawn more closely together by the disappearance of the man they had both loved. So they had decided to share a flat in London.

Now she was alone in the flat. Teddy Blaze, the Newbury trainer, whom she had urged for so long to leave his wife and marry her, and who had so often promised and failed to do so, rang to say that he was to be divorced. He was now free and available. He drove up to London at great speed and knocked at the door of the flat, loaded with champagne and roses. As Sue saw him standing there, flushed with his belated achievement, she felt the excitement drain away from their relationship like cooling bath-water. Not only could she no longer marry him, she could hardly bear to be taken out by him. In the restaurant they went to she sat mostly in silence, only criticizing him occasionally. At last she had to beg him, for his own protection, not to ring her or try to take her out again. When he wrote to tell her that he was engaged to marry a girl groom some twenty years younger, who lived in Didcot, she felt nothing but relief.

Since her friend had got married, Sue had taken over Jenny's job. She sat all day, dazed by the white walls and bored by the abstract paintings, trying her best not to become involved in the disastrous private life of Mark Vanberry, the gallery owner. In this she succeeded but, far too often for her own self-esteem, she came home to an empty flat to wash her hair and watch the television. On many such evenings she wanted to ring Jenny and laugh and gossip as they once did. What stopped her was not just Jenny's marriage – her amazed disapproval of Leslie had never come between them – but she had felt, curiously enough, more remote from her friend as she had come to find Leslie Titmuss more bearable. And now there was another reason: she had shown him Tony's photographs, she had had what amounted to a secret lunch with him. She had been manoeuvred, against her better judgement, into a conspiracy and she had promised to say nothing to Jenny about it. It was that small act of treachery that made Sue uncomfortable at the idea of telephoning. And Jenny didn't ring her. She was reluctant to tell Sue about Leslie's curious questions about Tony, and yet she didn't want to keep this latest development a secret from her friend with whom she had always discussed everything. So the shadow of Leslie Titmuss fell between them, and Sue was left wondering why on earth she had done what he asked her.

So, when the telephone rang one lonely evening, she half hoped it was Jenny and dreaded that it might be Mark Vanberry. In fact it was a somewhat husky male voice who made sure she was Miss Bramble and then announced that Atmos Films Limited was going into the production of historical and artistic documentary films. Would she be interested in joining the team? 'I was much impressed by the work you did on that beautiful programme "In the Shadow of the Triple Crown". Might I have the pleasure of taking you to lunch? Shall we say tomorrow, if you're free, at the Groucho Club? The name's Nubble. Arthur Nubble . . . Oh, and by the way, can you put me in touch with anyone else who worked on that magnificent production?'

The snow turned to slush which was washed away by incessant rain. Hector Bolitho Jones slid and skidded round his woods, shrouded in a yellow waterproof cape. He shook the drops from his beard as a dog shakes itself dry. The badgers emerged at night into a cold monsoon and scuttered back into their setts.

Although there were signs of buds on the branches and specks of green pushing through the black earth, Rapstone Nature Area was then no place for lovers. Through that month and the next Gregory Boland sat in the spare bedroom of his concrete-block house, surrounded by piles of maps, documents and transcripts of evidence, and wrote his report on the future of that particular countryside. During the bad weather Arthur Nubble completed his inquiries.

When the sun returned, making the soaked grass steam, two men in overcoats were to be seen walking past the great mulberry tree in the garden of St Joseph's College.

'It isn't so much a moral question,' Sir Willoughby was explaining. 'It's more a problem of educational technology.'

'You mean, dons shouldn't go to bed with their students?'

'It's not the bed part so much. It's what it leads to. A warping of the pupil–teacher relationship, favouritism in tutorials, sexually induced marking, and then, when it all busts up, tears in lectures and feelings of rejection that may seriously impair the performance at finals. That's why we don't find bed-hopping with pupils acceptable conduct at St Joseph's. Of course, there have been exceptions.'

'What exceptions?'

'Well. I can't remember exactly.' The Master became vague and avoided Leslie Titmuss's pale and persistent stare. 'But there must have been exceptions.'

'I wanted to ask you a few questions about one of your dons. Sidonia.'

'Well, he does seem to have become the flavour of the month. The last few months, anyway.'

'Has he?'

'I had a most extraordinary fellow here asking about Tony. This man said he was working for the *Fortress*. I suspected that was a lie.'

'It was.'

'You know about him?'

'He was working for me.'

The Master thought it best to conceal his astonishment and to say nothing.

'He was making certain inquiries for me about Sidonia.'

'This Mr Nobble?'

'Nubble. I suppose he made a prize idiot of himself, didn't he?'

'He knew absolutely nothing about Savonarola, and very little about Sir Isaac Newton.'

'He had his uses, filling in the background. I'm relying on you to complete the picture.'

In a moment of wild speculation Sir Willoughby guessed that Tony had been a crypto-Communist, a spy, a traitor, the fifth man, or sixth, and now, after his death, the subject of government inquiries. He was not to know that his crime was to have been the first man in Jenny Sidonia's affections.

'I don't see how I can help. I really didn't know a great deal about Tony's private life.'

'Nonsense! You know all about the private lives of everyone in your college.' Leslie stopped on the spongy lawn, apparently not feeling the east wind which was making the Master long for tea and anchovy toast by the fire in his lodgings. 'Is that where it's going to stand?'

'What exactly?'

'The Blane Biology Library.' Leslie was looking at a great expanse on which, he had reason to suppose, planning permission might be given. 'I've made some inquiries, the D.E.S. has a certain fund for educational developments of special value to industry and commerce.'

As in a dream the Master saw the tasteful building in Cotswold stone. In the hallway there would be a statue, wouldn't there, or at least a bust, of his good self? It would be, as he had no child, his single, magnificent claim to immortality.

'Secretary of State. Is there really any hope –?'

'I shall have, of course, to talk to colleagues.' Now Leslie gripped Sir Willoughby's forearm and turned to more immediate matters. 'For the moment I have just a few more questions about Sidonia. Number one. I expect you remember a girl who was a friend of his called Susan Bramble?'

CHAPTER TWENTY-FOUR

Gregory Boland worked long and tirelessly on his report. He tabulated the evidence and classified and reclassified it under various headings, 'Sewage', 'Traffic Volume', 'Rail Access', 'Population Density' and 'Commercial Opportunities'. He looked again and again at the beguiling drawings of children playing in the pedestrian precincts and he remembered the walks he had taken on the site, the cathedral hush in the middle of beech woods soon, perhaps, to be broken forever and to be broken by him. And yet, he told himself, being a reasonable man as well as honest, neither life nor architecture could stand still. The English, sooner or later, must face up to the fact that it was a myth that they lived in a series of delightful villages, strung like jewels across some rustic landscape. They would have to wake up and realize that they lived along motorway routes and by service stations in some vast and anonymous suburb which stretched from Land's End to John o' Groat's, punctuated by theme parks and shopping malls. If that was the future, was it after all so terrible? It meant jobs for many people, including architects and town planners as well as policemen, sewage workers and girls at supermarket check-outs. The country needed houses which, like motor cars, were a sign of healthy prosperity. Those who wished to spend their days in uninterrupted contemplation of the great crested grebe could, as Counsel for Kempenflatts had ventured to suggest in a peculiarly acid final speech, move to the Highlands of Scotland. Gregory Boland, who had come from the

Highlands, had no intention of going back there, however the English landscape developed.

And yet, and yet ... As Gregory fed more and more facts into his computer, hoping that the ingenious machine would come out with the answer he found it so hard to arrive at, as he remembered the stream of experts, planners, botanists, porers over archaeological remains, politicians and sociologists who had passed before him during that long hearing, he couldn't help remembering Dr Simcox. He hadn't at first taken to the Doctor, who seemed lacking in respect for the tribunal and to regard all the evidence, including his own, with the same amused detachment. But then something Fred had said returned to him: 'We're all at the mercy of strangers.' Gregory had protested at that, he remembered. It had seemed irrelevant to the proceedings. But now, thinking about it, he saw Fred's point; although it was one which would never be understood by a computer.

He, after all, had been born in a small country which had fallen into the hands of the alien English. The Scots, in Gregory's view, had done nothing to deserve such a fate and what crime had the inhabitants of Rapstone and Hartscombe and the countryside in between committed that they should be punished by Fallowfield Country Town? It was not their fault that three of the farmers who lived in their midst were prepared to sell the past to a hungry developer who, like some vulture wheeling in the sky, was only on the look-out for a defenceless body to pick to the bones. Their homes were not to be razed to the ground and their woods destroyed because they occupied the perfect site for a new town, but simply because it was there that Kempenflatts had found an opportunity to make money. Slowly, painfully and with minute attention to detail, Gregory Boland was coming to the view that he would decide against Fallowfield.

Such were the Inspector's thoughts when his wife knocked at the door, something she rarely did when the computer was wrestling for his soul, and announced a telephone call from the Ministry of Housing, Ecological Affairs and Planning. He went downstairs to have his ear filled with the voice of Ken Cracken, calling him as though on a loud-hailer.

'Boland. I suppose you've broken the back of the Fallowfield business?'

'Ay.' Gregory was, as always, cautious. 'I think I see light at the end of the tunnel.'

'And you've done a splendid job, by all accounts. How about a celebration lunch? Give yourself a day off and come up to town.'

'I don't think that would be quite appropriate.'

'Not to discuss Fallowfield, of course. That's entirely off limits. But we're up to the bloody neck in these applications now. We're looking for someone of real experience to become chief adviser in a brand-new planning department. Salary not yet fixed but appropriate to the responsibilities. And naturally your name came up in preliminary discussions. Think about it and give me a bell, why don't you?'

Once Gregory had mentioned this to Mrs Boland the result was inevitable. Was he to lose a last chance to gain some of the prosperity he had missed by not joining the Masons? So, a couple of days later, Gregory Boland entered the Savoy Grill to be lavishly entertained by Ken Cracken and his political adviser.

'What we're looking for is a bloke with a real knowledge of planning law and a reputation for being clean as a whistle. Naturally you were first on our list.'

'I am suitably gratified.' Although he had protested that he never drank at lunch-time Gregory had been persuaded to share the bottle Ken chose, the second most expensive on the list. 'The Ministry doesn't often get a chance to show its gratitude.' As he raised the glass of Pichon-Longueville and was filled with its costly benevolence, Gregory felt himself at the beginning of a new career. 'This is a treat,' he said. 'A rare treat.'

'What attracts us to you' — Joyce Timberlake was looking at the Inspector over the rim of her glass with wide-eyed admiration — 'is that you understand politics.'

'I'm an architect by trade.' Gregory was flattered but modest. 'I don't quite know where politics comes into it.'

'Comes into everything, doesn't it?' Ken was carefully weighing up the rival claims of profiteroles and bread and butter pudding on the sweet trolley. 'The trick, in your present inquiry, is to come up with the right decision at the right moment.'

'I thought we weren't going to discuss Fallowfield.' There was a slight rise of the Boland hackles.

'Of course not. That would be quite inappropriate,' Joyce reassured him.

'Improper,' Ken agreed.

'Entirely wrong.'

'Until you've announced your decision.'

'Which, of course, we're looking forward to with enormous interest.' Somewhat mollified, Gregory returned his nose to his wine glass. 'But it would be pretty short-sighted,' Ken went on, 'not to recognize the political climate in which all these decisions are taken nowadays.'

'You mean a general free-for-all?' Gregory put down his glass and resumed his severe expression.

'That's one way of putting it.' Joyce laughed as though he had made a joke. 'In government we like to call it the operation of market forces.'

'I'm well aware' – Gregory looked like one of his Wee Free ancestors winding himself up to denounce the Pope – 'that there are those in government who think it a sign of our national well-being that the whole of Southern England should be concreted over to accommodate banks, shoe shops, hairdressers, building societies and other light industries. It's surely my job to see that the outcome of this particular case is my free and independent decision!'

There was a silence while the product of so many elders of the kirk fixed his listeners with a glare of defiance, and then Ken Cracken sat back and clapped his hands in a loud gesture of applause which disconcerted the waiters.

'Damn good!' Ken raised his glass. 'Let's drink to your free and independent decision.'

'So long as that's perfectly understood.' Gregory Boland then drank to his independence.

'Of course,' Ken began again after a suitable pause for reflection, 'if you'd said all that about concreting over England a year or two ago I'd've entirely agreed with you.'

'A year or two ago the only song we sang was about the free market economy,' Joyce bore him out. 'It was all on one note. Fallowfield might have seemed the answer to all our problems.'

'But there's been a bit of a difference in the political climate, quite honestly, Greg.'

The Inspector looked warily from the Minister to his political adviser. What were they getting at now?

'The truth is' – Ken Cracken now leaned forward confidentially – 'Leslie Titmuss has become ozone-friendly.'

'He's come out for the rhino and broad-leafed trees, hedgerows, butterflies, chemical-free farming, unpolluted streams. The rumour is' – Joyce laid a strong hand on Gregory's cuff and smiled to indicate that she wasn't to be taken entirely seriously – 'that he's given up using a hair-spray!'

'Oh, he never used a hair-spray,' Ken corrected her. 'I don't believe he's got beyond brilliantine.'

'We're off the H in H.E.A.P. and on to the E.'

'It's not housing. Ecology's the buzz word nowadays.'

'Well,' Gregory told them. 'I'm very glad to hear it.' Indeed he was. As his mind was turning towards saving the Rapstone Valley for the badgers he was delighted that he would have his Secretary of State's approval.

'But the major political development in the last two years' – Ken now looked at Gregory in a way the Inspector found uncomfortably conspiratorial – 'is something entirely different. Not really anything to do with the environment.'

'No,' Joyce agreed. 'More something to do with housing.'

'I'm afraid I don't understand.' Gregory was again afraid that he might understand them too well. Ken Cracken waited ostentatiously until the waiter had cleared away the pudding plates – he had gone for the profiteroles with a touch of bread and butter pudding on the side – and then he leant forward to make it quite clear to anyone of the meanest intelligence that Gregory Boland was being invited to take part in a plot.

'The outstanding event of our time,' he said in a stage whisper, 'is that Leslie Titmuss decided to buy Rapstone Manor.'

'Mr Titmuss's house.' Joyce made it painfully obvious. 'So naturally he's a bit concerned about what goes on in his back garden.'

'I'm sure you're not suggesting, either of you' – Gregory thought he knew quite well what they were suggesting – 'that I should allow the position of the Secretary of State's house to have the slightest effect on my decision?'

'Of course not,' said Joyce, apparently horrified.

'God forbid!' Ken echoed her.

'No effect at all,' said Joyce.

'Your decision will be based, I'm sure, on sound environmental principles.'

'Fulfilling our duty,' Joyce intoned, as though it were part of a new and recently learned litany, 'to our planet earth.'

'Of which we've but got a lease for a short number of years.' Ken Cracken took up the response and then added, in a more businesslike manner, 'I'm sure the Secretary of State would be delighted if you made that the basis for your decision to stop the development.'

'The basis for my decision?' Gregory Boland, his eyes alight with the strength of his principles, looked at his hosts with scorn; in such a way the early Protestant martyrs no doubt faced the threats of the Inquisition. 'What's Mr Titmuss got to do with the basis of my decision?'

'Absolutely nothing,' Ken Cracken agreed with a smile. 'Provided it doesn't mean a new town being planted on top of him. If that can be avoided, I know he'll be extremely grateful. And we'll look forward to your joining us, as our new overall planning adviser.'

'I'm sorry. I'll have to go now.' So Gregory the martyr thrust aside temptation and stood up proudly in the Savoy Grill. 'I have a great deal of work to do. Redrafting my conclusions. You may tell the Secretary of State that he will have my full report before the month is over.'

'Worked like a charm,' Ken said when the Inspector had gone home to disappoint Mrs Boland and he had ordered a couple of Remy Martins to go with the coffee. 'We've certainly got the right character. He'll go to the stake for Fallowfield Country Town after that.'

'You handled him beautifully,' Joyce told her lover with admiration.

'Well, you've got a great deal of political talent yourself. As well as being an absolutely delightful screw.' Ken didn't bother to lower his voice for the benefit of the waiter who was warming two huge balloon glasses. 'Hardly worth going back to the Ministry this afternoon, is it?'

'Hardly worth it at all.'

So, on a bright and windy April morning Gregory Boland's report thudded on to his Secretary of State's desk, to coincide with a well-timed paragraph leaked to Tim Warboys by Ken Cracken, which had appeared in the *Fortress*. LESLIE TITMUSS TO JOIN THE HOMELESS? it was headed at Ken's suggestion, after Warboys had been assured that Leslie would welcome so dramatic a statement of his promised sacrifice.

Now, as I am informed, the Planning Inspector's report is to give the go-ahead for a new country town in the Rapstone Valley, will Mr and Mrs Titmuss of Rapstone Manor be out on the streets? Hardly likely. Titmuss made a sizeable fortune before he devoted himself to becoming one of the country's most outspoken and abrasive politicians. He won't be driven to sleep in a cardboard box. What is certain is that Leslie Titmuss, with the unshakeable integrity which has been a characteristic of his political career, will keep his promise to follow the public inquiry's recommendations. He is not likely to allow his own personal comfort to get in the way of what he considers best for England. Whatever his critics may say, that has never been the Titmuss style.

'Did *you* write this? It seems to have the Cracken ring to it.'

Ken and Joyce were entertaining committee members of his constituency party and had brought them out to admire the view down the river from the House of Commons terrace. The silver-haired women and red-faced men who helped Ken Cracken to his huge majority in the London suburbs smiled with adoration as their favourite Cabinet Minister came up to them. But Leslie was tight-lipped and furious as he held the folded paper under the nose of his Minister of State.

'I'm not a journalist, Secretary of State. And I'm here with my constituency party.'

'You may not be a journalist but you've got as many leaks in you as a rusty sieve. It's about time you and I had a word together.'

'Why don't I take you all to find a cup of tea? And a drink, of course. Perhaps you'll join us later, Ken.'

'I do realize it's very embarrassing for you,' Ken Cracken said as Joyce rounded up the party and they left, disappointed to be missing what looked like being an enormously enjoyable row.

'Not half as embarrassing as it's going to be for you, my lad.' I've got him, Ken Cracken thought. Now he's starting to threaten me. He looked away, down the water towards the dome of St Paul's and smiled serenely. Then he said, 'I don't know why you're so worried about that piece in the paper. I mean, it's perfectly true, isn't it?'

'True he's given the go-ahead to the town. Yes.'

'And true you promised to abide by his decision.'

'I know what you want, Ken Cracken.'

'I'm not sure I want anything in particular. After all, I don't live in Rapstone.'

'You may not. But you're thick as a couple of thieves with Christopher Kempenflatt. How much did he contribute to party funds last year?'

'That's ridiculous. All sorts of businessmen contribute to our party funds.'

'Oh, I'm not suggesting you're out for money. Although I'd like to bet you and that toothy little researcher of yours have got a summer fixed up on Kempenflatt's boat round the Greek islands. Just watch he doesn't push you in, that's all. If he doesn't, I might. I know exactly what you're after.'

'I wish you'd let me into the secret.'

'You want me to go back on my word, don't you? You want me to reject the Inspector's finding. You want me to make a decision to save my own back garden. Titmuss, you'll be able to tell them all in the bloody tea-room, is using his job to protect his own interests. How very unlike Ken Cracken, who is as pure as the driven slush.'

'I've no doubt you'll find a very convincing way of putting it. If you want to stop the new town, that is.' Ken was smiling imperturbably at his master's insults.

'Oh, yes? How would you suggest I do it?'

'Start "In view of all we now know about the environment, and having regard to this government's very real commitment to preserve the British countryside ..." How about something along those lines?'

'Do you want to write the speech for me? Then you'd be quite sure it sounded like a load of lies!'

'I really can't understand why you're taking this attitude.' Ken now assumed an expression of pained innocence, which didn't suit him. 'It seems to be a matter between you and Gregory Boland, the Inspector. If you want him to think again about his report ...'

'I think I'll leave that sort of monkey business to you.'

'I was going to say, you know as well as I do that the Inspector's as straight as a die. If you or I asked him to do anything he'd fly off in the opposite direction.'

As soon as he had said that, Ken Cracken regretted it, because his Secretary of State looked at him and asked, almost with admiration, 'Is *that* how you managed it?'

CHAPTER TWENTY-FIVE

On the day when the warrant for the execution of Rapstone Valley was leaked in the *Fortress* and while Leslie confronted Ken Cracken on the terrace of the House of Commons, Jenny was at work, as usual, in the garden. It was her best time of the year, full of promise but before the weeds took over, when the first blossom was starting to appear and she hoped it would be dealt with gently and not shaken down by the wind. She took out the sweet peas she had started in the greenhouse and planted them in the earth which had been prepared for them. Then she straightened up with the trowel in her hand and looked about her, noticing the changes, the opening of buds, the length of the shoots, since yesterday. She had a premonition of disaster, as though the whole landscape were about to be blotted out, as must happen at the moment of death. She blinked, told herself not to be ridiculous, and went in to start on the dinner.

When he had finished eating, Leslie pushed his plate away, and, instead of saying, 'Very tasty!' as his father always did, he smiled bitterly and said, 'Well. It's happened.'

She didn't ask him what had happened because she didn't want to know.

'The Inspector's report's come out in favour of Fallowfield Country Town. So far as he's concerned the bulldozers can move in tomorrow.'

Jenny felt her afternoon's vision return. She said, 'And what about as far as you're concerned?'

'I undertook to accept the result of the public inquiry. You'd want me to keep my promise, wouldn't you?' And when he said that, he turned on her with such a look of fury that she wondered what on earth she had done wrong, although she was soon to discover.

'I've got to keep my word, haven't I? Otherwise I'd be just a shifty politician. Not someone you could mention in the same breath as the wonderfully honest Mr Anthony Sidonia.'

'I don't know what you mean,' Jenny said, after a long silence.

'No. You probably don't.'

She didn't answer him, but collected the plates and took them out to the kitchen. Mrs Bigwell was coming the next morning but she washed up slowly and with enormous care, taking as long to do it as she could and trying not to think about what Leslie had said to her. When the glasses were polished and the saucepans scoured and put away, she went into the sitting-room where she found her husband watching himself being interviewed about the result of a by-election. The man smiling and making jokes on the screen and the other Leslie, slumped in an armchair, pale and angry, appeared as different people. She collected a book and went upstairs to bed. If she couldn't avoid an argument she could, at least, put it off for as long as possible.

She was sitting in front of the dressing-table brushing her hair when she heard his footsteps on the stairs. As soon as he had opened the door he said, 'He's got to be got rid of.'

She didn't ask him who or what he was talking about, but she sat still with the brush in her hand, wearing a nightdress and with her face clean of make-up.

'You've got to get rid of him,' he repeated.

'If you mean Tony' – she tried to smile – 'I think he's gone already.'

'He's not gone yet. He's been here. All the time since we've been married. I knew that in Rome. In that restaurant of his you took me to. Sitting between us. So you could compare me with him!'

238

'Why are you saying all this now? Please don't.' She looked at him, pleading. She was ready, even though he had gone so far, to forget what he had said.

It was her calmness that infuriated him. The way she sat there quietly, with her dark hair shining, dressed in white as though for some sort of sacrifice, forced him to attack her. He had so much information, such a huge weight of evidence which he had carried around for so long that he had to be relieved of it. He had to prove at long last that he was, in every sort of way, a better man than Sidonia, whose shadow had kept him in the cold.

'You're wrong about him. You've got it all wrong.'

He had meant to wait. When a time came, as he knew it would, when she would say, 'Tony wouldn't have done that', he could have presented his unanswerable case and banished this superior, smiling ghost forever. But Jenny never did speak the words he was waiting for, although he imagined that she always thought them.

So it had gone on, during the long period of investigation. Each night he had come home and been friendly, funny in his way, had praised her, appreciated her, even made love to her, and said nothing. But that evening was different. He had been beaten, cheated and forced into a position where he would have to keep his word. Sidonia, he knew she was thinking, wouldn't have found that difficult at all.

'Please,' she begged him again. 'I'm tired.'

He wanted to say, I'm tired also. Tired of your late husband. What he did say was, 'This won't take very long.' And then, as though he were dealing with a matter of politics, he said, 'I'll just run over the main points. His mother, for instance.'

Now she knew it was a nightmare. What on earth had Myra to do with Leslie Titmuss? She said, 'She was a dancer.'

'Don't you believe it. She worked in the wardrobe. Even then she was always pretending to be someone important. All her stories about dancing, the parties she went to, probably her lovers, they all came from another girl. A dancer who died. Do you think your Tony didn't know?'

'You mean Myra made things up?' Her smile was more infuriating to him than any look of shock would have been.

'Most things. Including the husband killed in the war. So far as I can discover she never married anyone.'

'So far' – she was looking at him, amazed – 'as you can discover? What've you been doing?'

'Finding things out,' he told her. 'I made it my business. Don't you think I had a right to?'

'Things about Myra. What on earth does it matter?'

'Not much. Except that I had to tell you. Sidonia comes from a family of liars.'

He had to tell her. Jenny wondered why he should have to tell her anything.

'When it comes to *his* lies, of course, it's difficult to know where to start.'

'I don't want to hear.' She wanted to cover her ears now, shut out his cold, deliberate voice.

'I expect you don't. You've *got* to listen, though. Now. It's only fair.'

'Fair?'

'Fair to me. You've never been that, have you? You're not going!'

She stood and tried to get out of the bedroom. He positioned himself between her and the door.

'How should I start? The affairs with students. He told you he didn't have them, didn't he? That was his way of making you feel special, specially wanted, until you'd passed the exams and got your reward. All lies. Blane told me. At least twice the college nearly got rid of him. Because of the girls who passed through his bed on the way to their exams.'

'Even if that were true' – she didn't believe him – 'what does it matter now?'

'Doesn't it matter? About him and Susan Bramble?'

Relief flooded over her. He was going to tell her nothing she didn't know already. 'Of course I know,' she said. 'Sue was Tony's girlfriend for years.'

'For years.' He looked at her and smiled. 'Years after you were married.'

'I know that's not true.'

'When he went to London to lecture, to go to dinners of the Historical Association and was supposed to be staying in his club. Such a gentlemanly, old-fashioned excuse, wasn't it? And when Sidonia went to do his film in Rome, the one your friend Bramble worked on. He didn't want you to drive down through France with the unit, did he?'

'I flew out to Rome. I was with him.' She hated herself for arguing, for admitting that Tony needed defending.

'You joined them. After he'd slept with your friend in all the hotels during a scenic trip through Europe. And then he lied to you about it. Come to that, they both lied to you.'

'You don't know!' Now she was trying to defend Tony. 'Anyway, how do you know?'

'I had a man' – for the first time he seemed defensive – 'a man to find out.'

'A man to find out things about Tony?' She found it impossible to believe.

'Yes.'

'You mean a detective?'

'Yes.' And then he said, as though this made it better, 'I couldn't rely on him. He's a bit of a fool, quite honestly. In the end you always have to do these things for yourself.'

'You did it for yourself!' She felt herself choking with anger, a feeling entirely new to her. 'You mean, you went round asking questions? Trying to find out that Tony slept with people and where he did it?'

She was attacking him now, but her blows were like those of a child. They didn't move him from his position or hurt him in the least. He smiled at her complacently, knowing, as he always did, that he was in the right. Sooner or later she would have to agree with him.

'I didn't just *try* to find out when Tony slept with people. I succeeded.'

'What for? Whatever *for?*' She was looking at him, not only angry but amazed, as though he were a creature from outer space.

'So you'd be free of him.'

It was a shock, of course, he understood. She'd come to terms with it. Sooner or later.

'Free?'

'All right,' he admitted. 'So we'd both be free. I did it for both of us.'

'You did it for me? I don't understand.'

'I'm sure you will.' Now he sounded like a doctor, promising her that if she took the medicine she'd get better quite soon. 'You will when you think about it. I'll leave you in peace, if you like. We can talk in the morning.'

'In peace? How can I be in peace now?'

'I'll sleep next door. I think you'll find the worst is over.'

He left her then, like a man conscious of a job well done.

Something was over, but what was it? Certainly not the worst, probably the best. Had Tony died at last, killed effectively by Leslie Titmuss? Was her marriage to Leslie over, to be only another memory, ending in a disaster more final than death? Had she a friend she could trust? Jenny stood alone in the middle of the bedroom floor, turned and saw herself in the dressing-table mirror, a pale figure who seemed as far from her as the smiling image on the television screen had been remote from her husband.

She would have liked, above all, to get into bed, to pull the pillow round her ears and try to forget everything Leslie had told her. That would have been to follow her instinct, not to meet trouble half-way but to take refuge from it, in silence, in a refusal to argue, in sleep. But she had to get away from Leslie. She couldn't lie down in his bed, in his house where he might come to her in the night, get in beside her and, failing to understand the enormity of what he had done, attempt to make love to her. She had to go. This need was stronger than her usual passion for avoiding trouble, so she began to dress quickly, to pull on jeans and a sweater, to find her bag, her keys and her money, and then she went down the big staircase, seeing no light under the spare bedroom door. She moved quietly, as though she were leaving a child who, after a great deal of trouble, seems at last to have fallen asleep. She crossed the marble-paved hall and then, still trying her best to make no sound, unbolted and slid open the heavy front door. When she stepped out into the darkness it was as though she were breathing clean and unpolluted air at last.

She took off the handbrake of her car and let it roll down a gravel slope silently before she started the engine. Then she switched on the headlights and saw the trees, the hedges just starting to turn green, the walls of thorn and twigs, all speed past her, lit for a second. At the head of the valley she looked out towards dark fields and woods and remembered that they were now to be obliterated in a tidal wave which her husband had not been able to control. But that, she told herself, was the least of the troubles of that night. The road was empty so she drove fast towards the lights on the motorway and the signs for London.

When she got to the flat she was surprised that it was not yet one in the morning. Leslie's revelations which seemed to have gone on forever must have been over by eleven and she had broken all records on her journey to London. Now she longed to avoid meeting Sue and had no idea how she could put the questions that had to be asked. Her heart sank when she saw the lights on in what had been their sitting-room, and when she rang the bell Sue came down to open the door almost at once. She looked suddenly older and much less pretty than Jenny had pictured her when she thought of the scene to come. Sue was wearing glasses, as she only did when she was reading or watching television on her own, and a dressing-gown which looked as if it were ready for the cleaners.

'Jenny! What is it? You look terrible!'

'Are you alone?'

'Worse luck. Come in. It's wonderful to see you.'

And when she was inside and Sue had closed the door Jenny, who could believe she looked terrible, said, 'Not so wonderful, I'm afraid. Not now.'

'What's happened?'

'Happened? Everything seems to have happened.'

'My poor Jenny. I can imagine. Has Mr Titmuss turned out awful? You'll stay here, won't you? What else can I do to help?'

'I suppose' – and now Jenny realized that she was asking for the last thing she really wanted – 'you can tell me the truth.'

CHAPTER TWENTY-SIX

Kev the Rev. thought an all-night vigil outside the Rapstone Nature Area would be the best way of dealing with the matter. He saw a great crowd of protesters holding up candles and singing together.

'We'd never get hold of enough candles.' Daphne Jones was practical. 'They've even given up selling them in Worsfield super-markets.'

'They've got those curly, coloured things people buy for dinner parties in the Hartscombe Hostess shop,' Mrs Vee remembered. 'But they'd be terribly expensive.'

'Not much good getting a crowd assembled together at night,' the herbalist said. 'That's not going to cause much inconvenience to traffic.'

'We could get a good few people together,' Mrs Vee thought. 'Our phone's never stopped ringing. But night time wouldn't be much use to television. What are your views, Chairman?' It was an emergency meeting of S.O.V. committee members, a solemn occasion after they had read the news in their copies of the *Fortress*.

What Fred thought was that he was back in his youth again, in the time of protest marches and all-night vigils. As the Reverend Kevin Bulstrode spoke he seemed to hear a more shrill, less elegant version of his father's voice. How many times had Simeon Simcox coughed the night away in draughty churches, or led singers down country lanes to put an end to apartheid or the Bomb – and these things were still obstinately there when the guitars had been put away and the churches emptied. All the same, Fred would have liked to tell them that Fallowfield Country Town would vanish into the mists of legend if only they could exorcize it with candles and protest songs. He said, 'It's up to Leslie Titmuss. He could still stop Fallowfield.'

'Absolutely,' Mrs Vee agreed. 'That's why we need to demon-strate. To show Titmuss we mean business.'

'Of course, he has said he'll stick by the inquiry's decision.' Mrs Wilcox was pessimistic.

'Then it's up to us,' Mrs Vee said cheerfully, 'to persuade him to change his mind.'

Fred remembered his father, in a rare moment of insight, saying that protests and marches might not do much for a cause but they certainly made the people who took part in them feel better. He also wished that Jenny had managed to preserve her loyalty to the group and they could have talked, stood together under the trees, held candles, sung songs or done whatever else came into their minds. These thoughts he immediately recognized as fantasies and did his best to dismiss them.

It hadn't taken Jenny long to learn all she needed, and far more than she wanted, to know from her friend, Sue Bramble. Sue might have been capable of years of silent deception but she couldn't lie when asked a direct question by her friend.

'Oh, damn!' she said. 'I suppose it's true. Would it be pointless to say I'm sorry?'

'Yes,' Jenny told her. 'Quite pointless.'

'You were always special to Tony. Absolutely special,' Sue said after a long and hopeless silence. 'I'm sure it didn't make any difference to his feeling for you.'

'I don't know.' Jenny felt she was in a dream from which there was still, perhaps, some hope of waking up. 'I don't know what difference it made. But I do know' – here she was certain – 'something's changed. Changed forever.'

'It's useless to say I'm sorry.'

'Yes.'

'But I'm truly sorry you had to find out.'

Jenny thought that if it hadn't happened, it wouldn't have been there for her to find out. But that wasn't the point either.

'What're you going to do now?'

'I don't know. I don't know at all.'

'But you can't go back to Leslie?'

'No. I suppose not.'

'Not to a man who sets on detectives.'

The detectives were the worst part about it. It was the thought of detectives, shadowy men in macs, Jenny imagined, lying in wait for her, thumbing through her past and Tony's, which had turned a quarrel into a nightmare.

'You'll stay here tonight, anyway?'

'No.' Jenny looked at her friend. 'No, I don't think I can.'

'Because you can't forgive me?'

'I don't feel I can do anything yet.'

'Then I'll move out somewhere. You can stay here on your own.'

'No. I'll go now, honestly. I need to think.'

'Can't you think here?'

Jenny looked round the flat and thought of all it had meant in their long friendship.

'No,' she said. 'I don't think I can.'

When Jenny left Sue Bramble, she couldn't make up her mind about anything, even where to go next. She thought of going to a hotel, and then decided against turning up without luggage at almost two in the morning. During her time with Leslie she had lost touch with London and there was no friendly front doorbell she felt she could ring. She stayed in the car because it was warm, because its familiar shell protected her and because driving was, after all, some sort of occupation. She travelled at random, taking turnings without thinking, until she found herself by the river. She drove along it and saw Big Ben and the Houses of

Parliament, which made her think of Leslie and then she accelerated, wanting to put him out of her mind.

Then she was in the City, finding herself among tall banks and office buildings, places where her previous life had never taken her. The streets were silent and deserted, as in a town that has been evacuated in time of war, but the area was so strange to her that she was lost immediately and took turnings which brought her back, after a long detour, to the river again, so she was driving in aimless circles. At last she turned northwards, through streets which were still alive with drunks and minicabs waiting outside all-night discos and couples quarrelling, and, somewhere in Kilburn, two gangs of teenagers chasing each other across a wide road. She saw bottles thrown and heard glass breaking. Later it was quiet again, among rows of sleeping houses with cars parked in front of small, trim gardens, decorated with plaster lions and sundials. She turned by a sign to a motorway, not caring particularly where it led her.

Jenny drove in the slow lane and container lorries surged up behind her, flashed their lights angrily and lurched past. After a while she pulled into a service area, parked and sat for a long time before she felt she dared get out of the car.

The café was still open, filled with muzak and the smell of frying. In the passage outside it a few tired men were playing with the Space Invader machines which squeaked and gibbered complainingly. Jenny sat in a corner, among empty tables. In the distance a Sikh family, the men in anoraks and turbans, the women with plastic macs over their saris, the children falling asleep among plates of egg and chips, were resting, on some endless journey. Nearer to her a grey-haired man and a girl who looked very young were talking in low voices and holding hands. Was it a father recovering his runaway daughter or two apparently ill-suited lovers escaping? Jenny knew she wasn't the only one with troubles, a thought which seemed to clear her mind a little.

She thought a lot about her grandmother Paget and the house

in St Leonards where the sea muttered all night and the doors and windows rattled in the wind. With so much of her faith shattered and still needing someone she could trust, the small woman in the floppy shower-hat who plunged into the waves on Boxing Day seemed the only person capable of filling the role. Granny Paget had, like Tony Sidonia, been dead for a long time and the house in St Leonards-on-Sea had been sold, or Jenny might have turned her car southwards. She would have liked, more than anything now, to be battling against the wind with her grandmother along the prom. As she thought of it, she could feel her mind clearing further. She would have told the old lady the whole story. It would have been received, no doubt, without any particular surprise, and over the 'slap-up tea' in the sitting-room afterwards, when the fire was lit and the circulation starting to return to her toes and fingers, she would have got her answer.

But what would the answer have been? She remembered Granny Paget's contempt for lies and 'fairy tales' and the brusque way in which she had dismissed her mother's failure to understand 'the importance of sticking to things'. She could also imagine what her grandmother would have had to say about men who imported detectives into their married lives. Jenny sat for a long time in front of half a cup of cold coffee thinking about these things. When she left the motorway café it was already light. She now drove with some idea, at least, of where she was going.

When she got to the Rapstone Valley there was a mist on the ground from which low hills and clumps of woodland emerged into the pink light of a landscape as in a Chinese painting. As she approached the road past the Nature Area, she heard an eerie sound which might have seemed, to a nervous ear, to be the lamentation of souls in torment. When she turned the corner she saw a surprisingly large crowd of people, some still holding candles which flickered in the daylight, surrounded by vans, cars and television cameras. Their banners and placards, fluttering in the breeze, read SAVE OUR VALLEY, SAY NO TO FALLOWFIELD and LISTEN TO US, TITMUSS. Blocked from going further, she stopped and rolled down her window. A man approached her, carrying pamphlets.

'We haven't all been here all night,' Fred told her. 'But they did a piece about us on the news and it's extraordinary the number who've come. Students from Worsfield, Hartscombe people on their way to work. Almost everyone who lives in the valley. Are you sure you're all right? You look exhausted.'

'I look terrible.' She remembered what Sue Bramble had told her. 'As a matter of fact *I've* been up all night.'

When he had put his head through her car window, Fred had smiled at her and invited her to breakfast. With the window open she realized how hungry she was and how cold. There was no reason why she couldn't stay a little and let more time cushion her from a final decision. She let him direct her into a lay-by and when she was parked he took her to a place where the landlord of the Baptist's Head had brought out urns of tea and coffee, bacon rolls and piles of sandwiches. Now they had moved a little away from the crowd and she was warming her hands on a plastic cup.

'If you were up all night,' he said, 'you should have joined us. You'd've had a marvellous time, singing "We Shall Overcome" with your teeth chattering. Oh, I forgot. You're not allowed to do that sort of thing, are you?'

'I don't know.' She looked down into her coffee cup. 'God knows what I'll be able to do now.'

She had said too much, out of tiredness and loneliness, and a longing to speak to someone who was alive and would listen. Fred felt a sudden and irrational hope.

'Why *now*?' he asked. 'Has something happened?'

'Something, I suppose.'

'With you and Leslie?'

She was too tired to be careful. 'Yes,' she said. 'With me and Leslie. Last night.'

'Is it serious?'

'I don't know. I suppose if anything's serious this is. I'll drink my coffee and go. I don't want to bore you.'

'Of course you won't bore me. Anyway, you can talk to me. People tell me things. I'm a doctor.'

She looked up at him hopefully. He knew she wanted to tell him her story. But no longer as a friend, still less, he was afraid, in spite of all his fantasies, as a potential lover. He had put a professional distance between them. If she confided in him now it would be for medicinal purposes only.

'I might want to tell you, sometime,' she said. 'I suppose.'

'Please do.' Now he thought the best thing he could do for her was to entertain her. 'I've become a bit of an expert on marriage guidance.'

'Marriage guidance?' She repeated his words in wonder.

'Oh, yes. I've discovered it's a most powerful aphrodisiac. I had a patient. I can't tell you who it was but . . .' Like many doctors and lawyers, those to whom confidences are given, Fred found it hard to keep a secret. He started to tell Jenny about Evie and Len Bigwell.

Leslie Titmuss had got up early as usual and found Jenny's car gone and although he went all over the silent house looking, he discovered no note, no message, nothing. He stood for a moment, uncertain, and then he told himself that she would be back. Of course she would. Where else, after all, had she to go? He went through the scene of the night before and saw nothing unreasonable or untrue in what he had told her. He had, he thought, scored a notable victory and freed her from an old deception. Of course she would return and they would be closer to each other because he would now have no rival. This is what he told himself as he waited for his driver. By the time he got into his car and started for London he was convinced that he was right.

On the road past the Nature Area he met the crowd of protesters. Their candles were out and they had stopped singing.

The Hartscombe herbalist thumped the black bonnet of the Rover as it slowed to get past and there were a few shouts. Someone called, 'Don't be the valley vandal!' and he gave them a pale smile and an almost royal wave of the hand. The demonstrators were too polite, or too much in awe of him, to stop the car, which accelerated past the last banner and a platoon of Curdles, who were cheering ironically.

He was now travelling too fast to notice the couple drinking coffee under the shadows of the trees. Had he done so he might have been perturbed to see his wife with Fred Simcox. For the first time during that long night Jenny was laughing. By making her laugh Fred had given her courage for what she knew she must do next.

CHAPTER TWENTY-SEVEN

INTERVIEWER: Mr Titmuss. You've announced that you're prepared to give planning permission for a new town called Fallowfield to be built near Hartscombe, where you have a home?

LESLIE: Yes. I said I'd leave the decision to the inquiry. That's the democratic way we do things in this country.

INTERVIEWER: It's going to cause a bit of an upheaval for you, isn't it? The town's going to be built all over your back garden.

LESLIE: You might say I'm used to upheavals. We caused a bit of an upheaval when we came to power, didn't we? Anyway, what do you want me to do? Change our free enterprise policies just because they might cause me a bit of personal inconvenience?

INTERVIEWER: Well, no. Of course not. But –

LESLIE: That was the old Socialist way, wasn't it? Preaching one thing and practising the other. Wonderful old clergyman I used to do odd jobs for when I was a boy –

INTERVIEWER [who knows this bit by heart]: Cutting nettles –

LESLIE: Cutting nettles was the easiest part of it! Cutting nettles was a holiday task compared with the other jobs that I had to do. Anyway, he never stopped his sermons about equality and the evils of capitalism. He could afford to do that on the private income he got from shares in the local brewery. Let me tell you this, my lad. Scrape a Socialist and you'll find a member of the privileged elite.

253

INTERVIEWER: Will you and your wife be moving, perhaps to somewhere more rural?

LESLIE: And you can say what you like about the present government. We're not a collection of hypocrites. We don't vote one way and live the other. No, I don't suppose I'll be moving. My roots are in that part of England. That's where my father was born, and my old mother of course. I expect I'll stick with it and see it dragged into the twenty-first century. There's a lot of wonderful opportunities ahead of us, you know.

INTERVIEWER: Does that go for your wife also?

LESLIE: I think you've had your interview now, haven't you?

At which the Secretary of State stood up, not before the tactful director had switched back to the presenter. Leslie, frowning and dangerous, marched out of the studio ignoring his interviewer's stumbling apology and inquiries from an anxious girl about his waiting car. Once safe in the back of the official Rover and on his way home, he realized his mistake. They had no reason to know of the quarrel and Jenny's disappearance. He had been foolish to get angry, and all he had done was to make an innocent question look damaging. 'I expect, my lad, she'll go where I go. That's what she usually does.' If he'd said that with the well-loved Titmuss chauvinism it would have stopped all rumours. In fact, at the mention of his wife, he had felt a rising panic. Suppose he had been wrong. Suppose Jenny had been foolish enough to refuse the challenge of adjusting herself to the truth about Sidonia. Suppose she had simply run away somewhere to hide from him and the uncomfortable facts he had been forced to tell her. Suppose that Jenny, unfairly and unjustifiably, was lost and gone from him forever, just as Sidonia was lost and gone from her? As he peered into a bleak and lonely future, Leslie felt something which was unusual for him. His hands were sweating and he was afraid.

So, when he reached his gates and saw, at the other end of the avenue of lime trees and in front of the green-grey walls of the house, Jenny's small, shining Fiat, a huge weight of anxiety seemed to be lifted. As had happened so often in his life he had taken a risk and the gamble had paid off. He had refused to compromise or keep silent. He had taken the positive – he would like to have said, the bold and dangerous – action and he had been rewarded. Jenny had come back. No part of her, he was now sure, would have to be shared with the dissolute and deceiving Tony Sidonia.

He dismissed his driver and went into the house. It was very quiet but the doors and windows were open. There was a fresh wind blowing through it as though someone had been trying to air the rooms after a long illness or a death. He called in all the downstairs rooms but got no answer. He went up the stairs. Perhaps she was asleep and hadn't heard him. He opened the bedroom door gently but he needn't have troubled. The room was empty. Then he crossed to the window and looked down on to a patch of lawn sheltered by tall yew hedges. And there she lay on her back, her arms and legs stretched out as though she had just fallen from the sky. He turned quickly and ran down the stairs to find her.

Jenny had slept for a while where she lay on the damp grass, grateful for the silence. She heard him call her name and she sat up blinking. He thought how pale she looked and how exhausted. 'I thought you'd be back,' he said.

'Yes. I came back. There's no point in not forgiving.'

'Forgiving?' He couldn't believe it. 'You don't mean you've forgiven Sidonia?'

'That's not important. I mean forgiving you. I was going to make some tea. Do you want some?'

She got up quickly and left him. He stood still for a while, trying to make sense of what she had said. When he knew that he was angry he followed her.

She was in the kitchen when he said, 'What the hell have you got to forgive me for?'

She had her back turned towards him, filling a kettle. 'What

255

you did to me. I don't suppose you could've thought of anything much worse. I don't want to talk about it any more.'

'Well, I do!' He was sure of himself, of course, and sure he was in the right. 'I suppose you kidded yourself I was all wrong about your late husband. You think I've slandered his blessed memory!'

'No. Not that. I went to see Sue.'

'And I suppose she lied to you?'

'No. I'm afraid she told me the truth.'

'So. What am I supposed to have done wrong?'

'I don't see that there's any point in talking about it.' She put the kettle on the hotplate of the Aga, where it began to spit and rattle. She tried not to hear him shouting, '*I* see the point! I've a right to know what you've got against me!' She felt him grip her wrist to hold her, so she couldn't escape. She thought he might free her if she told him. 'I had a life,' she said. 'It was mine until I met you. I was in love with a man. He might have tricked me. I don't know why he should have but I suppose he did. Anyway, I loved him. He's dead now. So there's nothing to be done about it. But to pay someone money to pry and peer into everything that happened to me! Behind my back . . .'

'Sidonia did things behind your back, remember.'

'Perhaps for love.'

'Why do you think I did it?'

'How can I tell? I don't understand you.'

'Because it was my right, that's why. I always came second.'

'You came afterwards. Did that give you a right to spy on me?'

'Not on you. On him!'

'On someone dead?'

'Not dead to you. That's what I told you. I'm not ashamed of what I did. Why should I be?' He looked at her, as though for reassurance, but she gave him none. Instead she pulled away from him and he let her go.

'All right,' she said. 'I'll have to be ashamed for you.' She found the teapot, warmed it and put two spoonfuls of tea in carefully, as though these small actions deserved her full attention. Then she started, as calmly as she could, to explain. 'I've thought about it all as much as I can –'

'And talked to your friend Sue Bramble, who cheated you?'

His voice was full of contempt and at once Jenny felt as protective of Sue as she had been of Tony. Blazing with unusual anger, she heard her voice, from what seemed a long way off, shouting, 'I think you did something awful. So awful that I still can't believe it. No one had the right to do that to me. No one! But I took a risk when I married you. A deliberate risk. I didn't really know what you'd be like. You've turned out to be like this. It's who you are.' She was quiet again now. 'All right. We'll try and forget this happened. Perhaps we can.'

'You want to forget about Sidonia?'

'About what you've done. If we're going to live together.'

He looked at her for what seemed a long time in silence. Then, 'You want to live with me?' He said it like a challenge.

'I want to stay with whatever we've got left. I don't want to run away.' The kettle was boiling and she made the tea, pouring it out through a strainer. 'It's important to stick to things. Not like my mother. I don't want to be like her.'

'You want to forgive me.'

'Please' – she had never felt so tired, she thought, in all her life – 'there's nothing else to say.'

'Did you go to the Doctor?'

'What?'

'Did you tell Fred Simcox your troubles?'

'Perhaps . . . I started to.'

'Oh, yes.' Leslie looked suddenly triumphant, as though he had found out something else unpleasant. 'And did he tell you to forgive me?'

'No.'

'Just the sort of bloody patronizing thing he would do. Tell him that when you next see him. I don't want to be forgiven.'

'I won't tell him. No one else has got anything to do with it.'

'Not by you. Not by him. Not by anyone. You understand?'

'Perhaps forgiven's the wrong word.' His fury seemed, she thought, to come from suffering and she wanted, now that they were to stay together, to console him.

'What's the right word? Overlook? Make allowances because I don't know any better? Maybe my feelings aren't quite as delicate as yours and your friends'. Oh, Leslie Titmuss, he wears the wrong tie and the wrong suit, but you've got to make excuses. He was tactless enough to tell the truth in a common sort of way. The poor bastard doesn't know any better, so we'll have to forgive him. You think I want to spend the rest of my life being forgiven by you? Do you think I'm going to sit here being *tolerated*?'

'You won't be,' she promised. 'We won't ever talk about it.'

'No,' he said. 'We won't talk about it because we won't be together. We can't be now.'

'Why not?' She was almost too tired to ask him.

'Because I'm not prepared to forgive you for forgiving me. That's why. For God's sake, can't you understand?'

He opened his hand then and, quite deliberately, dropped the cup and saucer he was holding. He moved to the table and sat, apparently calm. Jenny said nothing but fetched a dustpan and brush and swept the pieces up from the stone floor, grieving for the china that was broken.

'There's going to be a new town,' he told her. 'That's decided. You won't like it. Your friend the Doctor's going to hate it. I can't be sure I'll like it much myself. I tried to stop it for you, but in the end I couldn't. Perhaps that's the best that can happen. Things can't stand still, can they? It's no good being in love with the past all your life. That's what we're in power to tell people.'

She emptied the dustpan into the bin and put it away in the cupboard. She no longer wanted to hear about his power.

'So at least it'll be something different. You won't want to live

258

here any more, will you? Not when it's surrounded with super-markets and multi-storey car parks and all the things that you lot wish people didn't want nowadays.'

'And you?' she asked. 'Where'll you want to live?'

'In the future,' he told her. 'After all, I made it happen.'

CHAPTER TWENTY-EIGHT

There followed days of extraordinary stillness. The sun shone and there was almost no wind or cloud to be chased across the sky. The valley was silent and deserted as though preparing itself, in a period of withdrawal, for the onslaught of the bull-dozers. Driving between the hedges, Jenny had an unusual sighting of a hare. Knowing what was to happen she found she no longer wanted to look at the landscape that had become a home to her. If everything had to change, it was time for her to go.

'Are you sure it's what you want?' She and Leslie had been sleeping apart and when they met at breakfast they treated each other with the politeness of strangers.

'You haven't left me any choice,' he told her.

'I think I have.' His unfairness had a sort of daring about it which took her breath away.

'Either to be forgiven or forgotten? I'd best be forgotten.'

'I shan't forget you,' she said. 'I promise you that.' He stood up then to leave for the airport. He was on his way to another European meeting, this time in Luxemburg. He stood, tall and pale in his dark clothes, and she wanted, for a moment, to comfort him. But he looked at her in a way that gave her no encouragement. Then he turned from her and left the house.

Alone and because, in spite of all that had happened, it had become such a habit with her, Jenny telephoned Sue Bramble.

'It's Jenny.'

'Jenny! How are you?' Sue sounded nervous and falsely cheerful.

'All right, I suppose. Leslie's gone. It's all over.'

'What's all over?'

'Us.'

'I see.' And then, 'I'm only surprised it lasted so long.'

'That's not the only thing. This place seems to be over as well.'

'Your house?'

'Yes. They're going to build a new town all round it.'

'Oh, of course. I read about that.' Sue sounded as if she couldn't believe they were talking as though they were still friends.

'I'm coming up to London.'

'To the flat?'

'Yes. I've got to live somewhere.'

'Of course you have. I told you I'd move out. I'll go today. Oh, and I'll get it all cleaned up for you . . .'

There was a silence and then Jenny said, 'No need to do that.'

'No need to get it cleaned up?'

'No need for you to go.'

'Oh.'

'I don't really want to be alone. Not for a while. Please stay if you think it'll be all right.'

'What do you mean, if it'll be all right?'

'After that awful business of me finding out.'

'How on earth was that your fault?' Sue was incredulous.

'Well, I suppose none of it would have happened. If I hadn't taken on Leslie Titmuss.' Jenny's voice was very quiet, as though at the start of tears.

'Come up to the flat,' Sue Bramble said. 'I'll do my best to look after you.'

'Congratulations, Ken.' The Minister looked up from his seat in the first-class compartment of the B.A. plane into the smiling face of his Secretary of State. 'You've done very well out of all this, haven't you?'

'You mean out of the new town? I think you've done well, Leslie. Your reputation for selflessness is higher than ever.' Ken Cracken, in his general disappointment at the turn events had taken, allowed himself a touch of irony.

'Oh, I don't mean the new town.' Leslie settled himself down and fastened his seat-belt. 'That's all ancient history. I mean the reshuffle. Your new job, Ken.' He smiled again. 'Your great opportunity.'

'Opportunity?'

'Oh, yes. You're the new generation, after all. The young lad with the future before him. As for me, well, I've thought things over. Perhaps it's time I made a nuisance of myself on the back benches. Then I can have a real go at you lot in the government whenever I think you deserve it.'

'You're going to retire?' Overcome with amazement and hope Ken Cracken could do little more than repeat his leader's words.

'I made a mistake, it seems. I'd better be moving on, before I make any more.' If what he said was a confession of failure, Leslie Titmuss's smile showed no sign of it. What was the mistake? his number two wondered. Did he know he'd been outmanoeuvred over Fallowfield? All such speculation was drowned in the rising tide of his ambition.

'I suppose that *will* mean a reshuffle.' It was all going exactly as Ken had planned, with the ever-present help of his political adviser. Titmuss had been defeated over the country town and was retiring hurt, leaving a post for which his Minister of State was the obvious successor.

'I hope you'll enjoy your new job, Ken.'

'Thank you. I'm sure I will.'

'I had a word about you. In the appropriate quarter.'

'That was very generous of you.'

'I thought so. I pointed out your special talents. You do have special talents, don't you, Ken?'

'Well. I'm not sure which ones you're talking about.' Ken Cracken did his best to sound modest.

'Strategic, tactical talents. "Young Cracken," I said, "is a genius at guerrilla warfare. He lives and dreams ambushes and surprise-attacks. In his briefcase he carries a Para lieutenant's swagger-stick. He'll do well somewhere where the fighting is certain to go on forever." So you've got it, Kenneth.'

'Minister of Defence?' Ken was puzzled.

'Something that'll suit you much better than that. This is really active service. You're going to be number two at the Northern Ireland Office. Now, what time do we get back tomorrow? I've got an extremely important dinner date.'

'Oh, yes?' Ken Cracken spoke in the tones of a man who has just seen himself bound for oblivion. 'Who with? Someone beautiful?'

'Someone extremely beautiful.' Leslie got out his briefing papers and prepared to conceal his feelings for the rest of the journey. 'My mother!'

'I know. I promised you'd never have to move from here.'

'You did, Leslie. You promised me faithfully.'

'And I'm going to keep my promise to you, Mother.' Leslie Titmuss was being cooked dinner by Elsie in 'The Spruces' in what must have been one of the most dust-free environments in the world. Even the glazed crust of the steak and kidney pie looked as though it had been done over with Mansion polish. He paused to eat, deciding on how to put the matter in the most politically advantageous fashion. 'There is this business,' he said carefully, 'about the new country town.'

'Can't that be stopped?'

'I don't see how it can. I gave my word, you see.'

'You gave your word to me as well, Leslie,' Elsie Titmuss said with one of her sweetest smiles, and scored a hit.

'Of course, these things take years to build. Ten years at least.' Leslie Titmuss came back at her with an even more powerful smile.

'That's all right then. This place will see me out.'

'It might see me out too. I'm going to sell the Manor. No good rattling about that old mausoleum now, is it?'

'But Leslie. It was to be your home.'

'Not my sort of home, really. The sort of place where the old-school farts hang their tweed hats in the hall and sit for hours reading *Country Life* in the lavatories. That's never been my style at all. You know that, Mother.'

There was silence as they ate. Then Elsie said, 'Are you sure you have to be on your own, Leslie?'

'Yes, Mother. Quite sure.'

'That Jenny seemed such a nice girl.'

Leslie didn't answer.

'Not a ban-the-bomber, was she?'

'No, Mother. She wasn't one of those.'

'I suppose you're not going to tell me what was wrong then, exactly.'

'What was wrong?' He looked at his mother very seriously. 'She couldn't make a steak and kidney to touch yours, Mother.'

'Would you have another helping now, with the crust on it?'

'It's very more-ish.' She helped him to another slice of pie and he took a potato with butter and parsley. In the brightly shining room the clock on the mantelpiece ticked like a bomb and the china ornaments gleamed behind the glass door of the display cabinet. Elsie gave herself a minute second helping just, as she said, to keep her son company. She wanted to console him, even if he didn't want to be consoled. 'There wasn't somebody else, was there?'

'I suppose you could say that.'

'Another man?' She breathed in sharply.

Leslie's mouth was full so he nodded and then looked down at his plate.

'She didn't seem at all that sort of girl to me,' his mother told him. 'Appearances are deceptive.'

'Yes. I'll tell you what we'll do. If they do build this new town while we're both around, Mother . . .'

264

'*You* will be, Leslie. You surely will be '

'And you, most probably. We'll make them put in a new house, just where this one is. A new "Spruces". You'd like that, wouldn't you? And it'll be in the middle of town, you see. Handy for the shops.'

Elsie thought about it and then repeated, 'This'll see me out, Leslie.'

'Well, we'll have to see. There's a long time to go yet.'

'Perhaps you could live in it, Leslie. If you have to sell the Manor. I'd like to think of you settled.'

'Live in it? In Fallowfield Country Town?' There was something about the idea that seemed to amuse him. 'Well, yes. Perhaps I could.'

'I'm sorry,' Elsie said after another silence. 'About that other man.'

'Don't worry,' he told her. 'I think I've seen him off. I shan't be lonely. Not so long as I can keep working. Oh, and have dinner with you here, when I feel like home-cooking.'

'I don't know how Jenny could do that.' Elsie Titmuss pursed her lips in wonder and outrage. 'Not when she had you, Leslie.' Then she looked again at her son's plate and saw that he was down to his last mouthful. She lifted the spoon over the pie dish hopefully. 'Won't you take pity on this last little bit?'

'No, thank you very much. I couldn't fit it.' Leslie pushed his now empty plate away from him and said, as his father had before him, 'That was very tasty, Mother. Very tasty indeed.'

And Ever Afterwards

Then wilt thou not be loth
To leave this Paradise, but shalt possess
A Paradise within thee, happier far.

Paradise Lost
John Milton

CHAPTER TWENTY-NINE

Just over a decade later, the world had got considerably warmer. The sea rose, sloshing over many Pacific islands and flooding expensive houses on the coast of Australia. Ice-caps in the north began to thaw, leaving polar bears stranded, alone and hungry, on floating rafts of diminishing ice. The increasing temperature produced plagues of locusts and the ladybirds became intolerable. The biological clocks of many tortoises were put considerably out of time and the world's ornithologists sought in vain for Ketland's warbler or the burrowing owl.

Defeated on local issues, the Vees turned their attention to wider matters and the remnants of S.O.V. still met in their house for buffet suppers and talks on the ending of the world. One speaker broke the news to them that the ice was being melted not, as was popularly supposed, by the fumes of ever-increasing traffic; the damage was done, so he said, by myriads of termites, set at large by the destruction of the rain forests, breaking wind. 'Is this the way the world ends?' Fred asked with attempted solemnity. 'Not with a bang but a termite's fart?'

'Honestly, Dr Fred,' Mrs Vee rebuked him. 'Can't you ever take the universe seriously?'

Despite Fred's scepticism, the global changes affected Harts-combe. The punts tethered at the riverside rose and were known, in certain weathers, to float into the road. In what was left of the countryside, the harvest mouse was an exotic rarity, the nightingales had been decimated and the adonis blue butterfly was totally extinct. And, as inevitably as the Pacific Ocean advanced to kill the crops and displace the islanders, Fallowfield Country Town flooded the Rapstone Valley.

The change had started slowly. It was noticed that the narrow lanes became full of traffic. Then cars often had to back up to allow the passage of heavy lorries and building machinery. Then bulldozers came to tear up the hedges and flatten the fields for urban construction. These beginnings were greeted by a final flurry of S.O.V. demonstrations from which the Curdles were notably absent, for as the tide of Fallowfield advanced this family was washed to a new height of prosperity.

What had happened was this. With his new-found authority as Chairman and Managing Director of the family business, Len Bigwell had consulted Jackson Cantellow on the question of the lease of the rabbit hacienda from one of the farmers who was about to turn his arable land into car parks and supermarkets and high-priced housing estates. When he saw the lease, Jackson Cantellow pursed his lips and couldn't resist humming a triumphant bar or two of Haydn's *Creation*. What Dot Curdle seemed to have obtained, more by luck than legal cunning, from a farmer whose mind was clearly on other matters, was a tenancy protected by the Agricultural Holdings Act. 'And they can't shift you,' Jackson Cantellow rumbled in his most resonant bass. 'Except with untold gold.' So that was how the Curdles became converted to the 'country town conception' and could afford to buy the freehold of Rapstone Manor when the Right Honourable Leslie Titmuss put it on the market.

So the house remained unaltered, on the very outskirts of the town. The garden was given over to a high-density development of rabbit hutches, mainly containing angoras. The food-producing animals were left to the many subsidiary farms and freezer-packing facilities the Curdles had acquired in various other parts of Southern England. From their headquarters in the Manor the family branched out into other businesses, including double-glazing, patio doors, loft conversions and the covering of ceilings with whirling patterns of raised plaster – a form of folk art which had become enormously popular with the inhabitants of Fallow-field Country Town. The Bigwells had now produced three healthy children and Len, who had been elected to the town council in the Conservative interest, would become one of Fallowfield's early mayors. Grandmother Dot had retired from business and sat for much of the day dozing in the conservatory and dreaming of past lovers. Billy, her youngest child, having grown out of his period of juvenile delinquency, now ran the Cordon Bleu Lapin Frozen Dinners export department. He had fallen wonderfully in love with Sharon Wellings, the daughter of a Fallowfield dentist, who was still in her last year at school. They had met at an old-time Barry Manilow concert in the Fallowfield Arts and Leisure Centre and they carried on their affair secretly, it having been expressly forbidden by Mr and Mrs Wellings who disapproved of Billy Curdle as an older man with a criminal record and as such unsuitable company for young Sharon.

Rapstone Manor remained unchanged and isolated amid the ocean of new building, and so did the Rapstone Nature Area which had been privatized and become the property of Greener Than Green Ltd (Chairman and Managing Director Sir Christopher Kempenflatt), a concern which owned a number of other nature areas as well as maximum security prisons, mental hospitals and remand centres. Hector Bolitho Jones, ten years older and ten years more lonely, was still in charge and ran his kingdom in accordance with the strict rules laid down by Greener Than Green Ltd. The new regime was entirely to his taste as it was designed to make public access to the area brief and patrons were encouraged to spend as much time as possible in the café, the hall of animal waxworks and the gift shop at the area gates. Children, of course, were allowed to enter the area, but only at specified times, in supervised parties and if they followed the clearly marked Instructional Nature Trails. Their grandparents could also visit at certain times, but they were confined to Senior

Citizen Rambles. Young people were allowed in only in accredited groups and had to show their identity cards at the turnstile in accordance with recent legislation designed to stamp out Nature Area hooliganism. No one of any age was permitted to stray from the designated paths, sit or lie down, carve their initials on trees, sing, dance, picnic, drink alcohol, smoke or play any sort of musical instrument. As he looked over his domain at night, under a sky turned orange by the lights of Fallowfield, Hector Bolitho Jones was profoundly grateful that in his small world plants and animals reigned supreme. Men, women and children were second-class citizens.

Walking home one evening from having locked the turnstile, Hector saw an unwelcome scrap of litter on one of the trails. He stooped and felt sickened by the sight of a small packet which had once contained what his ex-wife Daphne, in a way which had distressed him, had called 'rubber johnnies', but which he preferred to give their proper medical title. The appearance of a condom here revolted him as a piece of obscene graffiti on a cathedral column might have outraged a Bishop. He went indoors to burn the offending object and in doing so forgot to repair a small gap in the fencing down by the stream, a job he had postponed once before. From that time he didn't merely dislike the human beings who polluted his Nature Area, he hated them passionately.

It cannot be said that Fallowfield Country Town, when it was complete, was quite the bright and shining monument to the success of Titmuss's England that its developers had promised. To pay back the loans raised from Jumbo Plumstead and other bankers, Kempenflatts charged the Fallowfield shopkeepers heavily. Those who had opened in high hopes in the glistening, mock-Georgian shopping malls, setting out their health foods and designer knitwear, their Country Craft table mats and their large selections of sentimental or suggestive greetings cards, found their sales inadequate to meet the soaring rents and soon went bankrupt. The big chain stores moved in. But they also found that the amounts they were required to contribute to Jumbo's interest charges made their businesses unprofitable. Many shops closed and remained empty. Some pedestrian precincts became deserted, being used as public urinals by those made pugnacious or nauseated by Fortissimo lager.

In the most expensive areas of the country town the roads had been privatized and the householders who lived behind locked gates had men from security firms always on the beat. 'The Spruces' didn't occupy such an area. The old house had stood for a long time at the end of a row of shops in Babcock-Syme Boulevard and, while she lived, Elsie Titmuss had worked doubly hard to keep it clear of dust from the construction work going on around it. Elsie died before the house was finally pulled down to be rebuilt according to the architects' specification for that part of Fallowfield.

During the period of rebuilding, Leslie Titmuss travelled a good deal, going to America, Canada and Australia, partly to promote his book of memoirs which he had called, summing up his childhood labours and what he still felt to be the daring and radical nature of his political career, *Grasping the Nettle*. He never saw Jenny and although his solicitors had offered her a large settlement she refused it. When he moved into the newly built 'Spruces', he was photographed crossing the threshold with a smile which might have been ironical.

Jenny and Sue Bramble shared the flat again and lived together almost as they had in the days before Leslie Titmuss sent his gift of the orchid. Jenny, wishing to find a reason for forgiving her friend, came to the conclusion that she wouldn't have known the truth if it hadn't been for Leslie's unacceptable way of finding it out, and facts unearthed in that manner were far better buried again. For a while Sue's guilt made her treat Jenny with exaggerated politeness and consideration, as though she were suffering from a fatal disease. At last Jenny told her to come off it and be in a bad mood if she felt like it, and their lives returned to normal. Sue went on working for Mark Vanberry at the art gallery and Mark, through the good offices of the lover of one of his ex-wives, found Jenny a job as a picture researcher. She advised publishers and magazines on illustrations and she found a good deal of satisfaction in tracking down paintings and drawings with some meaning to them, leaving the Abstract painters to Sue, who almost never rested her eyes on their work.

For Jenny, the past seemed to have vanished. Remembering Tony, her first husband, had for long been her main occupation. Now he had left her because she no longer knew quite what to think of him. Her time with Leslie seemed insubstantial also, a dream which began with their first dinner and ended when he awoke her with the truth about Tony. So, in her new existence, she spent very little time remembering things.

When Sue announced she was going to marry Mark Vanberry, Jenny was, at first, appalled. 'How can you? He'll get you muddled up with all those girlfriends and the wives who're always hitting him and making scenes and, honestly, Mark of all people! He's just got no talent for marriage.'

'Oh, dear, do you really think so?' Sue looked as though she might be dissuaded. 'I used to say exactly the same sort of thing about your Mr Titmuss.'

'Well, yes,' Jenny said. 'Exactly!' However, she knew that Sue wouldn't take her advice and, in point of fact, it didn't turn out badly at all. Sue was pregnant and Mark, as is the way with fathers in their fifties, became besotted with the baby. During the next four years she presented him with two other children, of whom he was also intensely proud. Mark began to look younger and less haunted. He was determined to stay alive in order to see as much of them as possible. He also put himself on an unusual diet of marital fidelity.

So the Vanberrys became Jenny's family. She stayed in their house and looked after the children when they went out or at times when Mark took Sue to America in search of more

Abstract art. Jenny remembered the children's birthdays, worried when they were ill and took them on expeditions into what was left of the countryside. On such trips she never went near the Rapstone Valley and she had no idea what Fallowfield Country Town looked like.

It would be wrong to say that Jenny was unhappy but, although she had one or two discreet affairs, she never fell in love again. Like Fred Simcox she had loved two people in her life, and that was as much as she could manage.

Fred thought that he had found a great value in Fallowfield; it reconciled him to death.

A benevolent providence, he thought, or told himself he would have thought if he had believed in such a thing, mercifully allowed everything to deteriorate during one man's lifetime. The summers got worse, the music noisier and more senseless, the buildings uglier, the roads more congested, the trains slower and dirtier, governments sillier and the news more depressing. Good things, glow-worms, barn owls, farmland, fish shops and girls who enjoyed being called beautiful, were slowly withdrawn. The process was no doubt a merciful one because, when he came to the end of his allotted span in a world so remote from the one he had grown up in, the average citizen was quite glad to go.

When he thought like this Fred realized what had happened. Titmuss and his colleagues had done what he would never have believed possible. They had made him a conservative.

He thought about this for a while and then told himself to stop indulging in such thoughts. Fallowfield Country Town was there and the Rapstone Valley was gone forever. People in Fallowfield would continue to fall in love, give birth, play with their children, lie in bed together on Sunday mornings, make up quarrels, come home singing from the pubs and enjoy occasional happiness. Sometimes, seeing its familiar glow in the sky as they crawled home along the eight-lane motorway, they would think of Fallowfield as home and perhaps find it beautiful. He told himself all this, but was not entirely convinced.

'Just as well they make these changes or no one would ever want to die.' Fred was explaining his ideas to his old friend Agnes, who had cooked him dinner in her flat in London. It was a pleasantly untidy room which smelt of her perpetual French cigarettes. It was the only place Fred knew that smelled as France did when he was young, Calais now being as odourless as Fallowfield Country Town. In this room Agnes lived, cooked, wrote letters, and often, after going out to prepare a directors' lunch or a Hampstead dinner party, stretched herself out on the hearthrug and fell asleep. 'My God,' she said, 'you really are cheerful tonight.'

'Although Leslie Titmuss lives bang in the middle of the Country Town, he seems to enjoy it. He doesn't give any sign of wanting to die.'

'And Mrs Titmuss?'

'Nothing more's been seen of her. Nothing.'

'You still think about her?'

'Not as much as I think about you,' Fred assured Agnes. 'I mean, I have so much more to think about when it comes to us. But sometimes she does cross my mind. Mainly, I suppose, because of the mystery.'

'What mystery?'

'Why she ever took up with Leslie. And why she left him. I don't know how he did it, but he had a few years of her life.'

'Does that make you jealous?'

'It gives him more of her to think about. That is, if he ever thinks about her at all.' He had no idea of what went on in the mind of the old back-bench M.P. who had once again become his patient. But then Fred had never entirely understood Leslie Titmuss. Even in Leslie's comparatively harmless old age the Doctor could only look on the politician as some sort of natural disaster, at which people would always shake their heads and wonder.

*

Of course Leslie Titmuss thought about Jenny.

When he told Ken Cracken, long before, on an aeroplane bound for Luxemburg, that he had been mistaken, he didn't only mean that he'd been mistaken about Fallowfield Country Town, although it was his defeat in that particular battle which had made him decide that the time had come for him to fire at his colleagues from the back benches. He meant that he had been, more deeply and importantly, mistaken about Jenny. He had thought that, bound together by the accident of their love, he had found an ally, a supporter, someone he could rely on for loyalty; but she had done the one thing which, if she had thought about it for a moment, she must have known would make their lives together impossible.

He was prepared for almost any other reaction to his fair and necessary destruction of the Sidonia legend. He expected her to be hurt, for a while. He thought she might be angry, again for a little while. She might have been desolated at the destruction of her past, until their lives together, starting again on a realistic basis, more than made up for anything she might have lost. But when she turned on him and forgave him, as though all the damage had been done by him and not Sidonia, he realized that she was, like Christopher Kempenflatt and his friends who, in their arrogance, had pushed him into the river, one of the enemy. As such she could never be trusted again.

But of course he thought about her and memories of her, seductive and appealing as she had been, flitted across his mind. He was defended from them, as an anchorite might be by his vows of chastity, by his perfect certainty that he had been in the right. And perhaps, although he had resented Ken Cracken teaching him the lesson, he had been right about Fallowfield when he made his speech, so long ago, to the building trade. No doubt it was just that the green welly brigade, the complacent and comfortable country-dwellers, should be defeated. He had always believed in the future, provided it was built on competition, free enterprise and consumer choice, and if the consumers chose Fallowfield, who was he to set himself up as a superior being with purer tastes than all those good people queuing at the supermarket check-outs who, at regular intervals, obliged him by voting Titmuss? So he often left his elderly housekeeper at home and did the shopping himself, pushing his wire wheelbarrow and comparing the prices carefully before he committed himself to an investment in frozen vegetables or washing powder. He was widely recognized and people would stop and ask him his views about all the problems that beset the world. He was never at a loss for an answer.

His health remained excellent. This fact didn't stop him calling in Fred from time to time, mainly for the purposes of argument. He also enjoyed making the Doctor drive out to the end of Babcock–Syme Boulevard and would always apologize for the pain it must cause a nicely brought up member of a wealthy Socialist family to see how the other half lives. Leslie Titmuss became white-haired and seemed, as the years passed, to have found a way of life that suited him. His blood pressure remained constant, although his teeth gradually deserted him. During his years without a wife he managed to recover his son.

Nick wrote soon after his father's resignation from the Cabinet. It seemed that he felt he could make contact again once Leslie was free of the embarrassment of power and there was no danger of him helping the librarian in his career. Leslie went to visit his son and Nick came to stay in 'The Spruces' for part of his holidays. On one such visit he brought a solid girl in spectacles called Margaret, a devout Christian whom Leslie enjoyed shocking by recommending that village churches should be leased out as bingo halls and leisure areas when not needed for divine service. Nick married Margaret and she gave birth to two extremely aggressive small boys in whom Leslie found traces of the charactcristics of his distant self, in the years before he started cutting down nettles. Fred, to whom these infants were shown proudly when he visited, felt his worst fears confirmed.

There would be a long line of Titmusses, stretching out to the crack of doom.

Billy Curdle and Sharon Wellings found it difficult to know exactly where to go. Her home was forbidden to him and although Dot Curdle welcomed all lovers enthusiastically at the Manor, Sharon dreaded the old woman's eagerness to discuss the details of each encounter. She also disliked being taken to the Mine Host Motel on the big roundabout outside Fallowfield, the place of assignation for many of Billy's former girlfriends. Sharon, except at the high point of love-making, embarrassed easily and one of the girls who operated the computer at the motel reception desk had been in the form above her.

'Where do you want to go then?' Billy asked her one night, anxious to get the matter settled.

'I don't know really. Couldn't we drive out to the country?'

'The country's here!' Billy told her in what he thought to be a moment of inspiration. 'No need to drive out. I'll show you where I used to go when I was a kid and watch the old badgers.' He didn't tell her that he used to capture them with terrier dogs and organize badger fights on the rabbit hacienda, as he had put that part of his life far behind him. So Sharon finished up her lager and lime and they walked together, past the huge computer sales and insurance company offices, down the shopping malls and through a middle-range housing estate to the road which ran round the Nature Area. They found a gap in the fence beside the stream where, it was rumoured, kingfishers used to nest.

Avoiding the official Nature Trails and Senior Citizen Rambles, they climbed in the moonlight across the chalk grass- land which was still, in that carefully preserved environment, the home of gentians, several varieties of orchid and many unusual snails. They moved, hand in hand, up towards the beech wood which was murmuring in a small wind. Billy led his girlfriend to the place where he remembered the badger setts used to be, but soon their interest in wildlife dwindled.

They lay on a soft bed of decaying leaves and began to undress each other.

On that night Hector Bolitho Jones had also been out to look for the remaining badgers, but these retiring animals stayed aloof. He was armed, as always, with his father's old shot-gun. He had never used this weapon; he hadn't troubled to renew the shot-gun certificate when his father died, and not even his wife had known of its existence. Now he walked quietly, carrying it in the crook of his arm, a man living in a small prison of countryside, who had almost forgotten his wife and daughter and who certainly had no friends. His eyes shone out over his beard in alarm, as though he feared that the surrounding buildings would close in on him.

Walking through the woods he heard a sudden sobbing cry which he knew came from no bird or small animal. It was a sound he remembered his wife had made, in their distant days of love-making. Standing still and looking through the trees, he saw something which filled him with cold rage and grim determination. He slid in two of the cartridges he carried, raised the shot-gun and he had, in his father's sights, two gently moving white bodies who were breaking all the rules and regulations of the Nature Area.

What became known as the Fallowfield Double Murder was never solved. The Warden gave the police every assistance but they never found where the shot-gun was buried. Most of the newspapers blamed local lager louts, of unknown identity, on the rampage. Others thought it the work of a sex murderer who might strike again. It was generally agreed that the Nature Area had become a health hazard and a place far too open to crime. Sir Christopher Kempenflatt, acting on behalf of his company Greener Than Green Ltd, received planning permission to turn it into a Space Age theme park. Hector Bolitho Jones still presides over it with his beard trimmed and wearing moon boots and a suit of silvery clothing. No one has been caught making love there again.

48

```
F        Mortimer, John
MOR        Clifford, 1923-

         Titmuss regained
```

$19.95